George Smith's
FLOWER
DECORATION

Still Life at Hovingham Hall

George Smith's
FLOWER DECORATION

English Classic Design

With photographs by Tim Megson

To Audrey

with every good wish

George Smith

10.6.90

Webb & Bower
MICHAEL JOSEPH

DEDICATION

*To Frida and Robert Chappell of Mount Pleasant, Bermuda
and to my many friends around the world who have given
me hospitality.*

First published in Great Britain 1988 by
Webb & Bower (Publishers) Limited
9 Colleton Crescent, Exeter, Devon EX2 4BY
in association with Michael Joseph Limited
27 Wright's Lane, London W8 5TZ

Designed by Peter Wrigley

Production by Nick Facer/Rob Kendrew

Copyright © 1988 George Smith

British Library Cataloguing in Publication Data

George Smith's flower decoration: English classic design
1. Flower arrangement   2. Handicraft
3. Flowers
I. Title
745.92   SB449

ISBN 0–86350–181–8

Typeset in Great Britain by August Filmsetting, Haydock,
St Helens

Colour reproduction by Mandarin Offset, Hong Kong

Printed and bound in Hong Kong by Mandarin Offset

CONTENTS

1 *A Backward Glance*

CHAPTER 1
BEAUTY ON A BUDGET

A BACKWARD GLANCE

A love of flowers is universal. Since earliest times their colour, form and fragrance have been appreciated both for personal adornment and interior decoration. Their symbolic significance has been used by all civilizations for religious festivals and secular celebrations. Throughout history flowers have placated deities, crowned victors, strewn the paths of princes and perfumed the bowers of lovers. They speak an international language which transcends all human boundaries of race and creed. The simplest posy received or given can convey a sentiment more expressive than any words.

This is a personal anthology of original arrangements based on my thirty years of flower decoration. It does not claim to be fully comprehensive, but serves to place on record, by the magic of the camera, some examples of a transient art. Most have been specially created for these pages. I hope it will be a source of inspiration to the many thousands who, like me, rejoice in floral beauty and take pleasure in its arrangement.

An appreciation of flowers is not enough to make them live, for once cut we must learn how to make such ephemeral beauty last. This process of life prolongment is called 'conditioning' and consists of getting water up the stem as soon as it is cut. Plants absorb moisture and nutrients from the soil via their roots by osmotic pressure. Once cut this flow of sap is stopped. The process of conditioning is to restart this flow and so overcome any air lock that may have formed in the stem cells. The sooner this is done the less opportunity there is for wilting.

Leaves and stems are covered with breathing pores or stomata. These open when the plant transpires resulting in moisture loss and consequent wilting. All tips about conditioning relate to this effort to restore turgidity.

HOW TO MAKE FLOWERS LAST

Ideally we should only cut plant material when it is charged with moisture as in the early morning, or failing that when dew falls in the evening. To carry a bucket of water to the plant is both cumbersome and impractical, yet we must try to pick and condition with the minimum of delay. When away from home place cut material in plastic bin liners to reduce moisture loss. This will be fine for foliage, but the more delicate texture of some flowers, such as delphiniums, may be damaged if they are left enclosed over long. Flowers and leaves vary enormously as to their moisture requirement and only practice and observation can teach individual needs.

Plants fall into two major botanical groups: mono-cotyledons and dicotyledons. The former have simple vein systems arranged in parallel lines. Monocotyledons drink water easily; some examples are bearded iris, lilies, grasses and most bulbous plants. The more elaborately netted and radiating vein patterns of dicotyledons present us with more difficult subjects such as roses, lilac, chrysanthemums and dahlias. An inspection of the leaf against the light is a quick guide.

Warm water will be absorbed more rapidly than cold. Therefore it has greater restorative value in the case of wilted specimens such as gerbera where cold water conditioning may fail. Always recut stems in difficult cases under water with a really sharp knife or secateurs. Blunt scissors serve only to seal the stem not open it. Remove any surplus burden of foliage to reduce transpiration. Badly wilted flowers and woody stemmed young growth should be boiled for one minute. I reserve an old kettle for this operation. Protect all portions from steam except the cut ends by wrapping in a cloth or paper. Submerge only an inch of the cut stem end. This drastic treatment has miraculous restorative powers when followed by a long drink in deep tepid water – cold water is less effective.

Total immersion of large leaves in a bath of water will help to harden them and can be used on flowers with a spathe-like sheath such as arum, anthurium and spathiphyllum. Those with coloured bracts or sepals such as hydrangeas, hellebores, clematis and bouganvillia can also be immersed but for shorter periods. Two hours should be long enough for most items or the leaf surface may become waterlogged and turn transparent. The woody stems of shrubs and trees should be split or scraped with a knife or gently crushed with a wooden mallet on a wooden block. Flowers which exude a milky sap or latex should be sealed quickly in a flame. Repeat this process when recutting during arrangement for poppies and euphorbia. All these materials will require a long drink in a cool dark place for several hours, preferably overnight. To arrange unconditioned material is a waste of time and plant material.

The final position of your arrangement will have a bearing on its lasting ability. Avoid draughts, central heating units, strong sunlight and any sudden increases of temperature, all of which will cause the stomata to open and wilt. The plant material we select is the raw material of our art so it is worth all the care we can give it. Avoid selecting more material than you need for profusion usually leads to confusion. Often an open spacious arrangement is more effective than a tight mass, so 'leave space for the butterflies' in your designs.

I have called this chapter *Beauty on a Budget* in an attempt to show that something beautiful can be made for very little cost from the simplest of materials. The latest trend is towards simple bunches of mixed flowers 'artlessly' popped into groups of vases of varying shapes and sizes. These casual designs are a Thirties revival when Oasis foam and wire netting were unknown.

My own flower arrangements began in this uncontrived way with bunches of buttercups and ox-eye daisies gathered from hay meadows. I had many a ticking off from the local land owner for wandering through his fields. Illustration 1 captures the spirit of those carefree childhood days with a collection of common wild flowers placed in the christening mug of an earlier George Smith. Displayed on a window-sill it brings the outdoors inside, gathered when summer was young and the air was full of the cuckoo's call. Marguerite daisies, hawthorn blossom, dandilion clocks and hawksbit combine with glistening yellow buttercups and pink clover; plantains and sorrel docks are spiked with grasses and powdered over with Queen Anne's Lace. Even these simple flowers seem precious now when frost and damp despoil the field-side pathways.

Some people may never wish to progress beyond such haphazard bunches thrust into any handy receptical, but then they are unlikely to ever open this book. Their way is what I call the primitive style and is a deliberate casualness

by those who dislike flowers arranged. As with any fashion there is always the anti lobby. My early efforts progressed to jam jars of bluebells decorating every available vantage point much to the dismay of those who had to dust around them.

Gradually a sense of design begins to emerge and this chapter attempts to exemplify these different design concepts without being over didactic. To place a set of rules over an art form can also inhibit natural creative talent. Little wonder we see so many stiff tightly packed triangles produced with monotonous uniformity. Guiding principles of balance and proportion are allied to all artistic pursuits and should be absorbed as if by osmosis. This is why illustrations teach more than any words. We are all copyists to a degree, but eventually latent ability will emerge and find its own expression. I hope that the following examples will be of help, in particular, to beginners.

SIMPLICITY

Snowdrops must be one of the best loved of all flowers because they appear after the seemingly dead period of winter, symbols of new life and fresh hope. Like many bulbous plants their fleshy stems are difficult to insert into Oasis. Small pieces of crunched up wire netting firmly anchored is the answer. However, too much can make it difficult. Illustration 2 illustrates a dainty arrangement on my desk made in a bronze urn, part of a collection of pastille burners. This elegant object, used to perfume early nineteenth-century rooms, has perforations through which the charcoal-ignited vapours escaped. Fitted with a small liner it makes a charming holder for the first flowers of the year.

Did you know there are over thirty kinds of snowdrop? Most of us are content to know the wild single one *Galanthus nivalis*, found in mossy churchyards. I prefer them to the double forms, but mixed together they carpet our woodlands, their grey-green spears offset by russet beech leaves, modest in their purity. These here are a more vigorous and stronger growing form called *G.n.* 'Atkinsii'. Try to arrange them loosely so that each flower shows its individual beauty foiled by ivy leaves.

With them I am using two plants chosen for contrast. Because there are few truly black plants in the garden *Ophiopogon planiscarpus nigrescens* always attracts the eye of the observant. A member of the lily family it has tough strap-like leaves of a sombre shade. The flowers of violet blue appear in late autumn followed by clustered sprays of black berries which glisten like beads of polished jet. In spite of its exotic appearance, this Japanese plant is hardy outdoors.

The willow family is a vast clan, but several species give to the arranger useful outline material in early spring. *Salix melanostachys* bears curious black catkins like blobs of soot on green stems. Most willows strike easily from pieces stuck in the ground, but be careful where you plant them for they also make big trees eventually, searching out drains with their thirsty roots.

A few white flowers of azalea and an anemone give focal emphasis without detracting from the simplicity which flowers of another colour would have done, whilst marbled leaves of ivy hide the mechanics. This is a stiff, maroon-stemmed variety from the Azores, *Hedera canariensis* 'Azorica Variegata'.

A MOSAIC OF WINTER LEAVES

When flowers are scarce and expensive a decoration of leaves can be effective, long lasting and full of interest. Illustration 3 shows a collection of winter foliage arranged as a wall collage. This could also be used as a flat table design with height added by slender candles. Two shallow baskets are placed overlapping each other to create depth. Each basket has an inner square basket which holds a thin layer of Oasis made by cutting one block sideways into inch-thick slices, lightly soaked. Wrap each piece in cling film food wrap. As added protection for the wall, line the baskets with thick polythene. Cover the Oasis sections with a piece of one-inch wire netting to prevent it falling forward. For a table design

this latter precaution is not necessary. Now you are ready to create your collage.

Gather an interesting selection of foliage, trying to vary the shapes, colours and textures. Wash them in tepid, soapy water to remove grime and then condition. Using a cocktail skewer to puncture the film insert each leaf on a short stalk. I have grouped these leaves in blocks of one variety to achieve stronger visual impact. Once in position, it is difficult to resoak the Oasis, but a regular misting with a fine spray will help to refresh the foliage. They all have long-lasting qualities. Top left and lower right are tinted leaves of *Mahonia japonica*. This winter discolouration, caused by exposure to frost or poor soil conditions, is more appreciated by flower arrangers than gardeners. Much confusion surrounds the name of this plant often sold as *Mahonia bealii*. The flowers appear in November and fill the air with the scent of lilies-of-the-valley. The leaves are pinnate, composed of up to eighteen pairs of leaflets and arranged in umbrella-like whorls. Several excellent hybrids have been raised by cross pollination with *Mahonia lomariifolia*, a rather tender species. The best known of these is 'Charity', but I much prefer 'Buckland' and 'Lionel Fortescue'.

Below the mahonia, centre left, are the dark maroon mat leaves of *Tellima grandiflora* 'Rubra'. This is a modest little plant in spite of its high flown name. Neat clumps of scalloped, hispid leaves are deeply veined with bronze. The

2 *Simplicity*

9

colour varies according to the weather, turning more coral pink and puce as cold increases. It is a joy to pick, long lasting and a good contrast to ivy and bergenias. It will make excellent soil cover under shrubs and trees. New leaves expand in spring with masses of nodding stems of green bells, anything but grandiflora!

Below these are the dark green leaves of the Irish ivy, *Hedera helix* 'Hibernica', over laid with yellow green leaves of *H.h.* 'Buttercup'. This ivy gives a splash of sunshine to the garden, more yellow in full sun, it will scorch if over exposed. All ivies are slow at first so be patient. Once established they make handsome plants and provide an indispensible source of materials, especially in the variegated forms.

At the top centre is a small wedge of an ivy given to me in Belgium. The leaves have rounded points to their triangular shape with a distinctive overlapping of the two lower lobes. *Hedera helix* 'Deltoidea' assumes beautiful bronze tints

offset by jade green veins. Perfect as a collar for snowdrops, it should be more widely grown.

The central panel is of *Hedera colchica* 'Sulphur Heart'. We used to called it 'Paddy's Pride', a name I prefer. No two leaves are the same, with yellow veins and generous splashes of lime green which mix and merge into deeper green.

Below these is a group of *Bergenia* 'Sunningdale' leaves, a most desirable clone. Several bergenias are invaluable as a winter substitute for the ubiquitous hostas of summer. They colour best when planted in an open position. *B.* 'Sunningdale' has smooth rounded leaves, slightly reflexed and of a leathery texture which do not flop and look miserable in frosty weather. The colour is almost as good as the liverish hues of *Bergenia purpurascens* which holds its slender leaves erect showing off the crimson underside. These are seen top right with both sides arranged alternately.

As a contrast to these bold leaves snippets of *Cupressus*

3 *A Mosaic of Winter Leaves*

4 *Winter Beauty*

macrocarpa 'Goldcrest', a golden form of the Monterey cypress, create a feathery carpet. Grown in full sun and lightly clipped it makes a golden sentinal in the garden. This woven tapestry of leaves is guarded by Chinese roof dogs bought in Bangkok.

WINTER BEAUTY

In late winter, an arrangement of leaves and branches will give long-lasting pleasure. Illustration 4 is a traditional design utilizing the leaves discussed in the foliage collage in Illustration 3. They are all hardy plants gathered in January, one of the most taxing months for materials. The container, a stoneware jar, is fitted with a large candle-cup holder. The half block of Oasis is strengthened by a cage of wire netting to take the strain of the heavier stems.

The starting point of the design is a few alder branches gathered by the river bank. Britain has a great heritage of wild plants which should not be despoiled by indiscriminate picking so gather only a little using sharp secateurs. I deplore the present method of hedge trimming by machine which leaves a mass of torn and mutilated branches. The subtle red-brown of the catkins is set off by the silvery undersides of *Elaeagnus macrophylla*, a handsome evergreen shrub indispensible for winter decoration.

Begin with the outline of your design working where it is to stand and allow the free flowing shapes to suggest their own placement. Foliage arrangements teach us to appreciate forms and textures more varied and subtle than those of flowers. Note how the sharp spikes of variegated Gladwyn, *Iris foetidissima* 'Variegata' and pinky brown *Phormium tenax* 'Sundowner' contrast with the delicate filigree of soft shield ferns, burnished *Mahonia japonica* and rusty backed leaves of *Rhododendron falconeri*.

Sometimes the underside of a leaf is more interesting than the upper surface. This is true of *Bergenia* 'Glockenturm' which shows off its beef steak red colour when used reversed. The tougher texture of *Bergenia* 'Sunningdale' can be seen near the centre right. Trails and rosettes of lime green ivy, *Hedera colchica* 'Sulphur Heart', lead our eye from the central zone to the sprays of *Euonymus radicans* 'Emerald and Gold' and downwards to the table cover of cocoa brown linen. A Bretby pottery leaf plate and majolica pig underline the rustic theme. This triangular style fits easily into most settings. The decoration will last for two to three weeks if the Oasis is topped up regularly with water.

BULBOUS FLOWERS IN THE PARALLEL STYLE

In early spring we welcome the first bulbous flowers gathered from the greenhouse or bought from the florist.

Their straight stems have rigid lines which do not yield to flowing triangular designs. From Europe has come the parallel style, a stylistic version of the landscape design, developed to accommodate commercially produced uniform material. Illustration 5 shows a simplified adaptation with flowers grouped as if growing. This is an easy style to copy and employs regimented materials in an economical way.

The most useful containers to select are shallow pottery dishes with undecorated surfaces or simple baskets. My container is an old letter tray fitted with a pyrex dish. This is filled with Oasis or three layers of two-inch mesh wire netting. Begin by placing the tallest flowers to the back on the left hand side. Here six *Narcissus* 'Ice Follies' are backed by the feathery texture of heather *Erica erigena* and balanced by the multi-headed *Narcissus* 'Sol d' Or'. The central cluster of *Hyacinthus* 'City of Haarlem' was cut from a bowl of bulbs. I find they last longer used as cut flowers once they have reached the tiresome top heavy stage.

The foreground is occupied by a pot of primroses and a clump of winter aconites lifted from the garden and returned after flowering. These items are placed in polythene bags to prevent them becoming waterlogged and concealed with bun moss. Additional interest comes from garden gleanings. Bold cream and green leaves of ivy, *Hedera colchica* 'Dentata Vareigata' and dark green *Hedera helix* 'Hibernica' add substance. Two rosettes of grey green *Euphorbia wulfenii* are tipped with maroon, a sign that spring is near.

A few sprigs of a Chinese shrub *Sycopsis sinensis* bear tightly packed flowers of golden red. It belongs to the witch hazel family *Hamamelidaceae* and its early flowers are especially welcome. By choosing tints and tones of creamy yellow a greater harmony of colour and unity of design will be achieved. Contrast comes from the violet purple cloth and blue background.

AN EASTER BASKET

Each season has its appropriate flowers. Daffodils, early tulips and primroses are associated with Easter with their cheerful colours and unsophisticated profiles. Illustration 6 is an easy-to-follow design for the novice with an amusing theme of eggs and hens.

Baskets make ideal flower containers and this one of rugged vines looks like a large nest. First fix a bowl or plastic saucer inside the basket and fill with crunched-up two-inch mesh wire netting. Secure any loose ends to the basket for stability. A wobbly start is usually a catastrophic finish! Select some outline branches of budding greenery for height and width. Here I am using *Physocarpus opulifolius* 'Luteus' a shrub with striking golden green leaves early in the year.

Tender leaves on woody stems will wilt if not fully conditioned. It is a waste of time and plant material not to do this.

5 *Bulbous Flowers in the Parallel Style*

6 *An Easter Basket*

A seemingly drastic measure is to crush the stem ends and then boil them for one minute in an inch of water taking care to wrap the branches in a tea cloth to prevent steam damaging the leaves. Then place them in deep tepid water for several hours. They will harden up and last many days if this rule is followed. However, draughts, sunshine through windows, central heating, etc can all play havoc with immature growth so be patient and prepared to give first aid to wilted material by recutting under water, reboiling and resoaking.

The flowers are a colourful selection including large red Darwin tulips 'Lefeber's Favourite' and yellow single 'Gudoshnik', flushed with red. More unusual are the multi-flowered *Tulipa praestans* 'Fusilier' ideal for the rock garden. The central tulips are early double 'Monte Carlo'. Double yellow daffodils 'Inglescombe' are amongst the last to flower. The primroses have been dug up, wrapped in plastic, and placed on top of the netting. They will be divided and returned to the garden later. Leaves of the wild arum help to cover the mechanics.

Although I have a strong dislike of accessories mixed in with flowers, I have bent my rule to include the clutch of eggs. They are artificial but so realistic as to defy detection. The splendid antique egg tureens set the mood enhanced by a table-cloth of red linen.

A SPRING GARDEN

Flower arrangements fall into certain distinct styles, so the ability to recognize these and apply them will be of help to you. For the past thirty years the formal triangular style has prevailed. I have been one of its chief exponents, the famous mass triangle, sometimes referred to as the eternal triangle! Not every flower lends itself to this formal treatment so other decorative forms have evolved; in particular the landscape or naturalistic style which has been practiced in China and Japan for centuries, expressed through bonsai, ikebana and painting. This sparser approach is well suited to modern homes where materials are limited. In its simplest form it has an affectionate place in the hearts of children with seed tray gardens and more ambitious Easter gardens for church or chapel (see Chapter 6).

In Illustration 7 we have a scenic design which relies only on a bridge of driftwood for atmospheric effect. Not for me are props such as Chinamen or gnomes with fishing rods. To make something similar you will need a base of wood or natural-looking tray. Small food cans, glass jars and plastic plant saucers are clustered together to hold the assorted flowers. As most spring flowers resist Oasis, these should be filled with wire netting over pinholders for impaling heavy or fleshy stems.

The driftwood is such a striking feature that it at once dominates the scale of the design. To hide it or over fill the arch would detract from its beauty. It rests on a slice of weathered cedar. Two slender branches of yew create little trees left and right. This is the golden form of the fastigiate Irish yew, *Taxus baccata* 'Fastigiata Aurea'.

In the left group are double *Narcissus* 'White Lion' with three dainty clustered heads of *Narcissus* 'Minnow'. The drumstick primula *Primula denticulata* is always the first of its family to bloom and introduces the complementary lilac blue. On the extreme left are the strange maroon flowers and triangular marbled leaves of *Trillium sessile*. I would not normally cut such precious and long-lasting flowers except to introduce them to you. These Wood Lilies or Wake Robin are slow to establish and for the connoisseur but always remarked upon. In front are three lilac blue wood anemones, a choice gift from Beth Chatto. *Anemone nemerosa* 'Robinsoniana' enjoys the same shady conditions and leafy soil as the trilliums.

The centre group is of an old-fashioned favourite *Primula auricula* 'Irish Blue' with a deeper maroon variety beyond. Auriculas have been grown and cherished for centuries. There were once specialist societies and elaborate stands and miniature theatres were made to display the pots of flowers indoors. Some have a mealy coating which explains the name 'Old Dusty Miller'. They will dwindle and fail if not split up every few years and replanted in compost-enriched soil; they are happy in sun or part shade. Picking up these maroon tones are the pendant bells of the Snakes-Head Fritillary once abundant in Oxfordshire meadows. *Fritillaria meleagris* has chequered petals of greyish plum. I also grow a white one with a greenish tinge. They produce dainty seedheads upturned after fertilization.

Crossing the woody footpath we arrive at the second group with yellow polyanthus and blue pansies. Rich blue feathery grape hyacinths are the less common *Muscari comosum plumosum*. Beside these are the Pasque Flower anemones *Pulsatilla vulgaris*, with silky buds of violet purple. I enjoy the seedheads that follow. Beside these are pink dead nettles *Lamium maculatum*.

Above and to the left are the tantalizing Lenten hellebores, fashionable beauties that tax my patience in an arrangement. *Helleborus orientalis* comes in a wide range of colours braving the winds of March. I have several lovely forms which shade from greenish white with maroon speckles through pinky plum to darkest wine. But they do not last well as cut flowers even after scoring up the stem with a knife, boiling the ends and soaking. They are safest in a cold church in deep water.

To the right are the nodding heads and broad leaves of Dog's Tooth Violet. More like a miniature lily than a violet, the name derives from their fang-shaped roots. *Erythronium* 'Pagoda' has canary yellow pendant flowers like some Orien-

7 *A Spring Garden*

tal parasol. An aristocratic plant for cool shady places. Beside and above are the yellow-petalled, orange-cupped flowers of *Narcissus* 'Scarlet Gem' and the sweet-scented Jonquil, *N.* 'Trevithian'. The whole composition relies on the grouping of each type as if they were growing in a garden.

FLOWERS WITH ACCESSORIES

The landscape style is a popular choice to express a theme or tell a story with flowers. Recent years have seen the production of such elaborate set pieces at flower shows that I fear we risk ridicule from the 'artless' school who favour the unarranged look. There must be a middle road. Much of the fault lies with flower show schedules. If competitors are asked to use flowers to express non-floral subjects then the end result will be a gimmicky plethora of extraneous 'props'. I am off on a favourite hobby-horse, but not alone. Sir Roy Strong had some trenchant words to say on this subject back in 1983 when he described the NAFAS exhibit at Chelsea as 'dubious evocations backed up with theatrical junk in tawdry variety, all of which showed a lack of respect of the medium'.

Having said that, may I add that if an object is truly beautiful and of material sympathetic to flowers, it can enhance them. But it must always have that touch of quality. The bronze geese in Illustration 8 demonstrate this point. They express nature and the atmosphere of a waterside

composition. The gap between the two placements emphasizes their inclusion, but they are not vital to the whole. Plant material must always predominate over accessories.

The outline tree is of an orange-barked, contorted, weeping willow, a rare form of *Salix* 'Chrysocoma' the Golden Weeping Willow. It is grown for its winter colour, but dressed in spring green it makes a tree of great beauty. I thin and shape ours each February to avoid a tangled mass of growth. Willow is hard to condition so split, boil and soak the stem end. It is anchored in a heavy pinholder in a shallow Japanese suiban of brown pottery.

Yellow Dutch iris strengthen the waterside theme with cheerful clusters of double yellow King Cups, *Caltha palustris* 'Flore Pleno'. This double form of our native Marsh Marigold has shining green leaves and revels in the boggy margins of streams and ponds. Some bold leaves relate in colour and texture to the geese. On the left a crinkled leaf of ornamental rhubarb unfolds its bronze-green hand. *Rheum palmatum* 'Atrosanguineum' has red undersides to the leaves and makes a dramatic sight beside water. Smooth narrow-shaped leaves of philodendron are culled from a pot plant together with the splendid variegated leaves of aspidistra. Tufts of bronze-green grass and washed river pebbles underline the aquatic associations. The lilac blue cloth extends the boundaries of this watery place. This design borrows much from the serenity and sparseness of Oriental arrangements.

8 Flowers with Accessories

9 *A Question of Scale*

A QUESTION OF SCALE

Many arrangers feel daunted by scale. Through the magic eye of the camera every arrangement can be made to appear the same size as the page. Whether they are miniatures or massive pedestals their basic design structure is the same, only their size varies. So often people say to me at a demonstration, 'that wouldn't fit into my home' dismissing an arrangement as being beyond their capabilities. If you can scale down a design, or scale it up, you will develop the ability to tackle almost any size of decoration. Every arrangement has its starting point and it is then that the scale is fixed. Certain factors help to decide this for us depending where and for what purpose we are arranging our flowers. Sometimes we pick something just for the pleasure of enjoying it at close quarters. These intimate, close-quarter designs are often the most personal. Illustration 9 is one such small-scale decoration.

These exquisite miniature iris come from the Pacific coast of the United States of America, a cross between *Iris innominata* and *Iris douglasiana*. At Heslington they grow on the edge of the border in well-drained soil and full sun, slowly creeping forward with grassy leaves sprouting from pinky basal clumps. In May their delicate flowers unfurl entrancing our visitors with orchid-like grace. Their colours vary from deep maroon through purple, lilac, pink, misty apricots and yellows. I swop them with friends to increase my collection, this lovely golden maroon being one of the best.

When an arrangement begins with a special flower I go in search of others to enhance it. This requires restraint and discrimination or soon my star performer will become part of the general chorus as many clamour for a role. The antique container with its plinth of golden marble streaked with maroon suggested perky faced pansies, their colours matching the iris.

For the outline I used two stems of *Primula bulleyana* with seedheads of *Tulipa turkestanica* which blooms in March. By June the pink tinged bells of tellima will stand in Oasis. At the top is Bowles' Golden Grass, *Milium effusum* 'Aureum'. It lights up any shady corner in the garden with intense yellow-green leaves and flowers which are the essence of gracefulness.

To the lower left are trumpets of *Mimulus glutinosus* from the greenhouse with clammy stems that are sticky to handle. On the other side are the five-petalled flowers of *Potentilla* 'Daydawn'. The violet blues of *Geranium himalayense* 'Plenum' runs through the centre introducing a contrasting note. These Cranes' Bills remind me of childhood botanizing amidst the limestone dales. I see them still beside the roadside on northern hills and recall many carefree days at Malham Cove. They are a large family worth better acquaintance filling in well amongst shrub roses. A single columbine contributes its cream and violet combination.

The foliage is selected to strengthen the colour scheme. Bronze leaves of *Heuchera* 'Palace Purple' harmonize with the bronze vase whilst blue-grey leaves of *Hosta* 'Buckshaw's Blue' add a neutral tone. A sharp accent of citrus yellow-green comes from the deliciously fragrant Golden Lemon Balm, *Melissa officinalis* 'Aurea' and a zonal perlagonium leaf. Try to stop thinking of leaves as greenery. They are not all green. Grey, blue-green, bronze, cream, muted reds, lime green and yellow are all foliage colours – how dull our gardens would be without them and our arrangements too.

A JUNE MEADOW

Sometimes two styles will fuse to produce a hybrid style. This has happened in Holland where uniform florists' flowers have been used to create a parallel style. Severe vertical lines are contrasted with a horizontal plateau in an abstraction of the landscape style. It looks both crisp and fresh when well executed. The more naturalistic approach is also popular. It is one of the easiest styles to follow because the flowers are arranged as if growing. I have christened this the meadow style.

For both styles you will require round or oval flat dishes, shallow pottery rectangles or large trays. In Illustration 10 I used a large wooden rice bowl from Nepal painted a glowing lacquer red. Lined with stout polythene to make it water tight, it is filled with wet Oasis. A plain shallow tray could be used with separately grouped containers.

This decoration is inspired by a walk in our garden in June with all the luscious freshness that that month expresses. Especially striking are the mahogany red iris 'Gay Trip'. Their sombre richness and velvet texture calls for the complementary cream and green of variegated leaves. *Hosta ventricosa* 'Variegata' is one of the loveliest of this noble family. The leaves are deeply veined and generously margined with cream. Each leaf is further distinguished by a curved tip to its broad heart shape. It holds its variegation all summer and looks most elegant when the violet blue flowers on long stems appear in July.

Along the boggy margins of our ponds grows *Iris pseudacorus* 'Variegata' with quivers of primrose yellow and green striped leaves reflected in the water. This variegated Yellow Flag is another essential plant for the arranger with long-lasting properties used here to foil the bearded iris. Another moisture-loving plant is the golden Meadow Sweet placed in the centre. This Queen of the Meadows, *Filipendula ulmaria* 'Aurea' is difficult to condition, but of such intensity of colour I can never resist trying. Plant it in light shade as the leaves are prone to scorch in strong sunshine.

The horizontal placements consist of *Physocarpus opulifolia* 'Luteus' discussed in Illustration 6 by now showing its creamy flower heads. Beside it are the acid green heads of *Euphorbia palustris* one of the spurge family. It exudes a milky sap when cut. Seal the ends in a flame to condition. The rich bronze leaves in the centre are of *Heuchera micrantha diversifolia* 'Palace Purple' from North America. The evergreen leaves are satin smooth above and rich purple beneath. Airy plumes of cream flowers are produced in late summer. It has an amazing vase life of up to one month in Oasis, rather like its lovely cousin *Heuchera americana.* They have woody roots stocks so do not divide up as easily as tellima which they resemble.

All these different yellow-green and bronze leaves make a strong complement to the orange-red of primulas, poppies and honeysuckle. The primulas are of the candelabra type, their stems dusted with a farinose white powder. *Primula* 'Ravenglass Vermillion' is aptly named, but also known as *P.* 'Inverewe' it is a hearty grower which compensates for the fact that it does not set seed. With it I have placed an apricot flower stem of *Primula bulleyana.* Oriental poppies can be a mixed blessing in the garden, leaving unsightly gaps in a border as they die down after flowering. However, everyone who sees *Papaver orientalis* 'Picotee' comments on its white ruffled petals edged with salmon-orange. It looks almost artificial outdoors, but steals the show inside. I have backed it with the rushy leaves of Bowles' Golden Sedge, *Carex stricta,* whose triangular flower stems end in brownish male spikes over cream female flowers. This beautiful wildling gives the meadow touch to the group together with scarlet red *Geum* 'Mrs Bradshaw' a brilliantly coloured garden variety of Water Avens.

10 *A June Meadow*

A FLORAL MOTIF

The posy of midsummer flowers in Illustration 11 was created as the design for a toffee tin. It would make an easy-to-copy centrepiece for a small dining table or as a gift for a sick person.

Attach a plastic four-pronged frog inside a five-inch plastic saucer with Oasis Fix adhesive. Impale it with a round of moist Oasis foam. The saucer should stand on a pretty plate as a protection for polished furniture. Seen from above it presents a floral motif, but should look attractive from every angle. Select a variety of different shapes and sizes of flowers, some flat leaves and fine fillers such as Lady's Mantle, *Alchemilla mollis*, and one especially bold flower for the centre.

Start by arranging the outer placements to follow the rim of the plate or an imaginary circle. If we view this in a clockwise direction we begin with the yellow umbels of

11 *A Floral Motif*

Allium moly at the twelve o'clock position. This is a useful low-growing decorative onion, not offensive in odour once arranged. Next is the lavender-blue of *Geranium incisum* 'Johnson's Blue', not unlike the Meadow Crane's Bill, *G. pratense*. It makes a pleasing foil for the clustered trumpets of Woodbine, *Lonicera periclymenum*. Pollinated by moths, this climbing wildling releases its heavy perfume at dusk. Next comes a leaf of *Hosta ventricosa* 'Variegata', it ends in a sensuous curving point distinctive to this species and *Hosta undulata undulata* opposite. It is one of the choicest of all this beautiful and varied genus.

A large head of *Clematis* 'Lady Northcliffe' was conditioned first by floating on water for two hours. Clematis can be tricky, if picked too young or too old they may fail to last. The blue-green of *Mahonia japonica* berries adds a note of contrasting colour and cascading movement. It is always a race to pick these before they turn purple and are devoured by greedy blackbirds. Three varieties of garden pink add their spicy fragrance starting with an old unnamed variety at the base of the picture up to the maroon and white stencilled faces of *Dianthus* 'Highland Frazer'. This grows in a pocket on our terrace and produces exclamations of delight from visitors. Another old and cherished variety is 'Musgrave's White' with a green eye to the fringed petals. These well-loved garden flowers were used to flavour cordials, hence the Elizabethan name of Sops in Wine.

At the lowest point we have *Chrysanthemum frutescens* 'Jamaica Primrose'. A half-hardy plant raised each year from cuttings. Mine came from Bermuda where it grows outdoors all year, a cherished memory of the donor, Miss Gladys Hutchins. The yellow-green of Golden Marjoram, *Origanum vulgare* 'Aureum' associates well with the marguerite daisies and the golden trumpets of a scentless honeysuckle *Lonicera × tellmanniana*. This hybrid is worth growing for its pale green foliage which sets off the elegantly poised flowers. It prefers a sheltered position and is less robust than our native woodbine.

Three roses span the posy diagonally. The deep magenta red one is 'Madame Delaroche – Lambert', a name that conjures up the image of a fine lady. The buds have elongated sepals heavily covered with moss. It looks as though it belongs on a Victorian chintz or wallpaper. The ravishing beauty of 'Madame Isaac Periere' has pride of place and leads to the shell-pink quartered petals of 'Fantin Latour'. A fitting memorial to the great French artist. Fleecy clusters of Lady's Mantle help to fill in between the more solid forms used with its own pleated leaves. A cluster of Pansy 'Ullswater' brings us back to the beginning. Also in the arrangement is a head of *Astrantia major* looking like a tightly packed Victorian pincushion surrounded by ten pink bracts. *Hosta fortunei* 'Obscura Marginata', golden lemon balm, *Melissa officinalis* 'Aurea' and cream ivy complete the background foliage essential to any good design.

A GIFT OF FLOWERS

Few presents give greater pleasure than flowers, especially when they are received ready to be placed in a vase of water. The tied bunch in Illustration 12 would be welcomed by any hostess as it is prepared for immediate enjoyment.

Such a bouquet begins in the garden. Armed with a large basket and secateurs, select one or two of each available flower and some interesting leaves. Gathered at random, a fascinating collection of multicoloured varieties will combine together, without robbing the garden. For a more studied effect gather with a colour scheme in mind. It helps if you know the recipient's colour preference or interior decoration. Here orange, yellow and purple with green form a triadic colour harmony. Its intensity is heightened by the purple background which contrasts strongly with the orange and yellow. Change the background and the mood of the arrangement changes too, for colour has a strong emotive effect upon our senses.

Gather a variety of shapes to include some pointed flowers or spear-shaped leaves, bold rounded forms for focal interest and fine fillers. A few broad leaves will form a collar or ruff. Fragrance is also important for I find the first thing a person does is to smell such a gift. Roses are an obvious choice as they are everyone's favourite. More subtle inclusions may come from scented geraniums, lemon verbena *Lippa citriodora* and sweet woodruff *Asperula odorata*, with its smell of new mown hay. All these release their fragrance when handled. A bouquet garni of fresh herbs would please a city-dwelling cook.

Remove the lower leaves and condition the flowers in the usual way. Take special care to dethorn roses or sprays of hips. There is nothing more startling than to grasp a thorn when giving or receiving. After a few hours in water the materials are ready to be assembled. Take a long strand of raffia and tie it firmly to the tallest stem at the point where you will hold the finished bunch. Add flowers one by one in a fan-shaped design gently binding them in with a deft turn of the raffia. It is natural material and undamaged by water, but allow for some expansion of the stems. The bouquet will gradually take shape with spears and points at the outline, soft filler shapes to cushion the rounded flowers placed towards the centre front and a collar of broad leaves at the base. The finished effect should look airy, uncontrived and fairly spontaneous – not like some badly bandaged hospital case!

The stems are an important element of the design and should be shortened to create a decorative and balancing addition to the composition. A well-constructed bouquet will even stand on its own stems, but this feat is not essential. A second strand of raffia may be used to tie all with a bow after the first piece has been slotted between two stalks to stop it unravelling. A more luxurious effect can be achieved by adding a bow of ribbon. Here the choice is important for it sets the seal on the whole presentation. Avoid the shiny water-repellant type beloved of florists and inseparable from Cellophane. The ribbon says almost as much as the flowers, so a good collection should be in every arranger's repertoire. Try pale blue petersham with garden pinks, Swiss dotted muslin with old rose buds, burlap or hessian with autumn leaves and berries. Scarlet velvet or satin associates with an advent gift of holly, ivy and mixed evergreens. Long considered tokens between lovers, old ribbons can still be found and make a treasured gift after the flowers have faded.

In this collection the *Lillium* 'African Queen' takes pride of place matching the golden roses 'Ann Harkness' and Dahlia 'Ormerod'. Cheerful yellow Helianthus, yellow Kniphofia and fluffy Golden Rod, *Solidago* 'Lemore' add a cheerful note. On the outline the spear-shaped leaves and orange flowers of Giant Montbretia, *Curtonis paniculatus*

match the pendant head of *Lillium henryii* lower left and a fiery red hot poker.

The more sombre tones of purple *Clematis jackmanii* 'Victoria', pokes of *Buddleia* 'Lochinch' and the drumstick heads of *Allium sphaerocephalum* add interest and complementary colour. Quite the prettiest inclusion is the airy mauve veil cast by *Thalictrum delavayi* 'Hewitt's Double', an elegant plant deserving wider recognition.

Another lightening touch comes from buff-coloured wisps of *Lasiagrostis splendens*. Splendid indeed, it is a joy to grow or pick. In mid July a fountain of delicate shining heads spun from pale green silk shimmers over arching leaves. By autumn it has closed up, but is still decorative and the leaves are rimmed with russet. Two ladies passing it in my garden were overheard to say, 'I think they must have left it there on purpose'. How right they were and I am thankful they were not tempted to weed it out for I prize it

12 *A Gift of Flowers*

above all other decorative grasses. At the centre right a bold head of leek flowers catches the eye with lilic stems to the fine mass of grey florets. Beside it are the starry yellow flowers of *Coreopsis verticillata*. This invaluable perennial is covered in yellow daisy-like flowers on wiry stems for several weeks in late summer.

A CIRCLE OF AUTUMN BEAUTY

Autumn brings the midas touch to all deciduous plants, changing them, as if by magic, from green to gold. Evergreens assume a new importance in the garden landscape as winter approaches. The circle of flowers and leaves in Illustration 13 has all the mellow beauty of an October day. As so many ingredients suggested themselves for inclusion restraint was required in the final choice.

The style of arrangement is dictated by the vertical habit of the strange leaves of a carnivorous plant from American swamps. *Sarracenia leucophylla* grows on marshy ground and suppliments its lack of nitrogen by trapping insects inside the modified leaves. A fine network of red-brown veins accentuates the eerie beauty of these green and white flared trumpets. Such subtle colouring calls for companions of equally muted tones.

The foundation is a green plastic circular trough sixteen inches in diameter filled with Oasis foam. Sold in various diameters it resembles an old-fashioned posy ring much enlarged. It should be lightly soaked with water and kept topped up. Because it is difficult to see how wet it is, I cut out a small wedge of foam at each side which also facilitates the topping-up process. It could be placed in a shallow basket or directly onto the table, provided sufficient foliage is used to hide the side of the trough.

13 *A Circle of Autumn Beauty*

Slender Reed-Mace, erroneously called Bull Rush, grouped on the left rise from tinted rosettes of *Euphorbia griffithii* 'Fireglow', a Spurge with orange flowers in spring. Placed centre back are parchment-coloured seedheads of *Hosta* 'Ginko Craig' a white-edged variety with beautiful violet-blue flowers. Beside these is a clustered head of *Veratrum nigrum*. The False Helleborine is a native of Alpine pastures and enjoys deep moist soil. A slow-growing variety, the whorls of pleated leaves are decorative enough, but when topped by a graceful spike of maroon flowers the effect is stunning. A plant for the connoisseur, I pick only the seedheads with the exception of the example in Chapter 3 Illustration 42.

Broad leaves of a large vine, *Vitis coignetiae* cover the base and foil a cluster of yellow spray chrysanthemums. Sprays of embryo Date Palm fruits create forward movement together with trails of a purple-leaved vine *Vitis vinifera* 'Purpurea' on the right.

Two very different evergreen ferns introduce contrast. On the left are the lacy filigree fronds of Soft Shield Fern. This form of a British native has an off-putting Latin name *Polystichum setiferum* 'Plumosum Densum Erectum'. It aptly describes an elite plant with densely feathered fronds of mossy verdure. In early May scaly brown croziers of new growth unfurl in a spiral motion to form whorls of delicate green fronds which persist until buffeted by wind or sat on by snow the following February. What more could anyone ask of a foliage plant? The upright wavy blades of Hartstongue Fern offer a contrast both in form and texture. *Phyllitis scolopendrium* 'Crispum' has frilled edges to the leaves like some Elizabethan ruff crimped with a goffering iron.

At the base of the Fly Traps is the deciduous Japanese Painted Lady Fern which attracts more covetous admiration than any other plant in our garden. *Athyrium Goeringianum* 'Pictum' is also known as *A. niponicum*. The leaves are a silvery-grey with a central band of mauve which makes it distinctive from all others. It can vary, however, so always inspect the form offered should you be lucky enough to find it for sale.

Touches of burnished bronze-red come from leaves of *Mahonia japonica* and a few starved leaves of Paddy's Pride ivy. Two stems of *Lillium* 'Mont Blanc' are balanced by an albino rosette of *Fatshedera lizei* 'Variegata'. This is a cross between Fatsia and Hedera and in my case started out as a small house plant. Now it covers a shady sheltered wall and makes a handsome feature. The rushy grasses which rise from the base are the arching leaves of *Carex buchanani*, a Sedge spun from burnished copper.

To complete the impression of a marshy pond a carved wooden frog from Bali seems poised to jump—effective here, though I dislike using accessories. One inclusion I would not recommend is the ink cap toadstools which later erupted black soot over their neighbours!

HALLOWEEN

Crisp autumn nights transform the green leaves of summer into a bonfire brilliance of glowing colour. This final fling of nature provides the arranger with a bonus of materials that coincides with Halloween. This festival of restless spirits is enjoyed by children on both sides of the Atlantic. Americans call it Trick or Treat and family porches are decorated with pumpkin lanterns, cobs of sweet corn and branches of dazzling coloured sugar maple.

I too enjoy this mellow season and Illustration 14 reminds me of my many happy lecture tours throughout New England in the Fall. To make an inexpensive container, hollow out a medium-sized pumpkin through a hole seven inches in diameter. Into this fit a seven-inch saucer filled with Oasis and tape it into place so that it rests neatly on top of the fruit.

Any colourful foliage could be used, the outline here is of beech turning golden yellow and brown. At this stage it cannot be preserved, but can be pressed carefully between newspaper. A few brilliant yellow and scarlet leaves of *Bergenia* 'Ballawley' give focal strength together with the scalloped mustard-yellow leaves of Lady's Mantle, *Alchemilla mollis*. On the right are yellow leaves of Angelica etched with green transformed in beauty as they die. The deep purple leaves of the Smoke Bush, *Cotinus coggygria* 'Notcutt's Variety' together with wine-red berberis give depth and contrast.

The long sprays of chilli pepper, *Capsicum frutescens* are a long-lasting buy if you can find them at the florists. The upper outline is of teasel *Dipsacus sylvestris*, appropriate here because of its association with witchcraft. This probably arose from the strange formation of the leaf axils which form a cup to catch rain water. This handy source of clean water was thought to be efficacious for eye complaints. The straight grasses are from the tall ornamental *Calamagrostis × acutifolia* which decorates the garden well into winter. The stem of yellow-green orchids can hardly be considered beauty on a budget, but as they were a gift, I could not resist their inclusion here.

The pottery witch, miniature broom stick and lighted lantern grouped on silver birch logs all help to create the atmosphere of this night of pranks and hauntings.

A TRIO OF TREES

The three trees in Illustration 15 are variations on a much used theme, each constructed from materials at their best in winter. They cost little and will last almost indefinitely. The first is a triple topiary tree of bun moss gathered from marshy woodland. Carpet moss could be substituted but it does not have the same tufted velvet texture. Select a ter-

racotta plant pot or decorative plant holder, in this case a rustic pottery Victorian fern pot. A thirty-inch dowel rod painted brown is firmly set in quick-drying cement, obtainable at home decorating shops. Line the container with thin polythene, this can be peeled off when the cement has set to free the pot for other purposes in the future. Ensure that the dowel rod is perfectly vertical, a spirit level and another pair of hands are needed. Place a few stones around the dowel and then pour in the wet cement. Leave to set. Plaster of Paris can be substituted but beware, it generates heat and could crack a porcelain cache pot.

Use an apple corer to make a hole through each sphere of Dryfoam in three graduated sizes, then slide them onto the dowel. Secure with Oasis tape at the desired level. The moss is pinned in place with hairpins as for the teddy bear in Chapter 9. Syringe the moss periodically to prevent it from losing its colour. A decorative topping of chopped pine cone scales covers the cement. Small wired pine cones could be substituted for the green moss.

The centre tree of twigs is more akin to sculpture than to flower arrangement, but fun to make. The stem is a straight branch of *Prunus serrula tibetica*, a cherry grown for its ornamental shining bark. This is set in an eight-inch clay pot with plenty of rocks and cement, topped off with polished pebbles.

The twig tree head is made from slender wands pruned each November from our pleached lime trees, *Tilia × europaea*. This process of pollarding or cutting back encourages young growth with brightly coloured bark. It is this green and red bark which gives the tree its special beauty. Secure half a block of Dryfoam or a sphere to the top of the stem and then cover with wire mesh for added strength.

Individual twigs are inserted inverted so that the thin sharpened end enters the foam. These may vary in length, the fun part comes at the end when each twig is snipped to the desired length. Use sharp secateurs so that the cut end is clean and white, adding contrast to the finished effect. Pieces of lichen moss are tucked in to hide the foundation. Sold by florists, this tundra moss is now glycerined to retain its spongy quality.

The third tree is a cone of fresh ivy leaves less permanent yet simple and attractive. Make a slender cone twelve inches high and five inches wide from one-inch mesh wire netting. It will look much larger when covered. Pack this with pieces of wet Oasis cut to fit, used pieces can be utilized in this way. Always store old pieces in a polythene bag to prevent them drying out. Fit the wire frame inside a five-inch plastic saucer used to catch surplus moisture draining down from the apex.

The individual ivy leaves are the glossy Irish ivy, *Hedera helix* 'Hibernica'. At one time all the houses in our village and Heslington Hall were covered with this vigorous climber. The Victorians believed that it kept the buildings dry. All that has now gone and our plant is severely trimmed each March. It has dark green five-lobed leaves beautifully veined, when washed and polished they make a handsome decoration.

Fix your cone to a pot or decorative stand, in this case a bronze tripod. Start inserting the largest leaves at the base and work upwards, overlapping and angling them to catch the light. Fresh flowers or clusters of berries can be added, but the all-green effect is entirely satisfactory. Imagine a pair of these for an overmantel or buffet table. Immersion in a bath of water will resoak the Oasis, drain and replace.

15 *A Trio of Trees*

CHAPTER 2
ARRANGEMENTS FROM THE GARDEN

Garden flowers and foliage have an individual quality which makes them easier to arrange than commercially produced blooms. Their natural curves and graceful lines make them doubly useful to soften the stiffness of uniform flowers. It is important to have a mental image of the finished design as you pick. This enables the selection of the right shaped materials and avoids unnecessary waste. It is a technique which only develops with practice. Most of us pick too much, profusion can lead to a confused result.

A DOUBLE PLACEMENT DESIGN

Many arrangers have been inspired by the Dutch and Flemish still-life painters of the seventeenth and eighteenth centuries. Their pictures were profuse yet the colours, light and shade were so skilfully handled that they avoided overcrowding the canvas. Illustration 16 attempts to emulate their style without strict adherence to contemporary flowers. The alabaster vase is Italian of elegant slender proportions. The choice of two designs, one above the other helps to minimize this feature.

Home-grown flowers of early May are augmented by rubrum lilies, stocks and spray carnations. The pendant bells of Crown Imperial, *Fritillaria imperialis* were frequently depicted at the top of a painting. In Renaissance times the lily, fritillary and iris were associated with the Virgin Mary and given pride of place. This can create a top-heavy effect, but the orange wallflowers in the lower group help to balance. Their colour also helps to unite the hot pinks, reds and magentas to the pale lemon-yellow, cream and gold. A flower with both colours such as the polyanthus serves as a catalyst to fuse a strident colour scheme. The blue curtains are a rich contrast, whilst the books repeat the colours of the pelmet tail.

The perennial yellow paeony comes from the Caucasus mountains. The unpronouncable name of *Paeonia mlokosewitchii* is often corrupted to Mollie-the-Witch by gardeners. In common with other members of the buttercup family, *Ranunculaceae*, it dislikes Oasis and lasts better in tubes of water. Its fragile beauty is worth waiting for. The other flowers include striped tulips, perlagoniums, azaleas, tellima and velvety pansies. They are arranged in shallow plastic saucers of Oasis. The pale apricot sycamore leaves are *Acer pseudoplatanus* 'Brilliantissimum' which makes a showy tree in early summer.

The glaucous rosette of the Urn plant, *Aechmea* is a pot plant placed to give depth and a touch of the exotic. In the upper section the pendant bells of Lady's Locket repeat the pelmet fringe. Rich colours and rhythmic lines create an opulent effect.

RUSTIC SIMPLICITY

Less flamboyant is the rustic arrangement in Illustration 17. Favourite white flowers have a simple freshness suited to this stable setting. The shallow basket liner holds two bricks of Oasis strengthened by wire netting. The outline consists of arching sprays of *Rubus tridel* 'Benenden' those single five-petalled flowers could be mistaken for a dog rose. It belongs to the raspberry family and is ideal for pedestal work in more formal groups.

The other blossom is *Malus hupehensis* a species of crab apple from western China. The scented clusters of white flowers are set off by rich green leaves. Two varieties of tulip form the focal area. The elegantly pointed flowers of 'White Triumphator' are balanced by three large blooms of 'Mount Tacoma', a paeony flowered type. Acid leaves of golden feverfew, *Chrysanthemum parthenium* 'Aureum' peep

16 *A Double Placement Design*

through felted grey mullein leaves and a central cluster of lillies-of-the-valley.

Three other flowers add a note of delicacy and lightness. To the top left are the graceful green bells of *Tellima grandi-flora*, discussed in Chapter 1. The second is the white form of Lady's Locket, *Dicentra spectabilis* 'Alba'. This is much admired in our garden and lasts a long time when cut. The wild cow parsley or Queen Anne's Lace gives to the whole a country charm that blends happily with the bricks of the barn. Created for a garden reception this type of decoration would look well in a marquee for an early summer wedding.

IN THE FLEMISH STYLE

Maytime brings a wealth of garden flowers almost bewildering in their variety. Illustration 18 was commissioned as a chocolate box cover and has nearly one of everything to be found in our garden. The base of the alabaster vase used in Illustration 16 is combined with a comport supported by three swans. As it is porous material a plastic saucer holds the Oasis.

A luscious pink tree paeony demands attention centre right. This is 'Souvenir of Queen Elizabeth', a regal hybrid which sometimes has thirty blooms. Striped Rembrandt tulips, early yellow iris and columbines suggest the Flemish school. These paintings were done over a period of time so they frequently included a wide spectrum of the seasons. Late May and June are the best times to try to imitate their style. Double yellow roses 'Gloire de Dijon' and single yellow 'Fruhlingsgold' are amongst the earliest to bloom with the rich crimson of 'Etoile de Hollande' used above the paeony and in the lower placement. Used instead of an accessory the lower placement helps to fill the canvas and

17 *Rustic Simplicity*

29

avoids a set triangular pattern which would conflict with the period feel of this design.

A framework of shrubs softens the outline including a cascading spray of an early huneysuckle, *Lonicera caprifolium*, lower left. This fragrant climber has grey-green leaves cupped around the cream flowers. Next to it hangs a spray of *Deutzia × kalmiiflora*, a useful small shrub with rosy lilac flowers. *Clematis montana* and *Azalea mollis* link the two placements. Deep purple double lilac and paler wisteria add depth of colour. The blue hydrangea is from a pot plant and comes from the florist together with orange and yellow lilies, stock and gladiolus. There are over thirty varieties of flowers in this multicoloured decoration, yet each flower has room to breath with space left for the imaginary butterflies to fly through.

A WALL BASKET

Early summer brings the opportunity for outdoor entertaining with flowers arranged more informally. We open our garden throughout this period to groups, by prior appointment, and this gives scope for arrangements in the garden loggia, where refreshments are served. Converted from a cartshed, three generous archways open onto the garden. Walls of whitewashed brick and sturdy beams make a rustic setting for a collection of baskets.

The basket in Illustration 19 is first secured to the wall with strong screws as it weighs a lot when filled with liner, Oasis and water. Plastic food cartons make good liners. The graceful outline is of *Pyracantha rogersiana* 'Flava' a spiny firethorn smothered with tiny flowers used with white

19 *A Wall Basket*

Campanula persicifolia and cream foxgloves. The three focal flowers are a modern rose 'English Miss' of immense size if somewhat shyly produced. Next to these are the paler flowers of an old Bourbon rose 'Souvenir de la Malmaison'. The name commemorates the home of the Empress Josephine. It is at its best in hot dry weather. The most arresting feature of the display is the ghostly grey-pink Oriental poppy, 'Perry's White', which is not really white because of the pronounced maroon stamen and black centres. Cut and seal them at once in a flame before immersing in deep water. I also reseal as I recut when arranging.

The starry pink flowers of Hattie's Pincushion, *Astrantia maxima*, pick up the subtle colouring. Two flowers of double white clematis 'Duchess of Edinburgh' hang downwards. This climber always attracts interest from visitors with its strange outer circlet of green sepels. The whole sugary confection is accented by lime green leaves of *Hosta* 'Granary

Gold' and white-edged *Hosta crispula*, the best of this variable tribe. Foaming lime flowers of Lady's Mantle, *Alchemilla mollis*, and seedheads of green *Angelica archangelica* add interest. This type of wall decoration is ideal for a large party where it can be seen above eye level.

MIDSUMMER ROSES

By midsummer the garden is at its best with hundreds of roses perfuming the air. These are the old-fashioned shrub roses so popular today. They do not have the repeat flowering qualities of their modern counterpart, but they make up for this in scent and personality. The shallow fish basket in Illustration 20 holds a heady selection of richly coloured flowers. Begin with the outline choosing pointed flowers such as foxgloves, dusky pink Martagon lilies and ruby red

20 *Midsummer Roses*

thistles. *Cirsium rivulare atropurpureum* is one of those posh weeds that I am occasionally given. It is a real gem and flowers for weeks. I have seen it sold as a cut flower in Japan. Each type of flower is grouped together to avoid a muddled impression.

On the left are crimson paeonies aptly named 'Shimmering Velvet', a vigorous variety which holds its head well and needs little staking. More ghostly poppies are grouped on the right with a quiver of golden oats, *Stipa gigantea*. Below these a stem of the neat-shaped flowers of 'Petite de Hollande' flow to the right. These exquisitely formed miniature centifolia roses, ideal for smaller gardens, are also known as 'Pompom de Dames' a name which suites it well. Three flowers of clematis 'Nellie Moser' introduce variety with lilac pink sepals marked with a maroon bar. They make a light contrast to the deep velvety purple of the rose 'Reine des Violettes'.

By far the most sumptuous of all are the central blooms of 'Madame Isaac Periere' with its powerful fragrance. Just above the handle is a sport from this rose 'Madame Ernst Calvat'. Another Bourbon rose 'Madame Lauriol de Barny' completes the trio. I am glad to have all these ladies in one basket for they are my three favourite roses: voluptuous, many petalled and richly scented. One cannot help speculating as to what these ladies of the 1860s were really like resplendent in crinolines and petticoats.

A PAIR OF BLACKAMOORS

As summer advances into July several flowering shrubs provide picking material. Chief amongst these are the cascading stems of *Philadelphus* 'Beauclerk', a single-flowered mock orange of sweet scent raised in 1938. Unlike the double

21 A Pair of Blackamoors

hybrids such as 'Virginal', it lasts well in water. It is important to remove the burden of leaves as one does for lilac to prevent wilting. It is a laborious task to defoliate, but the saucer-shaped flowers will last much longer. Crush the woody stem ends and stand in deep tepid water. An inch of boiling water will revive badly wilted sprays, followed by soaking.

It lends itself to pedestal designs and Illustration 21 shows a pair of blackamoors in the crimson and white morning room at Heslington. Carved from pine with painted gesso decoration these figures hold six-inch diameter plastic saucers. Other white and pink flowers contrast well with the curtains of crimson moiré silk. The Georgian alcoves frame the decorations set on semi-circular Chinese tables. The rounded windows dictate the style of inverted crescents.

The central roses are 'Doctor Van Fleet', a vigorous climber with glossy foliage so like 'New Dawn'. The flowers are palest pink with a fruity fragrance that sends me straight back to childhood days. 'Madame Lauriol de Barny' adds a deeper tone. It is a clear silvery pink with no hint of mauve. Pendulous sprays of *Escallonia edinensis* link the pink roses to the white mock orange. Wavy white-margined leaves of *Hosta crispula* hide the mechanics. The half brick of Oasis needs daily topping up as such full arrangements drink a great deal of water.

A REGENCY POSY

The overmantel is decorated by a garniture consisting of a fine English clock and two Regency vases in the Gothic style. Illustration 22 shows a close-up of one of these marble and bronze containers fitted with a liner and holding a small round of Oasis on an Oasis pinholder. The spicy fragrance of

22 A Regency Posy

34

23 *A Summer Bouquet*

old-fashioned pinks has made them popular since Elizabethan times. Star billing goes to the almost stencilled faces of *Dianthus* 'Highland Frazer'. Beside it is the double mauve pink 'London Pride' together with the fringed, green-eyed single 'Musgrave's White'. The clovey fragrance of 'Mrs Simkins' makes it a well-loved variety in spite of its habit of splitting the calyx.

Blue-grey foliages pick up the colour of the Chinese silk cushions and picture mounts. The firm-textured small leaves of *Hosta* 'Buckshaw Blue' and fleshy *Sedum sieboldiana* add depth. This succulent will root in water and can be potted up after the decoration fades. A few heads of *Achillea ptarmica* 'The Pearl' last well even if it is invasive in the border. An intimate posy like this can be attractive where more elaborate decorations might daunt the novice.

A SUMMER BOUQUET

Many of us feel reluctant to gather quantities of flowers for fear of spoiling the garden. I always set out with two large baskets and end up picking only a few flowers, but dead heading a lot! Try cutting just one or two only of each variety, arrange them in the hand and tie with raffia. These mixed bouquets given to gardenless friends, especially in the city, give tremendous pleasure. Illustration 23 shows just such a bunch gathered on a July morning placed in deep water and arranged that evening. If the weather is hot, carry the bucket to the plant so that it goes into water at once.

This is a catalogue of so many special treasures inspired by the prints of Robert Furber. This Kensington gardener produced a wonderful array month by month which were engraved by H Fletcher in the 1730s. The white and gold paeony centre left is 'Queen Alexandra'. In the middle the pink quartered petals of 'Madame Ernst Calvat' lead to a large creamy rose called 'Tynwald'. This vigorous hybrid tea was named to commemorate the millenium of the Manx Parliament. I prefer it to 'Peace'. Just above this is a dainty apricot rambler 'Phyllis Bide' grown from a cutting. Charming for a small garden, it lasts a long time changing colour as it opens. Below and to the right are the pink dog roses of *Rosa complicata* which is quite uncomplicated in its open-faced simplicity.

The double clematis 'Vyvyan Pennell' links the upper and lower placement beside the shell-pink rose 'Fantin Latour', immortalized in his paintings. The rich rose-madder of 'Madame Isaac Pereire' has no peer. The apricot orange of 'Iced Ginger' against the marble plinth leads on to an old-fashioned double perlagonium 'Apple Blossom'. The yellow scabious is that back of the boarder giant *Cephalaria gigantea*.

Passion flowers seem more at home in the greenhouse, but our plant has romped away since being planted in a sheltered corner. The tendrils last well and drink water easily. Here it leads the eye back to *Clematis* 'Victoria' and a pink honeysuckle, *Lonicera americanum*. This elegant climber is pollinated by moths and gives off its scent in the evening like other woodbines.

The arching stems of *Buddleia alternifolia* are studded with lavender flowers. My plant was grown from three small pieces saved from an arrangement. Quaking grasses, *Briza maxima*, heuchera and cream lupins together with campanula and white penstemons are all backed by hosta leaves. What would we do without them! Although this fine urn suggests a formal setting this type of decoration could look just as good in a pottery jug. I have a wide variety for quick 'one of everything' mixed bouquets.

A STUDY IN BLUE

The number of blue flowers to be found in the garden is somewhat limited, which makes any all blue arrangement seem special. The setting is a midnight blue bathroom, the dark background a dramatic foil to mirrors, gilt and crystal. The inspiration and scale came from the Chinese ginger jar lamp and other blue and white porcelain. Old pottery vegetable dishes, foot baths and water jugs all make copious containers filled with crunched-up two-inch wire netting. Illustration 24 shows a shallow transfer ware dish by Wedgwood. Arranged in Oasis are slender spikes of violet blue *Hosta ventricosa*, delphiniums, hydrangeas and various clematis. The small blue *Agapanthus umbellatus mooreanus* is a hardy version of the blue African lily and has been with us for over twenty years. The taller more showy Headbourne hybrids yield some selected clones the best being 'Profusion' and deep blue 'Torbay', both worth searching for.

Touches of lavender and indigo find their way in from *Clematis* 'Perle d'Azure' and *Clematis × durandii*. The flowers of the latter are four-petalled or more correctly modified sepals, deeply grooved and sturdy. It does not climb like most of its family. The steely blue of the alpine sea holly is especially beautiful. Mine was given to me as Donard's Form of *Eryngium alpinum*. The central cone is surrounded by a filigree lace calyx frill, steely veined and blue like the flower stems. It can be preserved in glycerine solution. On the left is *Geranium wallichianum* 'Buxton's Variety'. In the early stages it might be weeded out as creeping buttercup, but once the white-centred blue flowers appear it is a joy until first frosts.

The watercolour is of border carnations by Nancy Lindsay, a noted gardener of the early twentieth century. Because of the cream lampshade and parchment picture mount I have used albino shoots of variegated Apple Mint, cream ivy leaves and variegated periwinkle to lighten the blues.

36

AN ALL-GREEN GROUP

Foliage plays such an important part in the flower arranger's repertoire, that its value cannot be over emphasized. Seedheads, grasses and green flowers are combined with choice leaves in Illustration 25. They are arranged on a copper urn standing on a rosewood card table. I often have an all-green arrangement here and it is surprising how much our house visitors prefer it to a flower group.

August and early September are harvest time and remind us that there are good seedheads to use green or dry. Here the spiny seedheads of *Morina longifolia* combine with the humble foxglove. Both preserve well in glycerine (see Chapter 9). Ornamental onions include the rounded heads of *Allium aflatunense* with the clustered parchment turrets of *Allium bulgaricum*. A slender touch of brown comes from reed-mace, *Typha angustifolia*.

Ferns are a special love of mine and feature in this decoration. They have daunting names to the novice, but the soft shield ferns are amongst the easiest and the best because they are evergreen. There are many feathery or finely divided forms, the choicest being *Polystichum setiferum* 'Plumosum Densum Erectum', quite a mouthful! It grows in a spiral whirl forming a cosy nest of brown scales which protect next

24 *A Study in Blue*

25 *An All-Green Group*

year's growth, shown here lower right. Another elegant inclusion is the criss-cross Lady Fern, *Athyrium filix-femina* 'Victoriae'. The fronds are crested and overlap each other in a lattice pattern, unlike any other. Try to buy or exchange a good form as they vary considerably. The third fern is top left *Dryopteris filix-mas linearis* with a crisp hard texture giving a light effect. Although this is a Male fern and the latter was a Lady fern, I can assure you there is no fraternization between the species.

The glossy bronze leaves are of *Heuchera* 'Palace Purple', a relative newcomer to our gardens, which has airy panicles of cream flowers of great delicacy. It lasts an amazingly long time in Oasis or water, as do the tendrils of passion flower. With so many fine textures some solid form is needed. Here two hostas play a major part. The blue-shaded lime leaves are of my own variety *Hosta* 'George Smith'. This sport arose from a plant of *Hosta sieboldiana* 'Elegans'. It has now been registered with the American Hosta Society, who record all new varieties. I am indebted to the British Hosta & Hemerocallis Society for his honour. The other hosta is equally precious to me, the gift of the late Eric Smith. The leaves of *Hosta* 'Granary Gold' are an intense lime green in spring fading to creamy green as summer advances. It has a longer vase life than any other hosta; about three weeks.

The leaves of two golden yellow shrubs feature near the centre. A rosette of the flowering currant *Ribes sanguineum* 'Brocklebankii' comes from a shrub which will light up the garden with its acid tones. Two or three leaves of the Indian Bean tree, *Catalpa bignonioides* 'Aurea' give depth. I use the leaves individually as the shrub is slow growing.

Green flowers have a special fascination for flower arrangers. In the centre are pale green heads of *Hydrangea cinerea* 'Sterilis'. This lovely shrub is so much neater and up-standing than its floppy relation *Hydrangea arborescens* 'Grandiflora'. Tight green buds open to pale pistachio gradually expanding to bracts of ivory. In due course they turn over and change moss green, perfect for drying, so it is lovely at every stage. Near the apex of the arrangement is my first spike of a yellow-green form of *Phygelius capensis*, a tender South African.

Decorative grasses lighten the composition. I always add these last like throwing the veil over the bride when all else is ready. The top fountains are from an invasive water grass best banished to its own island, *Glyceria maxima* 'Variegata' has pink shoots and green and white striped leaves. Cascading down the centre are the coppery tresses of *Stipa arundinacea*, silky to touch and shining like new washed hair. This is a connoisseur's collection, but any all-green arrangement will give pleasure and last a long time.

A HYMN TO BACCHUS

Fruits add to an arrangement an extra dimension with forms and textures more weighty than flowers. They are sculptured objects with tactile qualities which make us want to

26 A Hymn to Bacchus

touch their varied surfaces. The bloom of grapes, the velvet of peaches, the smoothness of pears, all help the arranger to create designs with added interest.

Because of this weight, both visual and physical, I am using a heavy bronze vase in Illustration 26. This was the gift of the late Jean Taylor, a gifted arranger. Bacchus, god of wine, wears a crown of vines so small seedless grapes are an obvious choice. They have a fluid quality which adds rhythmic movement. Pomegranates, a melon, apple and plums all add to the abundance. The colour scheme pivots around the red of the pomegranate and the green of the melon with several tints and tones to devise a harmonic whole.

Absolute security of mechanics is essential so do not skimp on the wiring up of your container, in this case a bronze bowl resting on three acanthus leaves. First wire the grapes by the stalk and place top and bottom. Precautions to protect the table such as cling film or a velvet pad are advisable. This table is a demi lune seen in Illustration 33 opened up to form a tea table. Add the apples and other fruit using wooden skewers or cocktail sticks for support. I always find it easier to place the fruit first and then the outline.

The flowers and foliage are all from the garden and my selection is influenced by the complementary colour harmony. Tendrils of a large decorative vine, *Vitis coignetiae* connect the upper and lower groupings in a reversed S line, often referred to as Hogarth's line of beauty. This is further accentuated by the cream red hot pokers, *Kniphofia* 'Little Maid'. Notice how the felted underside of the vine leaves catch the light. By October this rampant Japanese vine will be ablaze with bonfire colourings as it clambers high into trees. Sprays of rose hips, *Rosa* 'Highdownensis', montbretia, red penstemons and creamy ivy complete the outline. A scentless honeysuckle, *Lonicera* 'Dropmore's Scarlet', curves downwards lower right.

The central flowers are peach waterlily flowered dahlias and the curious orchid flowered dahlia 'Giraffe'. The latter has quilled petals of golden yellow backed by dark red in a bizarre combination. Above this central placement is a cluster of 'Joselyn' roses; raised by Messrs Le Grice of Norfolk it honours Mrs Joselyn Steward, a noted gardener and formidable flower arranger. She is best remembered for her mammoth green arrangements known affectionately as 'Joe's Green Jobs'. Like many of Mr Le Grice's off-beat coloured roses, it looks better indoors than out.

Bold leaves of *Hosta* 'Frances Williams' add substance. This desirable variety occurred in a batch of seedlings in a Connecticut nursery field, a chance in a million find by Mrs Williams as usually such variegation occurs by 'sporting', that is to say an all-green plant will produce variegated leaves. My own variety occurred in this way. *Hosta* 'Frances Williams' is blue-green with a lime or gold margin depending on its exposure to light. When sheltered from rain its pruinosity remains intact, much as the bloom on hot house grapes.

Combinations of fruits and flowers look best on a buffet table where a cornucopia effect is in keeping. Away from the service of food and the dining area fruit with flowers can look self conscious and contrived. Such combinations are fun to try but mastery over materials is required to impart a still-life quality. You will gradually develop this ability to know what to put with what and when. Taste is such a variable commodity in all fields of self expression, no two people liking exactly the same things. There will always be arbiters of fashion as well as those who merely strive to copy. Fortunately flowers are so lovely that they require very little art to embellish them.

A COMPOSITION OF BASKETS

I have used the three bell baskets in Illustration 27 countless times. This type of combined arrangement with three or more placements is an ideal way of making several smaller arrangements into one bold display. It has many applications where a more solid pedestal design would look too formal. I visualize this design in a country church porch perhaps with a harvest theme, here it stands in the garden loggia. They are wired to a piece of driftwood which in turn is attached to a steel rod. This rod, part of a bouquet stand, screws into a heavy steel plate concealed by the basketry base.

The white-washed walls of the loggia call for a contrasting background to the light-tinted flowers. Dark green leaves of *Mahonia napaulensis* came from a sheltered Cornish garden, however, in our colder Yorkshire garden the hardier *Mahonia media* 'Buckland' could be used. Sprays of variegated camellia and soft shield ferns create a dramatic outline. Strong yellow spray chrysanthemums, citrus-yellow waterlily flowered dahlias 'Glorie Van Heemsted' and *Lilium* 'Mont Blanc' give cheerful yellow focal appeal.

Creamy lemon *Kniphofia* 'Little Maid' and *Lilium martagon* seedheads give transition. Most people think of red hot pokers as being just that, but they come in a wide colour range from ivory through yellow, lime green, peach to fiery orange-red in as many varied heights up to six feet. They need a sunny spot with rich soil well drained in winter. Natives of South Africa they resent being dug up and divided in autumn so save this job for spring. As cut flowers they turn upwards like lupins so try to place them more vertically than horizontally.

A COLLECTION OF AUTUMN JEWELS

In late summer most roses produce a second crop of bloom. These are often of a better colour than the first flush. They have strength and fragrance which combines well with the many gems of early autumn. The arrangement in Illustration 28 is all from the garden arranged at Hovingham Hall, near York. The broad sofa table balances the sweeping outline of pale blue clematis, a herbacious variety from eastern China. *Clematis heracleifolia davidiana* has clusters of hyacinth-like flowers, slightly fragrant, on arching stems. The leaves are coarse and should be stripped away to give a lighter effect.

Autumn crocus or more correctly Colchicums are grouped near the centre, their fleshy stems in tubes of water as they resist Oasis. These wide lilac and white chalice-shaped flowers star the meadow grass in early September. The common name is Naked Ladies because their clothing leaves of shining green do not appear till spring. The white *Colchicum speciosum* 'Album' is for me one of the most beautiful and keenly anticipated of all flowers. Mine grow under Sorbus trees which shed their cornelian red berries amongst their pearly perfection.

These white and lilac bulbous flowers prompted the inclusion of spikes of purple Kansas Gayfeather, *Liatris spicata*, *Penstemon* 'Stapleford Gem' which are shot with colours like pale opals, amethyst delphiniums and the rich garnet red of *Dahlia* 'Arabian Night'. The roses are 'Golden Melody' and 'Magenta'. I first planted the latter in front of a huge bush of 'Cerise Bouquet' which killed its dusky lilac-pink colouring. Although a modern rose, in effect a tall Floribunda, it has quartered central petals and is deliciously scented. It ties in the strong pink of the double hollyhocks which add an old-fashioned touch to the group. I do not find hollyhocks easy to grow yet they thrive with nonchalance locally in inhospital places by farms and cottages, I wonder why? They last a long time as cut flowers if you can bear to pick them.

In a mixed bouquet try to include some lime green for it seems to unite all colours. Here the annual tobacco flower *Nicotina* 'Lime Green', *Hydrangea cinerea* 'Sterilis' and cream red hot pokers give sharp contrast. The white

27 A Composition of Baskets

agapanthus stand away from the dark background. This easy, relaxed looking arrangement is at one with its surroundings picking out the yellow walls and soft blue upholsteries.

A HARVEST WALL BASKET

Where space is limited a wall vase is an effective way of raising flowers above eye level, especially for social gatherings. The wall basket in Illustration 29 was purchased in Mexico, typical of the selection woven in that colourful country. It is invaluable in the garden loggia with the added advantage that every placement is clearly outlined, resulting in an economy of materials.

Diagonal movement is introduced by the scythe and sheaf of wheat which lend an atmospheric quality to the composition. Boldly placed they suggest the harvest theme without overstatement and are symbolic of the passing year; the scythe has a rustic simplicity which harmonizes well with autumn flowers and berries.

Many autumn flowers have a rounded form, dahlias and chrysanthemums in particular, so try to look out for pointed shapes to improve your designs and avoid monotony. Here arching blades of New Zealand flax, *Phormium tenax* 'Sundowner', with slender reed-mace combine with three spikes of *Kniphofia* 'Dawn Sunkist'. This red hot poker is a larger version of 'Strawberries and Cream' and likely to be much sought after. Mine came from Maureen Iddon's nursery near Preston. The apricot-orange dahlias are medium decorative varieties 'Katisha' and 'Schweitzer's Kerkrade' combined with red bronze *Chrysanthemum* 'Crimson Yvonne Arnaud'.

Reversed leaves of rusty backed rhododendron and preserved beech foil the flowers without diluting the colour scheme. Green leaves would be less effective. The orange hips of *Rosa moyesii* 'Geranium' give transition from the strong central colour outwards. This type of design has many adaptations, but requires extreme care when topping up with water. I invariably overfill the old glass bowl which holds Oasis, wire and water; this is not important on the brick wall, but could be in the house.

29 A Harvest Wall Basket

SOME WINTER GLEANINGS

Winter flowers are few, but all the more precious for their scarcity. Even the smallest of decorations gleaned from the garden will brighten a dressing table or desk and give us hope for better days. It is hard to imagine that the flowers in Illustration 30 were all gathered on a bleak November day. At first glance they look more like March.

The iris we used to call *Iris stylosa* is now called *Iris unguicularis*, which does not roll off the tongue quite so easily. My old clumps of *I. stylosa* never bloomed before March, but now I have two selected forms which flower freely from November onwards. The deep violet-purple blooms are 'Mary Barnard' and the pale lavender-blue 'Walter Butt'. I grow it planted close to a south-facing wall in gritty soil. They flower better after a hot summer's baking. On dismal days I search amidst their grassy foliage for slender buds. These open quickly indoors giving off a delicate fragrance. Prompted by their fragile crystaline texture I am using a vase of Blue John quartz with accessories of polished amethyst and a sparkling geode.

The other flowers consist of *Viola* 'Clementina', double white daisies, *Bellis perennis*, and a few sweetly scented primroses. These come from a plant spotted in a friend's garden. When I asked her why it was in full bloom in November, she dismissed it as 'neurotic'. It is certainly different to ordinary wild forms and I am never without flowers all winter except in severe frosts. All primroses enjoy being split up after flowering and replanting in leafy well-drained soil in semi shade. Cheerful winter jasmine, *Jasminum nudiflorum*, will brighten any arrangement with its starry yellow flowers borne on green stems. The leaves are *Tellima grandiflora* and the mottled yellow-green leaves of *Tolmiea menziesii* 'Taffs variety'. This is the pick-a-back plant sometimes sold as a house plant, but hardy as ground cover under trees. Mature leaves bear a miniature plantlet so it is easily propagated to give to friends.

30 Some Winter Gleanings

CHAPTER 3
FLOWERS IN PERIOD SETTINGS

To arrange flowers in a beautiful home at once inspires arrangers, enhancing their work and adding life to the setting. Countless visitors to my home, Heslington Manor, have asked over the past two decades, if photographs of the interiors were available. This chapter serves to answer that request with the first eleven plates showing flowers in period settings.

SMALL SPRING TREASURES

Illustration 31 shows an elegant little bronze tripod container set on a black slate base. The perforated lid was to permit scented vapours to escape from this charming pastille burner ignited by a miniature lamp held in the middle of the stand. Guilded ram's heads and cloven feet denote its neo-classical origin, standing six inches high it makes a perfect holder for tiny spring flowers arranged in Oasis, but such fine stems require delicate handling. A small wooden skewer can be used to make a hole in the foam before the insertion of soft stems.

The twiggy outline is of an early flowering Japanese shrub *Stachyurus praecox*. It has pale yellow flowers in stiff dropping racemes. It grows in open shade and is a joy to pick, always exciting attention at a demonstration. Two sprays of *Spiraea japonica* 'Goldflame' show its early bronze colouring which later will be splashed with lime and mid green. This is an easy and decorative shrub for small gardens, rarely exceeding its welcome, reverted all-green shoots should be removed on sight.

Dainty bulbous flowers include the brilliant blue Siberian Squills, *Scilla sibirica*, and grape hyacinths. The strong yellow lily-like flowers are those of the Dog's Tooth Violet, *Erythronium tuolumnense* 'Pagoda', a graceful plant with reflexed petals like a Chinese roof line. It enjoys moist shade

and must not dry out when being transplanted. The leaves are pale green and unmottled unlike other members of this species from North American woodlands. A few clusters of *Narcissus* 'Minnow' add fragrance.

To the left of centre are two flowers of *Viola* 'Irish Moll' with velvet petals of an elusive shade of greenish brown. A treasured gift from the Dowager Countess of Mexborough, a few cuttings taken in August and over-wintered under glass ensure the continuity of this prize. Two yellow pansies create focal impact together with a double apricot-coloured primrose.

The most unusual addition is the central cluster of green ruffed yellow flowers of *Hacquetia epipactis*. The first buds of this relationless plant with a genus to itself are eagerly looked for in March. This plant from the late Margery Fish has honoured me with many seedlings with long roots like black boot laces. The ruff of green sepels persist all summer when the yellow flower has faded. In this respect it reminds me of the rare and lovely *Bupleurum angulosum*. They are both in the Cow Parsley family of *Umbelliferae*.

POT ET FLEUR

I am not sure why we use this French expression for a combination of cut flowers with growing pot plants, as it is unknown to the French! It is a useful design concept for the arranger seeking a more lasting effect. Most of us have an assortment of foliage plants about the home growing as isolated specimens. Juxtapositioned together in one container, places their varied leaf shapes, colours and textures into an interesting composition.

In Illustration 32 a large bowl of painted wood is lined with thick polythene for protection. Immerse the selected pot plants in water to ensure that they are thoroughly soaked and then drain. It is difficult to water a plant pot tilted at an angle so I prefer to gently knock the root ball from the pot. Arrange the plants in the bowl to create a pleasing design packing compost or moss tightly around each root ball. Plants enjoy this proximity to each other because it cuts down the moisture loss experienced when they are grown in isolation in centrally heated rooms.

In this example three brick-red azaleas are combined to make one focal group. The white and green leaves of Dumb Cane, *Dieffenbachia* 'Rudolph Roehrs' add contrast, together with the feathery form of the Cocos Island Palm, *Syagrus Weddeliana*. To the rear right of the bowl a dark red croton picks up the colours of the portrait. The fascinating Cat's Tail Fern, *Asparagus densiflorus* trails along the table to the left. This greenhouse plant is not a true fern, but belongs to the *Liliaceae* family and bears insignificant flowers followed by red berries. I have enjoyed using it in tropical Africa with sprays up to five feet long. At home it grows much shorter and more compact.

Cut flowers can be added arranged in concealed tubes of water. I prefer the green plastic cones used to elevate flowers in large arrangements. When these are not available, glass boiling tubes from the chemist or metal cigar tubes could be substituted. Bulbous flowers lend themselves most naturally to this treatment. Here bold velvety red Amaryllis lilies repeat the texture and colour of the lady's dress. They are elevated to give dramatic height with leaves of New Zealand Flax 'Sundowner'. Additional cut foliage is not permitted in competitive work, but at home we may please ourselves.

Outline twigs of sealing-wax-red dogwood *Cornus alba* 'Sibirica' show their ornamental bark together with burnished whorls of *Mahonia japonica* on the lower left. Seven scarlet gerberas 'Bismark' have deep brown centres adding a dramatic note backed by red-bronze *Bergenia* 'Sunningdale' leaves. To the left are grouped nine tangerine-orange carnations. The forced blossoms of Guelder Rose, *Viburnum opulis* 'Sterile' pick up the pale peppermint green of the dumb cane.

The portrait of an unknown lady is by Margaret Carpenter 1793–1872, a painter of the early Victorian period. Her work follows in the tradition of Sir Thomas Lawrence and she was a successful gold medalist of the Society of Arts. The four-foot six-inch mahogany sofa table came from the collection of Lord Deramore and is English Regency.

31 *Small Spring Treasures*

32 Pot et Fleur

HARMONY OF COLOUR

Our choice of flowers for any decoration is governed by several factors. For me colour is the strongest influence and one to which most artistic people will immediately relate. A good colour sense is vital to the arranger. The ability to blend and balance, contrast and control colours varies in each individual and is dependent on their level of sensitivity. Our taste in colour alters with age as does musical appreciation. Sadly, many people never develop their full potential in these creative spheres. Exposure to the best environment is important.

Colour application is influenced by light intensity, temperature and proximity or otherwise to the equator. The further one travels towards the Arctic poles the softer the colours of nature become. Subtle Scottish tweeds inspired by heather, lichens and moss are a joy to behold in misty moorland light, yet would appear drab under a tropical sun. By the same token the brilliant folk weaves of Central America would look garish amidst Nordic tundra. It is these factors which give each country its individuality and which add a special flavour to every region.

Given a ready-made colour scheme it becomes much easier to select flowers and foliage to harmonize. Illustration 33 shows the entrance to the drawing-room at Heslington with a fine satin wood folding tea table inlaid with marquetry swags in the manner of Robert Adam. The curtains of shrimp-pink and green slubbed silk and seal impressions mounted on acid green velvet dictate the choice of colour, in this case a complementary one.

The outline consists of two hardy shrubs valued for winter decoration. *Garrya elliptica* with leaden green catkins was introduced from Oregon and California in 1828. It is a lumpy shrub to arrange so seek out lower side branches that have some grace and remove any surplus uninteresting leaves. The copious pollen shed by the flowers onto polished furniture is its only drawback. There is a beautiful male clone called 'James Roof' with catkins fourteen inches long, which I do not as yet possess.

The olive green twigs used for height and width are of an ornamental Dogwood, *Cornus stolonifera* 'Flaviramea' grown for its bark as the leaves and flowers are uninteresting. Hard pruning in March will encourage new growth and brighter coloured wood. Other touches of lime green come from Leucospermum, a South African foliage in the *Proteaceae* family. Some large leaves of *Hedera* 'Sulphur Heart' and bronze-red mahonia help to conceal the Oasis and unite the design.

I could enjoy this mixture as it stands but several heads of apricot *Hyacinthus* 'Gypsy Queen' were available in the

33 Harmony of Colour

48

greenhouse. This variety is one of my favourites, with hyacinth 'City of Haarlem' and 'Amethyst' close seconds. Its lovely colour tones with apricot gerbera and soft peach 'Coral' carnations. A few 'Fantasy' parrot tulips and double freesias pick up the colour of the central rosette of a Mexican succulent called *Echeveria rosea*. The yellow-green flowers with pink calyces appear in February when the whole plant is shrimp-pink in colour. It is one of those special treasures that brightens the greenhouse and adds a distinctive touch to indoor decorations. The container is an elegant bronze tripod fitted with a seven-inch plastic saucer topped up daily with water to feed the Oasis.

PLANTS AND FLOWERS COMBINED

A fuller view of the drawing-room is seen in Illustration 34. This sunny west-facing room has double windows curtained to the floor, with pelmets inspired by a bishop's throne canopy. A mahogany box filled with plants is placed on the floor where it shows to advantage without obscuring the view of the room. For special occasions and during the house opening season, cut flowers and plants are combined to create a more imposing display.

The mechanics are a twelve-inch diameter tin, three inches deep, treated with rust-proof paint. This is fitted with an eighteen-inch back rod holding an assembly of tubes to elevate the flowers. A variety of foliage plants form the background. As their pots vary in size, they are built up on an assortment of wooden blocks so that all end up level with the rim of the container. Each pot stands in a flower pot saucer to facilitate their being watered *in situ*.

The tallest cut flowers are the stately Foxtail Lilies, *Eremurus × shelford*. These natives of the steppes of Turkestan and Iran are not easy to grow. They require a warm, well-drained soil rich in humus. I have been successful in the past but find they disappear after a time. *Eremurus bungei* appears hardier, but its flowers of brassy yellow are not as attractive as the apricot, bronze and pink and pale gold of the Shelford Hybrids. As cut flowers from the florist they can be costly but last a long time adding interest and distinction to a group.

Some generous sweeping branches of apricot Exbury Hybrid Azaleas and the yellow *Azalea mollis* soften the design. The latter tend to pop up as suckers from grafted specimens where they were used as root stocks. They give to the arrangement a naturalness of form and a fragrance which is unsurpassed. This gentle flowing design is further accentuated by garden tulips with curving stems that continue to grow in water. There are several different types of tulip which I grow for cutting. Amongst the longest lasting are the Viridiflora type with a band of green running up each petal. Here the variety 'Humming Bird' with acid yellow and

green petals is most striking. The creamy yellow flowers of 'Niphetos', a Cottage tulip and 'Maja' a Fringed tulip blend the various yellow tints. The Fringed tulips have a strange crystal-like growth on the tip of each petal perhaps more grotesque than beautiful.

A touch of the exotic comes from white Anthurium lilies with green spadix surrounded by a fleshy spathe. These strong textured flowers look almost artificial but will last a month in water. This compensates for their high price. Cream carnations, apricot 'Media' spray carnations and 'Bonnie Jean' spray chrysanthemums form the focal area. At the centre of the design is a yellow paeony with cool lemon petals set off by golden anthers and a pink stigma: *Paeonia mlokosewitschii* is one of the choicest plants in the garden, occasionally rewarding us with seedlings thanks to the sharp eyes of those who weed.

The bronze-green carpet, the colour of winter moss, oyster beige chair covers and peach cushions and curtains combine to create a room of restful elegance. The pale apricot walls and white woodwork reflect the sunlight with highlights of colour from lime green silk cushions and Victorian glass vases.

A RING OF SPRING FLOWERS

An effective way of arranging flowers, especially those with straight stems, is to group them in clusters as if growing. Illustration 35 shows a sixteen-inch diameter wreath ring used to make a table decoration. The influence of the parallel style discussed in Chapter 1 Illustration 5 is evident. More details of the mechanics are already explained in Illustration 13.

The flowers pick up the colours in the Oriental carpet with its pattern of pink, turquoise, burgundy and blue flowers and foliage. Two plants of hybrid primroses in blue and magenta are planted in the ring. Dig out a wedge of Oasis foam, remove the plant from its pot and any surplus soil and slip the root ball into a small polythene bag. Plant this firmly in the ring. The polythene bag is to prevent waterlogging of the roots.

Begin with the tallest placements; here five stems of *Liatris spicata*, the Kansas Gay Feather, are grouped on the right. A similar parallel effect is made by grouping pink *Nerine bowdenii* at different levels on the left. No attempt is made to conceal their stems which are an element of the design and set off the heads of glistening flowers. Three orchid-pink carnations are added between these groups which together establish the rear height.

A dense cluster of 'Amethyst' hyacinths and magenta cyclamen arranged with their own leaves create the next level, leading the eye down to the base. Clusters of early *Crocus tomasinianus* are concealed in small plastic flower

tubes because their stems are too soft to penetrate the foam. Blue statice and imported wax flowers repeat the colours if not the seasonal theme.

From the greenhouse are prunings of pale pink azalea which add a light almost balletic quality with some pale lilac freesias for transition. It is these transitional placements between the severe upright and low horizontal groupings which make it fit more easily into its traditional setting.

At the lower left angular twigs of *Viburnum × bodnantense* 'Dawn' give off a sweet perfume. This is an invaluable addition to the garden as it begins to bloom in November and continues until March depending on the weather. A hard frost can ruin the display, but it soon recovers in a mild spell. The cut blossom tends to drop indoors, but the fragrance is worth this failing.

The base of the ring is covered with purple and bronze leaves of *Tellima grandiflora* together with leaves of Canary Island Ivy. *Hedera canariensis* 'Variegata' is best known as a house plant, but is hardy on a sheltered wall. It assumes pink tints on the marbled grey green and white leaves as a protection against cold temperatures. Another name for the same plant is 'Gloire de Marengo'.

THE DINING-ROOM AT HESLINGTON MANOR

Converted from the old farm kitchen, the dining-room in Illustration 36 has the original characteristic quarry-tiled floor. Laid over this an Oriental-style carpet was the inspiration for the colour scheme. Aquamarine curtains with maroon pelmet linings repeat in reverse the ground colour of maroon with aquamarine foliage. The apricot walls relate to the central medallion of the carpet. The white of the cornice

35 *A Ring of Spring Flowers*

and ceiling is reflected again in the skirting board. As the room faces north-east, it needs warm colours and the cheerful accent of flowers.

On the left a carved wooden cherub holds a cornucopia of flowers. The tripod pedestal stands neatly in the angle of two walls. When filled with summer flowers it receives much admiration on open days. It is the easiest of all my arrangements because it is not necessary to fill the back in completely so the effect is always light and clear cut. In this example I must confess to having been rather carried away by the abundance of the season!

The metal tin with rod and tubes are as in Illustration 34 and are firmly wired to four small eye hooks in the top of the pedestal. Absolute rigidity is essential as it stands before the door of the drinks cupboard concealed in the projecting wall, so is subject to a certain amount of traffic. The overall dimensions are eight feet high by three feet six inches wide.

Wall garlands of fresh flowers and an Irish silver dish ring filled with flowers carry through the colour scheme for a special dinner party.

The outline is of sweeping stems of *Buddleia alternifolia* grown from cuttings. I was given three pieces by a friend and grew two large shrubs from them. His has since died so I was able to supply replacements. (Sharing cuttings with friends is an important way of perpetuating both. I can never be lonely in the garden as it is full of recollected friendships.) It flowers on wood made the previous year so unlike the majority of Butterfly Bush it should not be pruned in spring. The flowers resemble clusters of heliotrope on long almost leafless wands and are nearly as sweetly scented. Pieces taken off with a heel of wood root easily in a trench of sandy soil outdoors. This can be done in August when the weeping standard tree is lightly thinned.

Branches of White Beam, *Sorbus aria* 'Lutescens' are

36 *The Dining-Room, Heslington Manor*

reversed to show their pale celadon-green undersides. Together with *Hosta sieboldiana* 'Elegans' they foil a medley of mid-summer flowers. The tapered top of the design has foxgloves and spikes of *Campanula latiloba* with wide lilac-blue cup-shaped flowers set closely along erect stems. They last a long time in an arrangement and are an essential addition to herbacious borders of pink, mauve and blue flowers.

Strong focal impact comes from *Lillium* 'Stargazer' a showy hybrid between *Lillium speciosum* and *Lillium auratum.*.These are purchased from the florist, but they bloom outdoors in raised beds in late August in our garden. They associate well with a medley of old shrub roses.

I have already sung the praises of 'Madame Lauriol de Barny', a Bourbon rose with silvery pink fully double blooms, in Chapter 2. It looks at its best cascading downwards on long arching stems. Placed beside it are deep magenta blooms of 'Reine des Violettes' an aptly named Hybrid

Perpetual rose. At the centre of the decoration are a few wine-coloured blooms of a modern hybrid called 'Bill Lomas'. Named for a fellow flower arranger this rose raised by Fryers of Knutsford, Cheshire has all the colour, fragrance and form of an old rose yet it has incredible lasting qualities.

A PAIR OF WALL DROPS

A closer view of these dining-room flowers is given in Illustration 37 which shows a section of one of the hanging wall decorations. This is an easy and economical way to make a special effect for a party. The base is a slim batten of wood seventy inches long by two inches wide fitted with a small ring hook and hung on a screw plugged into the wall just below the cornice. The batten is concealed by a loose

37 *A Pair of Wall Drops*

piece of ribbon five inches wide and eighty inches long, pinned at the top.

Two pieces of well-soaked Oasis are used in each drop placed to catch the light cast above and below the sideboard lamps. Cut each piece two inches wide by two inches thick and four inches long. Wrap in cling film and then tape to the batten. The ribbon is fitted over these projections by cutting out a rectangular opening two by four inches. The Oasis foundation protrudes through the ribbon, but is supported by the wood. I have used aquamarine waterproof wreath ribbon because it is less likely to show any water spots.

It is easier to assemble the posies on the floor or a table, but larger trophies or plaques should be created *in situ* to achieve the correct angle of prospective. Choose only well-conditioned flowers with good lasting qualities. Old cabbage roses look marvellous for just one night, but lilies or similar firm-textured flowers, foliage or fruit can be expected to last much longer.

You will be surprised how economical they are to create as each flower shows in profile against the ribbon or wall. In this example I used a stem of orchids top left with a pendant head of *Allium cernuum* top centre. Below this are pelargoniums given to me by Mrs Spry of Coombe Bissett together with long-lasting Sweet Williams. Stronger focal interest comes from a velvety bloom of *Clematis* 'Violuceau' a beautiful burgundy semi-double hybrid. The rose with buds is 'Petit de Hollande' a compact growing Centifolia with a gorgeous madder-crimson 'Madame Isaac Periere' and 'Madame Lauriol de Barny'. A single head of *Lillium* 'Stargazer' is backed by firm-textured leaves of *Hosta* 'Halcyon' and leads down to the dusky beauty of 'Reine des Violettes' at the bottom. A cascade of lilac mauve *Buddlia alternifolia* is overlaid with a charming old *Dianthus* 'Highland Frazer'. The stencilled faces of this single pink always draw attention. One subdued pink starry flower of Hattie's Pincushion, *Astrantia maxima*, completes the right hand side.

On the left side is a spray of a beautiful blue grass *Agropyron pubislorum* with loops of its leaves, like a smaller version of Lyme grass it is really a Couch grass but not invasive in the border. One head of *Pelargonium* 'Apple Blossom' lends an old-fashioned touch to this midsummer medley.

The effect is completed by made-up bows of ribbon pinned to the top of the batten to conceal the ring hook. A gentle misting with water will help to prolong their life, although these examples were only intended for one night they did last a week with some replacement of the roses.

A VASE FOR THE GUEST ROOM

With so much emphasis on flowers arranged in floral foam, the vase in Illustration 38 will come as a refreshing change to those readers who still prefer to put flowers in water. This is how my mother and grandmother 'did the flowers' using tall flared vases and relying solely on the criss-cross of stems for support, occasionally defying gravity.

This brass tripod of classical design was probably an oil lamp base fitted later with a glass trumpet. It is easy to arrange without mechanics. The choice of flowers was inspired by the muted raspberry-pink bed hangings which are lined with a dusky pink described as 'Ashes of Roses'. They contrast with almond-green walls and white woodwork. This early summer bouquet is as romantic as the room, with flowing lines that echo the draperies.

A walk in the garden sparked off the idea of combining creamy yellow lilac blossom with pink flowers. *Syringa vulgaris* 'Primrose' is a shrub I look forward to each year with single fragrant trusses of great refinement and unique colour. As a cut flower it far outlasts the double white and purple lilac, but must have all foliage removed, the stem ends crushed and a long drink in a cool place. Here it is combined with a trio of three varieties of tulip 'Niphotis' a pale yellow Cottage type, 'Springtime' a green and white Viridiflora and the lovely Paeony flowered 'Angelique' of pale blush pink. A few cream *Lillium* 'Mont Blanc' are featured centre front.

Several useful garden plants supply flowers of interest. Graceful pale pink spikes of *Polygonum bistorta* 'Superbum' form the upper outline. The appearance of clumps of dock-like leaves in spring makes little impression until the slender tightly packed pokers appear in May. This Knotweed prefers damp soil and is tolerant of shade where it will make a long-lasting display with spasmodic repeat flowers in late summer. It is an improved form of the wild Bistort we picked as children in moist meadows. The young leaves were cooked as spinach mixed with mincemeat and eaten as passion dock pudding in West Yorkshire.

On the left is the exquisite pendant Lady's Locket in its white form. *Discentra spectablis* 'Alba' takes up the colour in the white cornflower *Centaurea montana* 'Alba' which though of weaker constitution than the blue Mountain Knapweed lasts a long time in water. Long trails of *Clematis montana* 'Rubra' link the vase to the table by graceful cascading trails. This can be tricky as a cut flower and is best floated on a bath of tepid water to condition. One or two yellow-green variegated leaves of *Hosta fortunei* 'Albopica' show it in all its early summer brightness.

Two varieties of Cow Parsley top off the arrangement in the way our grandmothers added gypsophila or asparagus fern as an indispensible lightening agent. About Whitsuntide the hedgerows are powdered white with Cow Parsley, *Anthriscus sylvestris*, which coincides with the white May blossom. Much more unusual is the pink Cow Parsley *Chaerophyllum hirsutum* 'Roseum' with branching stems holding flat-topped heads of dusky pink flowers, the perfect match to the bedspread. Together they add the bucolic note which accords so happily with the Swansea cow creamers and Staffordshire pottery greyhounds in a restful period setting.

FLOWERS WITH PORCELAIN

Floral beauty has been a source of inspiration to artists in many different media throughout the centuries. It is from these records that we know what was grown and appreciated by our forebears. In Illustration 39 we see part of an attractive china dessert service made at the Coalport factory about 1846. Each of the sixteen pieces has a different floral motif, a faithful representation of the flowers of that period. The early Victorians were already expanding their collections of plants in heated conservatories as well as out of doors. The

artist has captured in paint all the vibrant colours and dewy freshness of many well-loved favourites still identifiable today.

This arrangement attempts to recreate these exquisite combinations of the painter's art in a multicoloured assortment. The container, fitted with a glass liner, is a fruit comport from the service and stands on a folding dressing table. On the lower left is *Rosa banksia* 'Lutea'. I have waited seven years to be able to pick these sprays. It bears compact clusters of flowers in dainty posies, butter-coloured and quite unlike any other rose. Once mature it puts forth prodigious growth up to forty feet high. The flowers appear in May on wood two and three years old. This fact must be borne in mind when pruning which should be minimal. It needs a warm sheltered aspect in full sun. I have used it in South Africa and the South of France, but to get it to bloom profusely in Yorkshire it is quite a feat. With the rose is *Spirea*

38 *A Vase for the Guest Room*

39 *Flowers with Porcelain*

bella with dainty arching stems studded with pink flowers.

On the right a trail of *Clematis montana* leads our eyes to *Hebe hulkeana* 'Fairfieldii'. The gift of that clever plantsman Tony Lord off the National Trust Garden Advisory Board. It has long panicles composed of dozens of tiny lavender blue flowers which last a long time in the garden if not in water. Hebes are something of an acquired taste I feel, and because of their questionable hardiness are a somewhat neglected genus. They were at one time grouped with Veronicas. However this is a plant of unrivalled beauty originating from Dunedin in the South Island of New Zealand, home of so many hebes. It likes poor stony soil in full sun facing south or west, similar to its natural habitat on rocky cliffs.

The strongest note in this otherwise delicate mixture is from a hybrid tree paeony 'Montrose'. The Suffructicosa hybrids are sometimes called the Moutan paeonies. They originate in China where they have long been regarded as the King of Flowers. It is not hard to imagine why as the sight of these gorgeous blossoms with petals of crumpled silk is well worth waiting for. And wait is what you may have to do. My shrubs have been five years getting established and include rose pink 'Elizabeth', pale pink 'Duchess of Marlborough', salmon pink 'Lord Selbourne', 'Mrs Kelway' a superb white and the pale pink 'Countess of Crewe'. They should be planted with the grafted portion below ground to encourage root formation in compost-enriched well-dug soil. In mild springs their precocious growth may be damaged by a late frost. To avoid this, plant them facing west or even north so that the buds have thawed out slowly before the sun's rays strike them. I have been known to rush out late at night with a bed sheet to protect my precious plants!

Placed low at the rim is a velvety maroon pelargonium and next to this the double pink and white 'Apple Blossom' and a white and salmon one all from the greenhouse. The rose is our first 'Mrs Sam McGredy'. Double white lilac 'Madame Lemoine' and the deep purple 'Souvenir de Louis Spaeth' are much fuller hybrids than the single lilacs of the period, but I am not being a purist about such anachronisms. The general effect is the important thing.

Many other early summer flowers are included. See if you can identify them; they include blue pansy 'Ullswater', Pacific Coast iris, mauve *Allium aflatunense*, columbines, striped tulips, yellow globe flowers, anemones, cranes' bills, ceanothus and deutzias. There are over thirty different species or varieties. One plant rarely met with is the double form of pink campion *Melandrium rubrum* 'Flore Pleno'. The bright pink flowers are in the centre of this group. This old garden plant associates well beside our pond with *Primula pulverulenta* which has magenta flowers and *P. pulverulenta* 'Bartley Strain' a delicious pale pink with orange eye. They both appear above and to the left of centre, adding a pleasing splash of colour.

The outline includes *Tellima grandiflora* with delicate green bells, pink Lady's Locket and the pale blue silky flowers of Jacob's Ladder. *Polemonium caeruleum* is an early touch of blue in the garden, but seeds itself about rather too readily. I also grow the white one.

PINK AND YELLOW FOR THE PRINCIPAL BEDROOM

A wider view of the principal bedroom is shown in Illustration 40 with a cascading design of early summer flowers. Arranged in a shallow basket it reflects the colours of this room and the bedroom across the landing shown in Illustration 38. The two may be viewed together on open house days.

There are those who cannot abide a mixture of pink and yellow, but this is largely a question of degree. Chrome yellow and hot pink will combine under a tropical sky, but would be too intense in softer light. Here muted pinks and pastel yellows are blended together by a flower that is a subtle combination of the two. Sweeping trails of honeysuckle *Lonicera × americana* with pink buds and cream flared trumpets act as a catalyst to fuse the roses with the poppies. By emulating nature we can achieve many balanced colour combinations. A bi-coloured flower will often prove the answer.

The addition of lime green is also a help in colour combinations. Two leaves used repeatedly are the spears of primrose yellow and green *Iris pseudacorus* 'Variegata' with contrasting form of *Hosta fortunii* 'Albopicta'. The loss of their striking colour by midsummer makes them all the more precious during May and June.

Another keenly anticipated sight is the flowering of the shrub rose 'Fruhlingsgold'. Ten feet high and as much across, the arching branches are festooned with yellow flowers up to five inches in diameter each filled with a boss of golden stamens. Its perfume carries a good distance in the garden. Branches of blossom should be picked before fully opened although a reserve will continue the display opening in succession from butter-yellow buds and expanding to palest cream single flowers.

In the middle of the arrangement are the muddled double flowers of 'Gloire de Dijon', an old climbing rose with childhood associations for me. The deep cream of each bloom is suffused with buff and edged with pink. It has a delicious fragrance which compensates for its lack of vigour. To the right the clustered panicles of primrose lilac repeat this delicate colouring.

The Oriental Poppies are the principal element of contrast. No longer confined to the old orange-red type they come in a variety of lovely colours ranging from smoky whites through dusky pinks, cerise, white edged with orange, apricot and every tint of red. They must be picked just as the crumpled petals expand, seal the stem ends in a flame and give them a long deep drink. Properly conditioned they will last five days.

Here I have used two prized varieties grown from root cuttings. The soft dusky pink is *Papaver orientale* 'Cedric Morris', another of Beth Chatto's excellent plants. The buds appear in mid May and must be staked at that moment, if left too late the task becomes impossible as the clumps fall open especially after heavy rain. We use circular wire hoops with divisions. The leaves and flower stems grow through these supports making them invisible.

The deeper pink poppies centre right originate from a packet of Sutton's art shades offered by that seed house in the Sixties. I admired it in the garden of Dorothy Gullick of Coombe Bissett. From her gift I have subdivided many clumps. Try to determine where you wish to grow these plants for once established they are hard to eradicate. I suspect that Sir Cedric Morris' variety originated from the same source and was selected by that great artist for its off-beat colour in his garden at Benton End, Essex. Anyone who has seen his paintings will be struck at once by his marvellous appreciation and control of colour. How lovely that these people live on in our gardens commemorated by the plants they cherished.

To lend transition to the group I have added five stems of a Candelabra Primula which grows in the damp margins of our smaller pond, see Illustration 146. *Primula pulverulenta* 'Bartley's Strain' is the choicest of all the family with mealy stems and clean pink florets accentuated by an apricot

40 *The Principal Bedroom*

orange eye. It is an elegant hybrid from the more commonly grown crimson-purple type. I have picked these with some reluctance as their decorative value in the garden far outlasts their vase life. By including them here I hope I may encourage you to grow them. Frequent subdivision is important in order to maintain vigour.

A note of lightness comes from three interesting plants all similar in function, but very different in origin. On the outline are the drooping heads of a native sedge *Carex pendula*, identified by its triangular stems and chaffy brown tassels which open in clusters at the tip. I would not like to be without this statuesque plant of subdued charm which flowers for a long period in damp woodland.

The shining heads of Golden Oats, *Stipa gigantea*, are also included. It is an important accent plant for dry sunny places where a shimmering fountain of flower heads will delight the eye. It rises almost five feet high from a grassy evergreen hummock. It is best left undisturbed, but should division be necessary this can be done in March. The scaly seed cases persist all summer enhancing the garden with an airy exclamation mark to punctuate the border.

The third plant has become almost a weed on our light soil, but a very curious and useful one at that. *Allium bulgaricum* has long stems which end in drooping clusters of bell-shaped flowers shading from maroon to pale green. It has a long vase life and associates well with the pink poppies. The cut stems smell of perished galoshes, but this rubbery odour disappears once it is arranged. The florets turn upwards after germination and dry into straw-coloured clusters, each resembling the turrets of a castle in miniature.

A MASS DESIGN FOR THE ENTRANCE HALL

First impressions are often lasting ones. With this in mind a bold and welcoming arrangement greets visitors as they step through the French window of the terrace or the courtyard door. Illustration 41 shows a late summer design for an effective position in this spacious hall. Viewed from two different approaches as well as full on it must be well finished from every angle.

The container is a large oval pan of polished copper, a metal with fungicidal properties. It is fitted with a piece of two-inch mesh wire netting folded to form three layers. A snug fit for the pan, loose ends of wire are twisted around the two side handles for extra security. Wide mesh allows heavy branches easy entry and firm anchorage as they pass through each layer of netting. This attention to initial preparation helps to avoid instability later, too much crunched-up netting will hinder progress and too little will fail to give sufficient support. Experience is the best teacher as individual tastes vary on the amount required.

An eight-inch copper tube is soldered to the base of the pan set towards the back. Into this slips snugly a thirty-inch long steel rod. Twelve green plastic cones are taped to the rod to elevate shorter-stemmed flowers. Filled with Oasis and water they provide a rigid support for the top placements. Although concealed by foliage these mechanics intrigue visitors unaccustomed to such a large domestic decoration.

My choice of colour varies according to the season: starting with red and coral in colder weather through apricot, peach, cream and finally green and white in a heat wave which is rare! The pale green walls are the perfect foil, but the painting also has a strong influence. Painted in 1710 and in its original frame, the oval portrait shows Thomas Metcalfe feeding cherries to a grey parrot. This delightful boyhood study is repeated in the dining-room where his twin brother is depicted with a pet goldfinch. The sturdy oak chest provides solid support for this large design placed at one end and balanced by a pair of wooden church candlesticks. Impaled on spikes the large candles have a central depression which holds a night light burnt for greater safety.

The outline consists of Box Elder, *Acer negundo* 'Aureo-marginatum', a handsome Maple with divided leaflets liberally variegated with yellow and green. It opens with an apricot-pink tinge expanding to its full effect by mid-summer. It is superior in every way to the white and green *A.n.* 'Variegatum', a variety now superceded by a clone called 'Flamingo' which is tipped with pink at the growth tips. They are all prone to revert to all-green shoots which should be cut away on sight. It is combined here with sprays of Mountain Ash berries, *Sorbus aucuparia*, stripped of their leaves. The fruits of these Rowans never last long in our secluded garden and I look with envy at lush displays on roadside plantings where they persist into winter until hungry birds are forced to eat them regardless of traffic.

The arching plumes of Pampas Grass, *Cortaderia richardii*, create an open top. This elegant plant is the New Zealand Toe-toe and flowers before the more frequently grown, *C. selloana* of South America. The flower head is pale green of silky texture and finer in every way with a drooping habit on five-foot stems. Here it is combined with the brown fruits of Reed-Mace, *Typha angustifolia*, a slender leaved native plant now rare in the wild yet easy to grow by garden ponds. Strong contrast comes from the large leaves of *Hosta sieboldiana* 'Frances Williams', used to foil the flowers and hide the assemblage of tubes.

The inclusion of a complete pot plant can help to concentrate focal interest. Here Gusmannia adds an exotic note. First water the plant and drain. Then carefully remove it from its pot and place the root ball into a polythene bag. This is lashed to three garden canes. This tripod of sticks is passed through the netting mesh to ensure firm placement. It can be returned to its pot when the decoration has faded.

41 *A Mass Design for the Entrance Hall*

The flowers are mainly from the garden and include crimson Dahlia 'Blaydon Red' and semi cactus orange D. 'Ormerod'. Scarlet geraniums, 'Fragrant Cloud' roses, monarda and flame-red gladioli all pick out the colour of Master Metcalfe's coat. From the florist, tangerine carnations add focal weight with apricot 'Media' spray carnations.

Two striking heads of *Haemanthus katharinae* are from the greenhouse where they are annually anticipated. These Blood Flowers are native to swampy places in Natal, South Africa though some species grow on the arid veldt. They start to flower when atmospheric moisture is present, hence the name Rain Lily. The finest I ever saw were at the Victoria Falls where the constant mist suited them. Their large umbels were set with scarlet fruits, something mine never do. They last a long time in flower with a massed head of

coral-red florets with pronounced stamens. They are easy and well worth growing in a cool greenhouse. Several stems of beige and brown Vanda orchids complete the design adding a tropical touch to an otherwise very English country house design.

A STILL LIFE IN THE KITCHEN AT FAIRFAX HOUSE

The reconstructed kitchen at Fairfax House Museum, York provides an eighteenth-century setting for a decoration combining flowers, fruit and vegetables in Illustration 42. The scrubbed pine table, beige walls and wooden dresser have a puritan severity relieved only by the scalloped pedi-

42 *Still Life in the Kitchen, Fairfax House*

ment. This plainness foils a still-life design grouped with abundance on a rectangular pewter meat dish.

A ten-inch diameter plastic saucer is filled with Oasis placed over a heavy pinholder. I cover the pinholder with old nylon stocking before pressing the foam onto the pins. The fabric can be easily peeled away when the decoration is dismantled to clean the prongs. A layer of wire netting covers the whole, secured to the side handles. These firm mechanics are set left of centre to allow room for the heavy fruits and vegetables to sit on the dish clear of moisture.

The colour scheme of orange and lime green has subtle inclusions of maroon, grey-green and beige which accord with the painted dresser and fine display of domestic pewter. The tallest placement is of the blackish maroon *Veratrum nigrum* described in Illustration 13. It passes through the netting and foam and is impaled on the pinholder. Although a rarity I do not often cut from the garden it lends the right note of severity and contrasts well with *Lillium* 'Pirat' and stately hollyhocks. The latter, *Althaea rosea*, was a flower beloved of Flemish painters and seems as at home here as it does growing by our village farm gates. The single flowers are lined with a deeper colour which helps to emphasize their beauty. Two stems of a bronze Day Lily *Hemerocallis* 'Stafford' add a rich note of colour together with Giant Montbretias and orange-red Rowan berries.

A spiny Sea Holly picks up the colour and texture of the pewter. *Eryngium giganteum* is a biennial which seeds itself. It looks wonderful by moonlight when the collar of steely bracts around each flower reflects the silver light.

Gold 'Anne Harkness' roses lead the eye downwards to a cascade of fruits secured with wooden kebab sticks. These include green lemons, oranges, capsicum peppers, nectarines and a yellow-green melon. A striped vegetable marrow makes a strong statement with a shape repeated by dried cobs of decorative sweet corn and fresh corn cobs. Strands of garlic flow across the table repeating the decorative pediment of the dresser.

Highlights of lime green come from a head of celery, variegated *Hosta* 'Frances Williams' and a quiver of decorative Golden Sedge. This striking discovery by Mr Bowles in a Norfolk Broad is *Carex stricta*. The arching leaves of a giant thistle, *Onopordon acanthium*, give a substantial background. Another bold leaf holds our attention on the right. This is the Water Saxifrage with umbrella-like leaves on rough stems. A native of California this leaf of *Peltiphyllum peltatum* shows the burnished tints of autumn. Note how it adds repose to the composition and contrasts with the yellow and brown throated foxgloves of *Digitalis ambigua*.

Immediately behind are the strange brown flowers of Hare's Ear given to me by that connoisseur of choice plants Lilian Martin of Edinburgh. This Burpleurum has branching umbels of brown flowers made even more distinctive by chocolate-brown bracts. Long lasting in water it is as desirable as *B. angulosum* if not as showy. Two rosettes of a bronze succulent, *Aonium arboreum* 'Folis Purpureis', add interest, their fleshy texture in harmony with the fruits. This decoration could be freely adapted for a harvest supper or informal buffet party.

To the near right a simple basket of mixed herbs suggests the culinary function of plants with bunches of rosemary, sage, golden marjoram, mint and thyme all tied with raffia loops ready to be hung from the ceiling for drying.

A CONE OF FRAGRANT FLOWERS

Fragrance has been described as the soul of a flower and certainly flowers with no scent do not have the same appeal. Since medieval times the importance of sweet smelling herbs to strew the floors, nosegays and pomanders has been widely appreciated. Fresh flowers impart to a room scents that man-made essences fail to compete with.

Illustration 43 shows a conical decoration of flowers chosen for their scent in the setting of The Hon Anne Fairfax's bedroom at Fairfax House. A staunch Roman Catholic she never married in spite of many suitors. Her father, the ninth viscount, built this fine town house for his daughter. Both she and her father felt that each gentleman fell short of their standards and lacked the religious fervour considered vital to the match. Perhaps this floral tribute is for those who have passed unloved from the freshness of youth like a flower to the dried and withered beauty of pot-pourri. This is a sad room for me with its single pillow, little prayer book and rosary reminding one of a solitary life spent in devotion to high ideals.

The foundation is a wooden dowel set in a flower pot used for the moss tree in Illustration 15. Three pieces of wet Oasis are threaded onto the dowel and taped in place then covered individually with cling film to trap the moisture. A three-tiered metal stand could be used, but these are hard to hide. Begin by fixing the outline with clusters of lavender grouped in each section. Clusters of Doris pinks and tendrils of Passion Flower, *Passiflora caerulea*, create downward movement. Variegated leaves of an old variety of Pelagonium 'Lady Plymouth' are used to hide the foam.

The focal flowers are richly scented 'Fragrant Cloud' roses and single clematis 'Perle d'Azur', a Jackmannii hybrid of pale moonlight blue. Additional fragrant touches come from Sweet Bergamot used to flavour tea. *Monarda didyma* 'Cambridge Scarlet' flowers in August when many herbaceous perennials are past their best. It is combined here with cream spray carnations edged with maroon in the same combination as the bed hangings.

A ribbon of lavender and lilac shot silk is threaded through the flowers starting with a bow near the top and spiralling downwards to the lower right. It is held clear of the moist foundation on a double-ended stub wire. Always cover wires with gutta percha tape to prevent iron mold damaging the antique ribbon. A light syringing with water will help to prolong the life of the flowers, but when it eventually dries out the best can be saved as the basis of pot-pourri, shown lower left. See Chapter 9 for an old recipe.

GLADIOLI AND DAHLIAS, FAIRFAX HOUSE

Occasionally the flowers available dictate the style or arrangement rather than their setting. This chapter features traditional arrangements designed to enhance period rooms. Illustration 44 is an exception in that it has modern influ-

ences with flowers grouped in parallel. Gladioli or Sword Lilies are particularly rigid flowers with a vertical habit of growth. If placed in a horizontal position, from the sides of a pedestal and vertically they create a cross the arranger has to bear throughout the design. The only way they can look natural when used in this way is if they have grown with curves from being left unstaked. Avoid creating something resembling a semaphore signal!

Constance Spry, the mother of present-day flower arrangements, always stated 'never force a flower into a position it would not naturally assume'. In traditional work those words still hold good, though I often wonder what she would have thought of some of the designs of the past two decades. I feel she would welcome the new and more natural approach becoming apparent today. However, flowers growing upwards from shallow containers owe more to the

43 *A Cone of Fragrant Flowers*

Eastern influence of landscape art than to the classical urns of Western designers.

The walls of the library at Fairfax House are a warm creamy peach which enhances a combination of soft pink and lemon-yellow flowers. The central parallel group of gladioli are balanced by the rounded forms of roses and dahlias. The rose is the vigorous hybrid tea 'Tynwald', with enormous double fragrant flowers. The dahlia is a small cactus type called 'Richard Marc' which combines both the pink and yellow of the gladioli. Both the products of hybridization, these flowers have the same subtle combination of colours.

Garden materials lend a transitional note to the design

with elements that also give it its individuality. At the right, a slender group of Tibetian Cowslips, *Primula florindae* follow the vertical line of Giant Mullein and the straw-coloured seedheads of *Allium bulgaricum*. They all have interesting stem; in the case of the primula they are coated with a mealy powder which greatly enhances the seedheads that follow. It is an easy plant for moist soil and follows the main display of the Candelabra Primulas. The mullian, *Verbascum chaixii*, has stems studded with yellow flowers each with a mauve eye. They open intermittently up and down tall stems. The whole plant dries off in autumn to yield branching seedheads for a giant dead group.

Downward and forward movement comes from sprays of

44 *Gladioli and Dahlias, Fairfax House*

45 *A Pair of Orange Trees*

lime green *Berberis thunbergii* 'Aurea', a painfully slow grow-ing Barberry distinguished by its intense colour. It shows up here against the mahogany sofa table. It is backed by chocolate-brown leaves of *Heuchera* 'Palace Purple' and the individual leaves of Indian Bean tree, *Catalpa bignonioides* 'Aurea' improves in colour as summer advances, but has a habit of dying back at the tips each spring which produces a rounded bush rather than a tree. The heart-shaped leaves are attractive used on their own leaf stalk.

To the extreme left and right of the rectangular dish are small greeny yellow red hot pokers. This unnamed seedling from Mrs Piper of Codsall turns up at the tips repeating the jaunty movement of the Chinese fish. Ears of green wheat help to underline the horizontal placements. Placed on a carved wooden stand the effect is light and graceful.

A PAIR OF ORANGE TREES

Illustration 45 illustrates a pair of topiary trees decorated with fresh clemantines made for a party at Middlethorpe Hall Hotel. Designed to fit an overmantel they flank a mirror in the library of this Queen-Anne mansion near York. Easy

and economical to make they are a variation on examples described in Chapter 1, Illustration 15.

Set into plastic pots their trunks are of × *Cupressocyparis leylandi*, the over-planted Leyland Cypress. Straight bran-ches with attractive bark look more natural than dowel rods especially when associated with fresh foliage. Impale one third of a brick of well-soaked Ideal Oasis on the top of each stem. This is a stronger quality of foam than Standard Oasis. Cover with a thin polythene bag and tape this to the tree trunk. This will trap moisture that might otherwise dribble down the stem and reduce evaporation.

Small snippets of greenery pushed into the foam fill out the tree; in this case *Osmanthus × burkwoodii*, an attractive evergreen with fragrant white flowers in April and glossy myrtle-like leaves. I use it here because it resembles citrus foliage, but boxwood, Portugese laurel, Cuppressus and holly could be used. Small clemantines, a type of tangerine orange noted for its strong colour, are impaled on wooden food skewers placed equidistantly amidst the greenery. Many variations are possible – try small kum kwat fruits, red cherry peppers or even white gardenias for a gala occasion. The finished trees stand in a pair of French tolé canisters well suited to the neo-classical setting of this elegant room.

CHAPTER 4
MODERN DESIGNS

WITH SCULPTURE IN MIND

I hesitate to use the word modern for this chapter heading because it may be argued that all post-war flowers arrangements are modern, that is of present and recent times. However, it is a term applied by flower arrangers to decorations which place the emphasis on design with mass and line boldly defined and strongly contrasted within the element of space. Transitional material is minimal because it reduces the impact of each ingredient by softening their form.

These stark designs have their setting in contemporary buildings where expanses of textured wall space, plate glass and steel supports call for decorations with a sculptural quality. The plant material of temperate zones is not as suitable for these styles as that of the tropics and sub tropics. In countries where bold material abounds so do the best modern arrangers. I think in particular of the brilliant designs of South African arrangers where access to dramatic material has been applied to such exciting effect.

This lack of bold material is a challenge to our imagination and should encourage the arranger to develop 'the seeing eye' as we call it. The arrangement in Illustration 46 began with the discovery of an interesting piece of hawthorn growing in a hedge. Almost circular in form it required a saw and two pairs of hands to extricate it from its tangled surroundings. Black with age, the coarse bark at once suggested the contrasting texture of a handsome hand-thrown pot of large dimensions. The branch sits perfectly astride the container lent to me by the gifted arranger, Di Fargus. I could enjoy the two without further embellishment, the gnarled form of the wood encircling the vase in a diagonal spiral.

The flowers are red Amaryllis, *Hippeastrum* 'American Express' chosen for their size and colour. Red is the most advancing colour and a complement to the turquoise blue of the glaze on the stoneware container. Three large dried fan palms accentuate the diagonal movement with pleated forms used to frame the focal flowers. Their neutral colour accords with the base of the pot.

Such a strong design would be suitable placed in the entrance of a modern building, lit by a concealed spotlight to emphasize its sculptural qualities. The flowers are concealed in tubes of water and will last a long time, a welcome economy for the month of January. On a smaller scale paper-white Narcissi could be massed together to welcome the New Year combined with pine branches, a symbol of longevity. The pot and the wood offer possibilities for many variations on this theme yet remain a dominant constant in themselves.

THE VALUE OF SPACE

The organization and distribution of space is an important feature of modern designs, illustrated by the *pot et fleur* in Illustration 47. Space can take an open or enclosed form, both will add interest and give value to mass forms. Ascending movement is achieved here by placing one arrangement above the other. Two Chinese wall baskets with flat backs, reminiscent of bicycle baskets, are lined with thick polythene to hold pot plants and cut flowers. The upper smaller one is supported on a plank of cedar wood also used in Illustration 104. Two wreaths of vine of graduated size are attached upper left and lower right. They enclose space and add width to the whole composition.

Unity is achieved by keeping to only white and green flowers and foliage with the shining silver of pussy willow catkins. Appearing in February, these harbingers of spring create upward lines in the open spaces. Two pots of white primroses and a cineraria plant are packed snugly into the baskets with bun moss. A fragrant touch comes from a plant of white Jasmine, *Jasminum polyanthum*, a deliciously scented climber for the cool greenhouse or conservatory introduced from China in 1891. It is trained round a wire hoop which prompted me to entwine trails of ivy around the vine wreaths, so integrating them into the design. The ivy is *Hedera canariensis* 'Azorica Variegata', a slighty tender variety as its name suggests. The waxy maroon stems are set with five-lobed leaves blotched with a high proportion of white.

Four stems of *Hippeastrum* 'Nivalis' create strong focal interest with glistening white petals emphasized by a green throat. Resistant to foam their fleshy stems are arranged in plastic cones filled with water. This also applies to the forced white lilac, a tricky subject to condition if the stems are not split or scraped. Recondition stems as they are shortened for arranging.

Bold contrast comes from leaves of *Mahonia × media* 'Buckland' arranged in the same vertical plane as the willow. Of the several hybrid crosses made between *M. japonica* and *M. lomariifolia* I find this to have the most handsome foliage. It makes a statuesque shrub in open woodland with large whorls of leaves crowned by clusters of fragrant flowers in December. At the base of the decoration a coarse linen cloth repeats the rich green, but contrasts in texture. A pale lime green background picks out the throats of the Amaryllis lilies. The design has a rustic charm which belies its dramatic height and vigorous movement.

46 *With Sculpture in Mind*

MOVEMENT AND STABILITY

Sculptural mass and space play important roles in the lively arrangement of Birds of Paradise in Illustration 48. The unique flowers of the Strelitzia are remarkably like the crested head of some elegant crane with spiky orange petals and blue anthers which burst from a grey-green beak. This distinctive profile makes them difficult to combine in a mass design with other flowers yet perfect for a modern line used on their own. Named in honour of George III's wife Queen Charlotte of Mecklenburg-Strelitz, *Strelitzia reginae* was introduced into Kew Gardens in 1773 from South Africa. One can imagine the excitement and admiration it must have caused when it first bloomed.

A free-standing piece of grey driftwood is placed beside this hand-thrown pottery vase. The tough stems of the flowers and their paddle-shaped leaves are held by crunched-up wire netting. Split leaves of New Zealand flax, *Phormium tenax*, are formed into loops and placed at angles to catch the light and enclose space. They add to the tension of the diagonal movement.

The floral arrangers of New Zealand are extremely creative with this tough-leaved plant, as are the Maori race who put it to many uses. Whilst on a visit to this beautiful country I learnt many tips and tricks to split, loop, shred and shape this pliable straight leaf. It comes in a variety of colours including green, cream, peach and purple-bronze. Sadly it has not proved as hardy in Britain as was hoped. It does best in dry winter conditions with copious water in summer. In its native setting it flourishes by river banks in frost-free areas.

At the pivot of the design a cluster of clementine fruits repeat the orange of the flowers and base cloth. A further two are cradled in the wood to improve the visual balance with their strong accent of colour.

This simple yet arresting design relies on the asymmetric

48 Movement and Stability

70

placement of the flowers and their dramatic profile for its effects. The mass of the wood coupled with the smooth neutral pot help to ensure a visual stability at the fulcrum point. Created from tough long-lasting flowers it could withstand draughts, heat and strong sunlight which would prove detrimental to more delicate materials.

EXPLOITING THE THIRD DIMENSION

One of the few positions in my home that lends itself to the display of a modern design is this antique card table set against the plain green wall of the entrance hall. The ormulu wall bracket, once a candle holder, is the only ornate feature in Illustration 49.

In the profusion of springtime an arrangement of vertical severity places the emphasis on six tulips and tropical leaves. The containers are a pair of Japanese bronze-red lacquer trays the colour of the hall curtains. Depth and interest are achieved by elevating one above the other on a rosewood base which harmonizes with the rosewood table top.

The third dimension is further increased by placing one saucer of foam to the back on the left and the other forward to the front on the right. This exploitation of the available depth is lost by the two-dimensional eye of the camera. Always try to imagine you are working within a cube of air and fill only two thirds of the visual space, in this case dimensions set by the limits of the table, bracket and ceiling.

The tallest point is fixed by a stately spike of *Eremurus* 'Shelford Hybrids', the Fox Tail Lily, strengthened by sticks of green bamboo. We have great clumps of this bamboo in the garden much valued for its stems, though I have failed to make the leaves last when cut. Two strelitzia leaves show their pink midribs taking up the subtle coral-pink of the cluster of 'Artist' tulips striped with the characteristic green of the Viridiflora type. A cluster of dark croton

49 *Exploiting the Third Dimension*

71

leaves black-veined with coral link the trays, table and tulips by colour repetition.

A pleated leaf of Chinese Fan Palm, *Livistonia chinensis* placed on the upper left links with another placed on the right with radiating spikes which draw the eye to three slender 'Humming Bird' tulips cut so that their heads are on the same level. This parallel bundling is hard to do when one has spent thirty years teaching others to graduate heads at different levels. Three cream and green aspidistra leaves connect the two groups with a rhythmic forward movement. A cluster of zonal pelargonium leaves 'Golden Fleece' introduces a note of lime green banded with bronze that picks up the lime green spurge on the left. *Euphorbia polycroma* is an exciting accent of acid green in the spring garden, but when picked it has a maddening habit of turning upwards in an arrangement.

The horizontal line of the table is accentuated by groups of bamboo stems arranged forward front and to the rear. A few sandstone pebbles add a tranquil note, their smooth rounded form suggests water. This double grouping owes much to the influence of the Orient where such designs are created to suggest an imaginary stream for fish to swim between two banks. It relies on understatement, quality of material and harmony of colour for its effect – all good ingredients of modern design.

COLOUR, FORM AND TEXTURE

Colour, form and texture are familiar words to the flower arranger, frequently used to describe a decoration. We must fully understand them to appreciate their application. Illustration 50 relies on all three for its effectiveness helped by the element of space and a plain background.

Colour has a universal appeal and is the easiest to understand. A good sense of colour is a natural gift and varies from person to person, but it is also a science that can be learnt. A beam of light passed through a prism produces a refracted band of colours called a spectrum. This band consists of six colours: red, orange, yellow, green, blue and purple as seen in a rainbow. The first three – red, orange and yellow – are termed advancing because they strike the eye with a greater force. The latter three recede and are the colours of nature. By arranging these six colours equidistantly in a circle we produce a colour wheel like the face of a clock with red opposite green, yellow opposite purple and orange opposite blue. You will notice that the advancing warm colours are each complemented by a cooler receding colour.

Three of these are the primary colours red, yellow and blue. If we mix any two of these together we produce a secondary colour. For example, red and blue in equal quantities give purple; yellow and blue produce green; and red and yellow mixed give orange. These secondary colours are

extremely useful to the arranger; look at Illustration 12 with its purple, orange and green triadic harmony plus a little yellow to lighten all the purple.

When we speak of colour harmony we mean colours which produce a tranquil effect. Colours which lie adjacent on the wheel such as orange, yellow and green produce an analogous colour harmony. Colours which lie opposite each other produce complementary harmonies and three colours which are equidistant in a triangular pattern produce a triadic harmony. Many of them have a seasonal application in flower arranging, such as red ribbons with evergreens at Christmas, yellow daffodils and purple crocus in springtime and blue cornflowers with orange marigolds for summer.

Colour also affects our emotions. Red, the colour of fire, is hot and demands attention, beware of ladies who wear only scarlet! Yellow is bright and cheerful and suggests sunshine, ideal for a sick room or nursery. Blue is cold and receding; green soothing and tranquil. We can exploit these emotive qualities by applying them to our designs so conveying different moods or messages.

This is a simplification of the theory of colour. Black, produced by the total absence of light, and white, a mixture of all colours, are regarded as colours in this context. When white is added to a pure hue or colour such as red, pink is produced. These lighter colours are called tints of that pure hue. Black added to a hue gives a shade. For example, black added to red will produce maroon, a shade of red. As with all terminology we sometimes hear it used in a confusing way, the most common example being pastel shades. This is a contradiction of terms because pastel has come to mean pale. We would be more correct to speak of pastel tints.

When white and black are mixed together grey is produced, its depth or lightness varying according to the proportion of each. Grey mixed with another colour tones it down, we speak of greyed tones. These are subtle and elusive tones which suggest antiquity. Once rich colours toned down by the dust of ages and faded by sunlight are found in our heritage of stately homes and churches. It is often helpful to use grey foliage when arranging flowers in such settings to make the combination more harmonious – study Illustrations 65 and 66.

In Illustration 50 red gives added impact to an exciting design of Parrot's Beaks, *Heliconia humilis*, shiny anthuriums and gerberas. Careful inspection of the heliconias will show that they are edged with green, a green showing quite a lot of blue. The blue-green broccoli is the same colour yet vastly different in both form and texture. The same green is found in the two strelitzia leaves placed vertically at the back.

What do we mean by texture? This is the tactile surface of an object. We experience it first as children by touching, later with the eye when our senses already know the feel of different surfaces. How often at flower shows have I seen the admiring public touch the flowers to see if they are real.

50 *Colour, Form and Texture*

Unfortunately this is frequently detrimental to the very texture they wish to explore.

Changes of texture add interest to a design almost as much as changes of form or colour. They are less obvious because they are more subtle. Here the shiny red peppers repeat the texture and colour of the anthuriums helping to creat unity. Yet they contrast with the velvet textures of the gerberas just as the nubbly surface of the broccoli contrasts with the smooth strelitzia leaves. These changes of texture are just as necessary as the more obvious changes of form.

The form or shape of each ingredient combine to create the total design. In this example there are many striking changes of form which add to its general excitement. The outline of split coconut husk makes a rhythmic statement which directs the eye inwards to the explosive cluster of cream grasses. Although neutral in colour both make a strong contribution. Note how the cream grass picks up the colour of the centre of the anthuriums. Horizontal placements of dried fungi echo the browns and creams of the speckled stoneware bowl by David Lloyd-Jones.

This vibrant and visually exciting combination of unusual material owes much to the influence of the modern Italian school of floral design. My frequent visits to lecture in Italy have given me a great appreciation of that artistic and exuberant nation. Their great creative ability with fashion, food and flowers is a rich source of inspiration to all artists and an expression of the warmth of the Italian personality.

MOTHER AND CHILD – A DOUBLE PLACEMENT

The idea of two placements within one design is not new. We have only to study the paintings of still-life artists in the seventeenth and eighteenth centuries to see how they used this device to complete the composition of their canvas. Restricted by rectangular dimensions they filled the lower spaces with fruit, flowers out of water, birds' nests, etc. Today the arranger faces similar confines set by the dimensions of the show bench or within the home.

The background is always important. A dark one will enhance light flowers and visa versa. Thirty years ago we had backings of corrugated cardboard on the show bench, which we considered a great innovation. Then came the niche, an

51 *Mother and Child – a Double Placement*

allotted space of predestined size into which no other competitor might trespass. The result was a series of peep shows viewed full on which resulted in long delays at public viewing time. Now we have the island unit, a free-standing area without backing. It requires the maximum ingenuity from the exhibitor and extreme concentration from the judge lost amidst a plethora of floral monoliths!

Illustration 51 was created over a decade ago yet is as stylish today as when it appeared in *Flora* magazine. Two containers of lilac-grey pottery are linked by a free form base of wood. The background of chocolate brown enhances the looped strips of coconut palm and cream basketry cane. I was given this long palm husk on the eve of departure from the United States of America. The only way to get it into my suitcase was to soak it in water and then cut it into strips lengthways. Flower arrangers will go to any lengths to get their treasures home. It has since been round the world with me and proved versatile material. Here three strips form a three-dimensional frame for pink anthuriums and lilac heads of decorative onion. *Allium karataviense* has broad basal leaves of glaucous green. The flower head of tightly packed starry florets forms an umbel the size of an orange. It

grows on thick stems about nine inches high which recommends it to the edge of borders or the rock garden. Best planted in groups the seedheads prolong the decorative effect. Young rugose leaves of *Hosta sieboldiana* 'Elegans' hide the mechanics and add a subtle note of grey-green to this predominantly pink, beige and brown composition. Strong visual tension exists between the upper and lower arrangements created by lines of bleached rattan purchased from handicraft shops. The spherical effect of the upper encloses space whilst the lower repeats this movement, but with a broken line of cane.

The design was inspired by the *Mother and Child* sculpture of Henry Moore and influenced by string inclusions in the work of Barbara Hepworth. These two great abstract sculptors of the twentieth century are a rich source of inspiration to students of modern floral design.

INSPIRED BY LOTUS FIELDS

The arrangement of pink flowers and brown lotus pods in Illustration 52 appears simple in concept. A series of parallel

52 *Inspired by Lotus Fields*

stems topped with upward-facing flowers or seedheads forms the basic design. Closer inspection will show that it consists of three separate groups united by foliage. They seem to grow from a favourite rectangular container of fawn pottery, shown more fully in Illustration 8.

This is an example of a style already touched upon in Chapter 1, Illustration 5. The parallel grouping or bundling of stems is still new to Britain and originated in Continental Europe. I predict it will become much more popular because of its freshness, simplicity and ease of assembly. The flowers literally grow from the water arranged on pinholders concealed by leaves of *Pelargonium tomentosum*. This heart-shaped scented geranium has been cherished by gardeners since it was introduced in 1790. Over-wintered in a frost-proof greenhouse the emerald green leaves are covered with velvety hairs irresistible to the touch, in this case without detriment to the texture.

Leaves of tinted tree paeony foil the central cluster of 'Pink Delight' rose buds, a florist's variety. Slender spires of pearly pink Penstemon 'Hidcote Pink' came to me originally from Wallington in Northumberland. It is probably a hybrid of garden origin and flowers over a long period until cut by frost.

Three pink and cream Cymbidium orchids introduce a note of the exotic. They are among the most long lasting of cut flowers which compensates for their cost. Behind are the wavy leaves of Hartstongue Fern also used in Illustration 13. The rigid outline of *Phyllitis scolopendrium crispum* is ideal as a backing although not entirely reliable as cut foliage, so resoak leaves that wilt.

The curious perforated seed capsules of Sacred Lotus resemble the rose of some outsize watering can and are imported stemless from the Orient. *Nelumbo nucifera* has fragrant pale pink flowers which rise from the water amidst umbrella-like leaves. It is upon this flower or leaf that Buddha sits, hence its high regard in the East. To mount the seedheads pass a stub wire through a seed hole and out near the stalk scar at the back. Hook the wire over and pull from the back to bury the hook into the fleshy pulp so that it is invisible. The wire support can then be pushed into a hollow bamboo cane to give a false stem. Grouped with pink gerbera 'Hildegard' it reminds me of the masses of lotus flowers I saw growing in Thailand with beautiful green seed pods.

This style of design has many applications and can be tried with any straight-stemmed flowers for height. The fun comes when using shorter items as lower ground cover. So many plants that I have long eschewed as being too fussy suddenly take on new value. Grouped together from front to back in an arrangement they create different textures like paths through a landscape.

CORPS DE BALLET

Clear or tinted Perspex is one of the most exciting of modern materials for containers, giving to the flowers an etherial quality which frees them from conventional surroundings. I have several custom made to my own design. The stand in Illustration 53 of clear lucite tubing mounted on a heavy base is the most versatile. By adding extra lengths it can be extended up to sixty inches and dismantles for easy storage or travel. Small round platforms fit into each tube with plugs of Perspex. A four-inch plastic saucer filled with Oasis is taped to each platform.

This colourless container gives me complete freedom of design and choice of material, but experience has taught me that lightweight flowers of pale tints look best. Against a dark background this looks dramatic. Here five 'Honetta' white anthuriums with a pink spadix suggest elegant flamingos. Placed horizontally they generate arresting movement in both directions across the vertical stand. This line is further accentuated by clusters of fresh green bamboo cut at an angle to heighten the streamlined effect. Left over stalks of gerbera could be used if bamboo is not available.

Three centrally placed arrangements counterbalance at the junction of the stems with the tubes. These consist of pale pink gerbera 'Clara' and the clustered double heads of *Pelargonium* 'Apple Blossom'. This old variety of zonal geranium always reminds me of a ballerina's tutu. Layers of greenish white petals expand to pale pink and change to deeper rose with age and sunlight. It can be grown outdoors in pots or bowls in summer, but looks best protected in a cool greenhouse.

Two varieties of hosta are included because of their white and green variegation. The broader green margined with white is *Hosta crisupula*, the most striking of the white-margined cultivars. However, it has many impersonators and is frequently confused with *Hosta* 'Thomas Hogg'. I find *H. crispula* sulks for a year or two after division and only a sheltered well-manured position will enable it to show its superior qualities. If over exposed to wind and weather the leaf edges become badly scorched and discoloured.

The other variety is a robust form of *Hosta undulata uni-vittata* with a broad central band of creamy white edged with green. The leaf forms a spiral twist which adds grace to the design. This is an ideal plant for massing amidst trees and shrubs in shady areas of the garden.

In order to reduce the shiny stems of the container I have draped trails of Spanish Moss from each group. This strange plant *Tillandsia usneoides* is epiphytic; it grows on other plants but does not seek nourishment from them.

It makes a spectacular sight hanging in long pendulous tufts many feet long from trees which line the streets of such cities as Savannah, Georgia. Within the plantations of the Deep South it is an abiding feature and for me a reminder of

gracious people who still have the old world courtesy of Melanie and Ashley Wilkes in *Gone with the Wind*. These strands were gathered in Bermuda where salt-laden breezes prevent it becoming established in any but the most sheltered gardens.

A SPLIT-LEVEL CENTRE-PIECE

Illustration 54 shows a table centre-piece adaptable to countless variations of plant material. Two clear Perspex (Plexiglass) sheets support each other by means of a central groove cut half-way down the top of the smaller sheet at the same length up from the bottom of the taller piece. Slotted together at right angles they stand on a circular base raised on four small feet. This original design packs flat in a suitcase and although Perspex is heavy to carry, when I arrive in some distant country it is a comfort to have a familiar container.

Three sets of short tubes act as holders for three pairs of fifteen-inch candles, the easycare table cloth exactly matches their deep peach pink. Unity of colour, elegance of line and distinctive plant material all combine to create a sophisticated centre-piece which would add glamour to a modern table setting.

A Perspex plate four inches in diameter clips on to the taller section to hold a saucer of foam. A lower saucer sits on the base in one of the quarters diagonally opposite. Five-inch holes cut low in the Perspex allow stems to radiate through and across so the flowers appear to spring from within the Perspex. The upper group is balanced by this asymmetric placement. Two smaller holes cut one in each sheet add interest and permit driftwood or tendrils to be threaded through. This simple yet versatile design has been much admired in many countries and I hope has inspired some of my audiences to copy the idea.

Peach-pink gerbera 'Beatrix' named for the Queen of the Netherlands, are used as focal material but pride of place goes to clusters of black succulents. *Aeonium arboreum* has branching stems terminating in flat rosettes. I was given this dramatic variety by Madame Marnier de la Postal from her husband's fantastic garden on Cap Ferrat. He called it 'Tete

54 A Split-Level Centre-Piece

du Noir' but 'Black Head' sounds less attractive when translated. *A. arboreum* 'Folis Perpuria' is found in the Canary Islands, Morocco and Ethiopia. In summer it grows in a large pot on our terrace and draws visitors like a loadstone, the hotter the weather the deeper its colour. Tufted egrets of black foliage add elegance in the same curious colour. Described in Illustration 2, *Ophiopgon planiscarpus nigrescens* also enjoys a similar position outside, but is hardy, retaining its sombre shade all winter. Contrast of colour comes from the golden green leaves of *Pelargonium zonale* 'Golden Fleece', a foliage plant bedded out with yellow, orange and apricot perennials. I nip out the double pink flowers to increase the supply of leaves and improve the impact of the colour scheme.

Placed top left and lower right are the apricot to cream tinted pokers of *Kniphofia* 'Dawn Sunkist', described in Illustration 29. This choice variety flowers in September and is worth waiting for. A few florets of *Alstroemeria* 'Ligtu Hybrids' pick up all the colours used with peach petals, lime green throats and black stencilled veins. It really pleases me when I find nature has come up with the same colour scheme! Airy panicles of brown-stemmed cream-flowered *Heuchera* 'Palace Purple' add the finishing touch of grace.

BACKGROUND AND LIGHTING

An arrangement can be made to look very much better by the way it is lit and because of the background against which it is presented. In Illustration 55 a simple design of white flowers takes on a more dramatic quality because of the purple background and table cloth.

Reserved for emperors, purple is a spiritual colour which commands both attention and respect. One of the three sec-

55 *Background and Lighting*

ondary colours it is a mixture of red and blue. Purple with a high proportion of red gives magenta, a colour used for the clerical robes of primates and bishops. Where blue has the higher proportion a more receding purple is evolved, a colour called hyacinth blue. Add white to this and the most beautiful tint of purple is created, a soft lavender blue called Claire de Lune or moonlight. This is one of the three great colours used in Chinese porcelain together with celadon green and ox-blood red – an example of a highly refined triadic harmony evolved by Oriental artists hundreds of years ago.

Used in such quantity purple could dominate this arrangement, yet by skilful lighting it stands out in clear profile. Two heads of Nile Lily, *Agapanthus umbellatus* 'Albus' are placed parallel to two chunky brown candles of pitted texture. These relate in colour to the basket of unstripped woven osiers.

A horizontal line of leek heads *Allium porrum* is balanced by New Zealand Flax leaves split and curved into loops. They give the effect of a bow and underline the interwoven texture of the container. Drooping panicles of white Butterfly Bush give strong focal accent together with three white 'Angora' dahlias. *Buddleia davidii* 'White Profusion' is a feature of our white border in August when it is spangled with peacock and red admiral butterflies. The russet seedheads which follow are also an interesting feature.

Arranging flowers is allied to painting, and depth can be achieved by adding darker flowers as if etching in the shadows. Here the deep purple of *Buddlia davidii* 'Black Knight' underlies the horizontal leek heads. In the centre the velvety blooms of clematis 'The President' strengthen the focal area. Contrast of colour comes from the yellow-green leaves of the Indian Bean Tree, *Catalpa bignonioides* 'Aurea' used individually in order not to rob such a slow-growing tree. The finished result is a design of simplicity, but also of strength emphasized by the strong plaited form of the basket and the rough texture of the leek heads and dahlias.

Placed on a low coffee table or on a buffet table this arrangement of white flowers would look most effective in the evening. Try to ensure that your arrangements receive good light, either from a table or standard lamp, which will increase their impact. Candles add a magic of their own as well as a note of festivity, but always ensure they will burn clear of the plant material.

a dull November day when we feel the need for the sunshine colours of yellow peppers, grapefruit and orange tangerines.

This analogous colour harmony begins in the blue sector of the colour wheel with two slender bottles of Mdina glass. Made near the Silent City they are prized mementoes of my visits to the Malta Flower Club. Beside them stands a flagon of Swedish glass in a lovely greenish brown, the colour of seaweed. These elegant and varied shapes enhance the composition giving it the quality of a still-life painting.

Turquoise blue, a blue mixed with green, is used for the cloth and background thus creating a setting which emphasizes the yellow and complementary orange of the fruit. Three placements of pure green – a grapefruit, rhododendron leaf and pepper – link the turquoise to the lime green flowers. The rayonnanthe chrysanthemums and sprays of miniature cymbidiums reflect the traces of yellow-green in the lower bottle. The chrysanthemums are a late indoor variety called 'Green Goddess' and will only produce this remarkable colour in low daylight conditions. A cluster of red-brown twigs and rounded leaves of *Bergenia* 'Glockenturm' pick up the marking on the orchid's lip.

From these lime green colours we move to the pure yellow of box or bell peppers, *Capsicum annum* centre front and the spray or ornamental Chinese peppers, *Capsicum frutescens* lower right. They flow from this Thai basket as if from a cornucopia, the silken cord handle continuing the line. The basket was a gift from the Lookout Mountain Garden Club of America, Tennessee. At the centre we reach the rosy yellow of pink-fleshed grapefruits and the pure orange of tangerines.

Fruits or flowers arranged without leaves would be a bald affair. Looped leaves of *Phormium tenax* 'Variegata' lead our eye over the back of the basket whilst the reversed tan colour of *Rhododendron faloneri* and bronze-red *Bergenia* 'Glockenturm' consolidate the focal area.

This is one of my favourite plates in this book because I enjoy creating still-life designs. It employs economy of material yet conveys a sense of abundance. Each crisply defined placement is satisfying to the eye and worthy of inclusion in the composition. I arrange from the heart rather than from the head so colour harmony is instinctive rather than analytically premeditated. However, I hope my readers will try for themselves some simple object grouping with a specific colour scheme in mind for good colour harmony is essential to our art.

STILL LIFE IN THE MODERN MANNER

We do not always need flowers to make a colourful decoration. In winter when flowers are scarce and expensive the green grocers' shops are filled with a wealth of beautiful fruits rich in form and texture. Illustration 56 was created on

FOR THE MUSEUM OF MODERN ART

I do not know of any herbacious perennials that start to flower at the beginning of winter, except *Eryngium proteiflorum*. Delaroux's Mexican Sea Holly requires a sunny well-drained soil and is unremarkable until it starts to flower in October. From a rosette of barbed strap-like leaves arise eighteen-inch long stems terminating in a cone of tightly packed flowers guarded by an armoury of steely bracts. This metallic collar etched from platinum and suffused with green is more curious than beautiful, yet makes a fascinating addition to the total effect. Often spoilt by frost I was lucky to have three blooms for Illustration 57 in mid November.

The triangular pot of almost Aztec severity, the texture of sandpaper, is shaded from green through brown to beige. To compensate for the small foot a heavy rock ensures that its centre of gravity is stable. Over this is fitted a block of Dry-foam. Two bold pieces of dried Royal Palm collected in Venezuela give inward curving height. *Roystonea regia* is native to Cuba and has sheathing leaf stalks which wrap around the trunk at the summit of the tree. Periodically these ten-foot long leaves are shed, together with its supporting

sheath of cream fibrous membrane. This can be cut into strips, soaked in water, then fashioned into fantastic shapes and dried. See Chapter 7, Illustration 107 for another example.

An ascending curve of tan-coloured clipped palmetto palms foil the sea holly arranged in concealed tubes of water. Bleached pods of a tropical tree cascade over the rim of the vase. At the centre five 'Grannie Smith' apples mounted on food skewers pick up the green of the flowers, pot and background. The antique chenille texture of two large heads of Crested Cockscomb *Celosia cristata* were once deep magenta now dried to a lovely tone of ox-blood red.

Exciting movement and rhythm comes from tendrils of Morning Glory gathered in Bermuda. Whilst we strive to grow this azure trumpeted convolvulus in pots the subtropical gardener wages war on the ever-advancing bindweed.

56 *Still Life in the Modern Manner*

Ipomoea and Pharbitis belong to a vast tribe of rampant climbers which left unchecked will cover everything in sight. The bare vines make interesting line material which associates well with the other dry elements. This design, accentuated by dramatic lighting, would make a striking decoration for the atrium of a museum of modern art.

ADVENT PURITY

In Illustration 58 creamy white and green flowers, foliage and candles convey a sense of purity for Advent. By using only flowers of the same tint a composition of elegant simplicity expresses this pre-Christmas season of penitence.

The container is a stand of bronze-green Perspex (Plexi-glass) designed to pack flat. Two upright plates of different heights slot into a rectangular base. Two horizontally placed pieces of different lengths, but the same width and thickness, slide into grooves cut in the uprights. The central cross plate ensures rigidity to a versatile unit which can be arranged in many ways at three levels.

Slender stems of white *Liatris spicata* 'Alba', the Kansas Feather Flower, continue the line of the cream candles used in parallel. Counterpoised against these verticals is a pair of asymmetrical arrangements composed of upward-pointing buds of *Lillium longiflorum* and downward-curving sprays of *Euphorbia fulgens*. This tropical shrub has fiery orange flowers, but white and yellow varieties exist. It is a native of Mexico as is the Poinsettia, *Euphorbia pulcherrima*, both have insignificant flowers but are surrounded by colourful

57 *For the Museum of Modern Art*

bracts which give the same effect. When cut they exude a milky sap which should be sealed in a flame.

Five Slipper Orchids emphasize the horizontal line, their white standard petals offset their green pouch. Once called Cypripedium they are known as Paphiopedilum, a name less easy to say or remember. Their poise and refinement add much to the design.

Creamy green ivy leaves and sprigs of Blue Fir, *Abies nobilis* 'Glauca' tell us that Christmas is near. This long-lasting fragrant tree is the basis of many festive designs in Chapter 9. Clotted-cream carnations complete the picture. The decoration has an air of distinction which comes from unity of colour, crispness of line and perfection of material for which I am constantly indebted to my florist. The base cloth of coarse green linen supplies a contrasting texture to the glossy container; the introduction of obvious contrast is necessary in a monochromatic design.

A CHRISTMAS GIFT

Our gardener Allan Buckle is skilled at weaving wreaths of home-grown vines and has combined three to make this shallow basket. He uses three varieties to make the circlets I need for Christmas presents decorated in a variety of ways. The largest leaved and most rampant is the Chinese Vine *Vitis coignetiae*. Pruned in November after its colourful leaves have fallen, the rich brown stems and curly tendrils give the basket character. Less attractive but prolific is *Vitis riparia* 'Brant' with bark that tends to split. The ornamental purple-leaved *Vitis vinifera* 'Purpurea' used in Illustration 13 is less vigorous but has the added advantage of lasting well when cut, plus decorative fruits.

Three circlets of equal diameter are placed one above another then wired together. A twelve-inch plastic saucer filled with foam sits snugly within the nest of wreaths. Large

59 *A Christmas Gift*

cones from the maritime *Pinus pinaster* are wired to make them sit upright. Pass a heavy gauge wire half-way round the lower scales then twist the two ends together. With a pair of pliers tighten towards the stem scar to ensure the cone is held firmly. Use the two wire ends as a double-ended mount by squeezing them together.

Branches of blue fir spray out horizontally from an under-planting of bun moss and glossy rounded leaves of *Galax aphylla*. These tough long-lasting leaves are imported from America where they grow wild in the Smokey Mountains. They are hard to find on sale in Britain but indispensible to American designers. A superior evergreen fern sprouts from behind three white candles. *Polystichum braunii* has glossy evergreen leaves which turn bronze with age. Like many ferns propagated by division it is slow to increase and consequently difficult to find except with fern specialists. Beside it are placed the brown fruiting spores of the Ostrich Plume or Shuttlecock Fern, *Matteuccia struthiopteris*.

Two groups of Slipper Orchids sprout from clusters of striped *Liriope muscari* leaves used to offset the bareness of their stems. The colour, waxy texture and poise of these elegant Paphiopedilums sets them apart from other flowers. Stubby and slender candles pick up the white of their standard petal whilst the taffeta ribbon bow reinforces their main colour. Clusters of fresh berries add a note of festive red and bring to the recipient an extra touch of luxury – cherries in December. Note how the red cloth exactly matches and restores the balance of red in the composition.

A WINTER STILL LIFE

Out of the context of the kitchen even the humble cauliflower takes on decorative possibilities, after all it is a flower. You must on occasion dare to be different. The bulk of the still-life group in Illustration 60 is a bundle of twigs supported in a basket of rope vine. These prunings of our pleached lime trees are pollarded each November as their tips of sealing-wax red glitter in the winter sunshine. A neat binding of hessian ribbon holds them in place, their tops cropped level.

On the right concealed tubes of water hold a spray of albino ivy. It will last a month in water but never root for it is without chlorophyll to manufacture food. Long catkins of *Garrya elliptica* cascade downwards with a mass of pale green catkins. The leaden green leaves are uninteresting and better trimmed to improve the effect of the flowers. This native shrub of Oregon prefers a south or west position against a wall, however ours survives and flourishes in a north-east corner of the garden. It should not be pruned unless overgrown and then only immediately after flowering in early March. The flowers are borne on the well-ripened wood of the previous summer.

Beside this group stands an old knife box filled with pebbles for stability. It supports a string of garlic and has a primitive quality in keeping with the vegetables. The cauliflower, a member of the *Brassica* family, is an unopened inflorescence or flower bud; as it is stemless three wooden skewers ensure support in the kitchen utensil.

On the left a curly head of Endive is a cut-leaved form of chicory, *Cichorium endivia*. Once regarded as medicinal, in the variety 'Crispa' the deeply dentate leaves have a mass of Medusa-like curls. The exquisite colour is the result of blanching. Two oyster fungi are much-travelled treasures with a rugged form and texture in contrast to the unopened mushrooms impaled on cocktail sticks.

This bundle of twigs illustrates how one form can be massed together to create another. It has a sculptural quality which I find satisfying even undecorated. To summarize modern design: simplicity of material and severity of line are both important. It is, however, that touch of the unexpected that adds the indefinable quality we call distinction.

CHAPTER 5
IN THE GRAND MANNER

Historic houses with their stately settings give scope for arrangements in the grand manner. Though few of us live in such great buildings, the advent of the flower festival has given many arrangers the opportunity to decorate on a scale beyond every-day experience. It is this very scale which is most daunting, calling for extra-large containers and especially sound mechanics. Utilize existing fixtures and fittings wherever possible, for extraneous objects rarely accord with the existing decor.

Britain has the best collection of historic houses untouched by conquest or revolution in the world. Many of the finest are rich in floral inspiration from the neo-classical period of the eighteenth century. An appreciation of history coupled with a sense of period are essential to the arranger in order to capture the spirit of the past yet impart to the setting that feeling of a lived-in home. Only flowers, people and family pets can achieve this effect.

A PEDESTAL AT FARNLEY HALL

The Music Room at Farnley Hall illustrates the need for dramatic scale as the eye travels upwards to the plaster frieze and coved ceiling. The pedestal in Illustration 61 was once a six-foot mahogany bed post. Mounted on to a platform base and with a square top, I bought it for a few pounds many years ago. The mechanics consist of a large metal bowl sixteen inches in diameter into which is soldered a hollow metal tube eight inches long. A thirty-two-inch long steel rod slides snuggly into this tube. On to the rod are securely strapped with Oasis tape, a selection of graduated plastic cones, filled with wedges of Oasis. These cones are used to elevate the flowers and to extend the length of short-stemmed material. The tin is firmly wired to the pedestal so that this combined weight gives complete stability thus pre-

venting any forward movement as gravity takes a hand. Never skimp on this initial preparation as there is nothing more frustrating than insecure mechanics when part way through the creative process.

Next comes the selection of the plant material. The outline is usually of branches of foliage or blossom. It is advisable, if possible, to gather your own material rather than rely on offers of material picked by others. This will often be too short or the wrong shape, for rarely can two people visualize the same finished effect. Pay especial attention to the conditioning, large wilted branches are not easily removed and replaced once the decoration is complete. Graceful downward curving material will be needed to avoid the flowers appearing like a coloured lollipop on a stick, disconnected from their surroundings. Here sprays of white beam approximately five feet long make a bold statement. The underside of *Sorbus aria* 'Lutescens' is pale celadon green and even more attractive than its upper surface. The focal flowers must be of sufficient boldness to hold the viewer's attention. Here *Lillium auratum*, the Sacred Lily of Japan, have heads which face both ways; they require careful placement so they can be made to face full front. The area between the outline and the focal flowers is one of transitional shapes. Try to organize your pointed flowers such as gladioli to form the top of the design graduating down to more rounded shapes.

Bold leaves such as grey-blue *Hosta sieboldiana* 'Elegans' are ideal to hide the rod and tubes. Peach-pink dahlias repeat the wall colour and large double stocks exactly match the antique rose-pink of the Aubusson carpet. The grouping of flowers within the whole composition creates paths along which the eye subconsciously travels. Pale pink carnations, roses, cream chrysanthemums and blue agapanthus with blue globe thistles, *Echinops rito*, all echo the pastel tints and tones of the room. A note of contrast comes from the purple leaves of *Prunus cerasifera* 'Pissardii' adding depth just as a painter adds shadows to give the third dimension to a picture.

The most interesting feature of this Palladian room is the collection of watercolours by Turner. The artist was a frequent guest and left it to his hosts, the Horton-Fawkes family. It forms a unique record of the interiors and the landscapes of Airedale in the early ninteenth century.

FLOWERS AT FAIRFAX HOUSE, YORK

The City of York takes pride in its many fine buildings. One of the most notable is the town house of the Viscount Fairfax completed in 1762. At one time a cinema and then a dance hall it has been painstakingly restored by York Civic Trust. It houses a superb collection of eighteenth-century furniture amassed by the late Noel Terry. The house is enhanced by the furniture which in turn is displayed to perfection in a contemporary setting. I was privileged to take the late Arthur Negus there and he was most impressed and enthusiastic.

Illustration 62 shows one of a pair of beautifully proportioned pedestal stands or torchères designed by Thomas Chippendale to hold candelabra. It makes an ideal stand because of the stability of the wide tripod foot. Placed on the upper landing it affords a view of the elegant staircase. The pale blue walls and delicate plaster moulding suggest an orange and blue complementary colour scheme. The carpet has apricot-orange border motifs. The flowers are arranged in a smaller version of the tin used in the previous plate also fitted with a rod and cones for elevation. It sits snuggly inside the hexagonal gallery top which is protected from possible water damage by thick polythene.

61 *A Pedestal at Farnley Hall*

The outline consists of a shrub rose with glaucous foliage and apricot-orange hips. *Rosa moyesii* 'Highdownensis' is not unlike its parent *Rosa moyesii*, but has carmine-pink flowers as opposed to red with a profusion of flask-shaped hips. Sprays of Mountain Ash berries stripped of their leaves reinforce the autumnal theme.

Three large orange decorative dahlias 'Quel Diable' create strong focal impact. The medium decorative 'Katisha' dahlias taper off lower left developing the transition to the outline. On the right three stems of *Lillium henryi* with pendant flowers on arching stems repeat this movement. This is an easy species to grow having persisted twenty years in our garden. Apricot-orange gladioli are placed at the top together with the arching flowers and leaves of *Curtonus paniculata*. This Giant Monbretia used to be called *Antholyza paniculata* hence its common name of 'Aunt Eliza'. The flower stalk is maroon which sets off the tubular flowers of burnt orange. The pleated leaves are useful air dried, pressed or preserved in glycerine solution.

Blue flowers are not particularly showy in a pedestal because of their receding colour, but are used here to harmonize with the walls. The dainty blue *Agapanthus mooreanus* is combined with the steely blue thistle heads of *Echinops rito*. This thistle dries well for winter decoration if gathered before it opens. Perhaps the real conversation piece is the *Eryngium alpinum*; this steely blue sea holly has a collar of fine lace which sets it apart from all others. The European eryngiums have rounded leaves on long pedicels as opposed to the striking New World species which have strap-like serrated leaves. An outstanding example being *Eryngium proteiflorum* used in Chapter 4, Illustration 57.

All the flowers are foiled by blue-grey hosta leaves of the *Hosta sieboldiana* 'Elegans' type. I have grown them from seed gathered from *Hosta* 'Frances Williams' so they vary

62 *Flowers at Fairfax House, York*

89

63 *The Formal Dining Table, Fairfax House*

somewhat in their colouration and leaf shape. The late Eric Smith did much work on the hybridization of the smaller blue-green hostas and a few of his *Hosta* 'Halcyon' are also included with a long cut life. They also form the basis of the dining table decoration in Illustration 63.

FORMAL DINING-TABLE DECORATIONS

Dinner-table decorations can be made in a wide variety of styles, the natural complement to food and wine. They always arouse comment and sometimes controversy at exhibitions. Because they are to be viewed from all sides and every angle by seated guests, certain limitations are imposed. The popular teaching that they should be low in order not to impede conversation is sensible, yet the most memorable tables I can recall are those that broke this rule. Aim at creating three main levels of interest: high candles for preference, lower flowers and then napery and place setting. At banquets and large formal tables flowers arranged much higher than eye level can look dramatic and in proportion. On such occasions guests will not be speaking across a wide table, but to the guest right and left of them.

The majority of tables are for exhibition purposes and I have included two examples in this chapter. The place setting should be limited to dessert with bowls of fruit, dessert plates, fruit eaters and port or madeira wine glasses the only necessary accessories. Illustration 63 shows the table at Fairfax House set for six people with Chinese export plates from the Nanking cargo rescued from the sea bed. The centrepiece is a silver palm tree which matches the fanciful candelabra with their paw feet and reptilian engraved legs, reminders of the British rule in India. Both are of a later date than the mahogany sideboard and fine Georgian knife urns. The pair to the pedestal supports a gourd-shaped Chinese vase.

A seven-inch plastic saucer is attached to the palm tree. Use a red hot poker stub wire to pierce four holes just below the rim of the saucer and attach with silver reel wire to the palm fronds. Dainty powder blue delphiniums echo the wall colour teamed with a selection of garden flowers. The small border carnations tone with 'Apricot Nectar' roses, rowan berries and some delicate maroon wild grasses. Touches of blue are supplied by the dainty *Agapanthus mooreanus* whilst bowls of peaches repeat the colour of dahlia 'Sondeveg' and pale gerberas the tint of the candles.

A FORMAL TABLE AT RUDDING PARK, HARROGATE

The dining-room at Rudding Park was the brilliant assemblage of Sir Everard Ratcliffe, a connoisseur of beautiful things. Illustration 64 records the contents displayed for an

64 *The Formal Table, Rudding Park*

exhibition in 1971, sadly they were later sold and all dispersed. The table is set with a magnificent Worcester dessert service of twenty place settings. Down the centre of the table are porcelain ice pails, bowls of fruit, silver pineapple stands in the form of palm trees and candlesticks.

The Regency centre-piece and matching three-branch candelabra by Paul Storr are filled with flowers set well above the heads of seated guests. A candle cup holder replaces the central candle. The blocks of Oasis sit proud of these holders enabling the flowers and foliage to be arranged flowing downwards.

I used similar splendid pieces at Badminton House for the visits of Her Majesty the Queen and the Royal Family between 1968 and 1980. For those twelve years the Duchess of Beaufort asked me to create the flower arrangements for the Three Day Event. The experience taught me many things. Always check your table just before and to ensure that the mechanics are covered, view the finished result from every angle, especially sitting down.

In this centre-piece, slender cream butterfly gladioli with crimson throats combine with pale pink carnations and pendant trails of Love Lies Bleeding in green and red. The chenille-like flowers of amaranthus last a long time and dry to a soft beige. Tendrils of purple grape vine, *Vitis vinifera* 'Purpurea', ladder ferns and Bells of Ireland, all help to add individuality. *Molucella laevis* is a native of Syria and can be grown as an annual. It can be difficult to germinate, but when well grown the green bracts surrounding the flowers are most unusual. First strip off the foliage. It will take glycerine solution turning to a parchment-cream colour.

A BLACKAMOOR OF AUTUMN BRILLIANCE AT HOVINGHAM HALL

In illustration 67 the brilliance of autumnn flowers lends itself to the mellow setting of old books and a fine Oriental rug. The gilded blackamoor container, one of a pair, is fitted with a six-inch flower saucer and placed on a Regency library table. The fine bronze horse in the alcove reminds us that the first Sir William Worsley built Hovingham Hall to house his horses as well as his family. An enormous riding school and three stone vaulted rooms intended as stables bear witness to his enthusiasm for all things equine.

The arrangement consists of an outline of berried shrubs, the most graceful being *Euonymus latifolius*, a decorative member of the Spindle Tree family from Europe. In September the branches are hung with rosy pink fruits which split to reveal orange seeds. By October the whole tree has turned a brilliant maroon red. Even in winter its outline gives me pleasure. With it are sprays of the fearsomely spiny *Berberis* 'Buccaneer'. The translucent fruits shade from green to scarlet red on arching stems. I have since rooted it

out having decided that it was so frightful to handle it did not earn the large space it occupied. I think one has to be rather ruthless about garden occupants from time to time, especially if they do not fully earn their keep.

The roses are second crop 'Super Star', a vivid colour hard to place in the garden, and the climber 'Meg' with single apricot-orange flowers. Interspersed amidst the mixed dahlias are *Dianthus* 'Doris' and one or two red hot pokers. This design would be very imposing on a buffet table as it lifts the flowers well above the level of the food.

STILL LIFE AT HOVINGHAM HALL, YORK

As an alternative to a formal dinner table the buffet table offers tremendous scope, from quite simple everyday living to the rich bavaura of Illustrations 65 and 66 (see pages 94 and 95). These two still-life decorations were created for a twenty-foot long refectory table at Hovingham Hall, York, the birth place of HRH The Duchess of Kent. They are an elaborate collection of associated objects evocative of the still-life paintings of the seventeenth century; a favourite style for me which offers exciting plant associations juxtaposed with objects of beauty or curiosity.

The triadic colour scheme of crimson red, grey-blue and orange has additional neutral tones of beige and brown united by the background tapestries. Large copper pans, two charcoal braziers and gilded altar candlesticks give weight and interest to the composition. An oak bench below the massive table holds a mandolin and vellum sheet of antique music. With such lovely accessories to set the scene it is easy to combine flowers and foliages with richness of form and texture.

Great height is achieved by using whole plants of *Onopordon arabicum*. This biennial is a tricky subject to condition and needs to be boiled for a minute then left standing in deep water for two days to harden. Avoid immersing the felted grey leaves picked from first year plants. Large clipped palms *Chamaerops humilis* 'Argentea' and branches of Blue Atlantic cedar *Cedrus atlantica Glauca* add breadth.

The inclusion of pot plants gives an exotic quality without the necessity of cutting them. Water the plant well, knock it gently from its pot and place it in a polythene bag. This makes it easier to incorporate in the arrangement and the plant can be returned to its pot later. The variegated pineapple, *Ananas comosus* 'Variegatus', pink-leaved paper plant *Caladium bicolor* and maroon *Begonia rex* are all treated in this way. Large dried leaves of a giant Bay Grape, *Coccolobis pubescens* are used to conceal the root ball. I first saw this enormous tropical shrub at Cypress Gardens in Florida. These leaves were purchased in Belgium, soaked under water they return to a malleable state and can be fashioned into interesting shapes.

In both compositions fruits add an extra dimension to the still life. In Illustration 66 a cut water melon, cherries, dried bottle gourds, oranges, okra pods and dried *Gunnera manicata* cones are linked together by tendrils of bleached wisteria vine. A lobster so beloved of still-life painters, was first boiled, cleaned and the shell carefully glued together with string to animate the legs and claws. A little poster paint added cosmetic appeal.

The flowers are blocked together to give impact from a distance. Pale parchment yellow iris, tangerine orange carnations and crimson amaryllis pick out the fruit colours. These two designs, complementary to each other, are amongst my favourites, full of interest and with a freedom of movement. They incorporate many individual sections each of which could be used as the prototype for a smaller composition on a buffet table.

FLOWERS AT SUTTON PARK, YORK

Yorkshire is a county rich in country houses and one of the most attractive and best maintained is Sutton Park, the home of Mrs Reginald Sheffield. It is filled with exquisite furniture and links with her husband's ancestors, the Dukes of Buckingham. The entrance hall has an interesting picture of Buckingham House before it was sold to George III by Sir Charles Sheffield, Bt, to become a royal palace, offset by walls of Chinese yellow.

The flowers in Illustration 68 stand on a gilded pier table with a *faux* marble top of siennese gold. The alabaster comport supported by dolphins is fitted with a plastic liner because of its porosity. Arranged in late summer the outline utilizes seedheads and grasses to offset the solid rounded form of chrysanthemum 'Apricot Julie Ann'. The tallest

67 *A Blackamoor at Hovingham Hall*

93

65 *Still Life at Hovingham Hall*

66 *Still Life at Hovingham Hall*

placements are of a majestic grass *Molinia caerulea altissima* in flower. It reaches five feet in the herbaceous border, a splendid exclamation mark turning to burnished straw in late autumn. Here it combines with slender reed-mace preserved in glycerine, see Chapter 9. Branching seedheads of yellow mullian, *Verbascum chaixii* and dried heads of astilbe tone with the parchment colour of the vase.

Bold leaves of *Hosta fortunei* 'Obscura Marginata' are used to pull the design together with focal weight. A lighter note comes from the silky seedheads of *Clematis recta*, a herbaceous species which requires stalking with brushwood in the garden. The masses of airy white flowers are invaluable in July though equally appealing to field mice which can decimate their display. An alternative would be the wild Old Man's Beard, *Clematis vitalba*, a rampant hedgerow climber

in southern counties of Britain. Orange cactus dahlias 'Symbol' and medium decorative 'Schweitzer's Kerkade' strengthen the colour combination. Dahlias have a bad reputation for being short-lived cut flowers. However, if all surplus foliage is removed and they are conditioned well before being arranged, they will last almost one week.

THE MORNING-ROOM

From the entrance hall we enter the library and pass into the morning-room, an intimate panelled room with an interesting collection of treen in many decorative woods. The flowers in Illustration 69 illustrate what can be done with large chrysanthemums, in this case the champagne-coloured

68 *Flowers at Sutton Park, the Entrance*

variety 'Julie Ann'. The container is a bronze Warwick vase standing on a walnut table. Above hangs the portrait of the young Earl of Mulgrave, later Marquis of Normanby. Set in a contemporary frame and flanked by the fluted pilasters of the panelling the decoration has to fit certain limits. This emphasizes the necessity always to work *in situ*.

The large blooms are softened by a variety of interesting garden material. Sweeping sprays of *Weigelia florida* 'Variegata' create the outline together with cream ivy. Two almost indistinguishable hydrangeas lend a note of pale green. On the lower right is *Hydrangea arborescens* 'Grandiflora' which has a lax habit of growth and loose flower heads which are frequently rain damaged as they touch the soil. Left of centre is the much better but rarer *Hydrangea cinerea* 'Sterilis', a sub-species with rounded heads and more

upright habit. With green tassel-like flowers is *Itea ilicifolia* from western China with elegant pendulous racemes crowded with greenish-white florets in August. It prefers acid soil and requires a sheltered position. Our plant has been slow to establish, but is growing against a dry west-facing wall.

To the left of centre are the curious spikes of *Digitalis ferruginea*, a perennial foxglove with tightly massed snuff-coloured flowers that match the Earl's coat colour. Included to lighten the arrangement are the spherical seedheads of *Allium aflatunense* and the straw-coloured clusters of *Allium bulgaricum*. They scatter their shiny black seeds leading one to suspect an infestation of house mice. A few wispy heads of the Spanish Golden Oats, *Stipa gigantea*, complete the outline.

The central foliage is a good form of *Hosta fortunei*

69 *Flowers at Sutton Park, the Morning-Room*

'Marginato-alba', a plant superior in every way to *H. albomarginata*. But you could be forgiven for being confused amidst this variable and often mislabelled tribe. Such plants are rarely offered for sale, but exchange hands between hosta enthusiasts. The variegated figwort *Scrophularia aquatica* 'Variegata' has spikes of brown flowers which are best removed to encourage the branching side shoots used here in the centre of the arrangement. To the right fronds of the Ostrich Plume Fern, *Matteuccia struthiopteris* add a note of elegance. This moisture-loving plant will run and form new shuttlecocks of fresh green leaves in spring. Like most ferns it will only last when mature and should have its stem tip singed before a long drink in deep water.

AN ELEGANT DRAWING-ROOM ARRANGEMENT

The home of Mrs Sheffield reflects her taste in every room, but none better than the elegant drawing-room with its choice collection of French furniture. Walls of cool apple green are offset by draped curtains of oyster beige silk with salmon pink lined festoons and deep fringe. The sofas are piled with silk cushions in a medley of peach, cream and turquoise, several with beadwork embroidery.

Such an exquisite setting calls for light feminine flowers and prompts the choice of a three-tiered stand placed inside a Minton tureen of turquoise blue. Short-stemmed flowers make up this airy design to be seen from all sides. The flowers are in tints of peach and apricot-pink with lavender-blue and magenta for contrast. The outline is of Purple Loosestrife, *Lythrum salicaria* 'Robert' is a plant for pondside margins. The pointed blossom of *Buddleia* 'Loch Inch' so beloved of butterflies, is mixed with magenta dendrobium orchids to add an exotic note. The rounded flower shapes grouped in clusters include an old single variety of dahlia called 'Sarah Peach', salmon-pink zonal pelargoniums, peach 'Gerdo' roses and a polyanthus rose 'Doris Ryker', both florist's varieties. A small magenta pom-pom dahlia gives contrast. Tucked in to give depth are lilac-blue hydrangeas from that useful variety 'Generale Vicomtesse de Vibraye' stripped of their leaves.

Green foliage is deliberately omitted to heighten the colour combination. Metallic maroon grey *Begonia rex* leaves are teamed with *Heuchera macrantha* 'Palace Purple' and short sprigs of *Berberis thunbergii* 'Atropurpurea'. The plum-purple berberis benefits from a severe pruning every few years in spring. This encourages long wands of new growth which will be mature enough to pick by August.

On the outer limits of the design are the dainty lilac flowers on wiry stems of *Thalictrum delavayi* 'Hewitt's Double'. It prefers cool deep soil where its finely cut foliage gives a fern-like effect.

A CRASHING RED BUFFET CENTRE-PIECE

An all-round buffet table centre-piece can be a challenge. To create something imposing, yet not solid, has various solutions. A container that elevates short-stemmed flowers to several levels can look attractive and add a note of lightness and gaiety to the occasion. Illustration 71 illustrates a wooden stand made for a large evening party at York City Art Gallery. Similar ideas could be worked out with a tiered construction of glass cake stands in graduated sizes. These can still be found in second hand shops and jumble sales. A more elegant version could be made in an alabaster vase as in Illustration 95 or a metal pagoda as in Illustration 111.

In Illustration 71 I have used a wooden stand made from six chair back spokes fifteen inches long, a three-quarter-inch dowel rod could be substituted. The three circles of wood are sixteen inches, twelve inches and eight inches respectively three-quarters of an inch thick. Three small wooden door knobs make the bun feet. Painted a glossy brownish red to imitate Chinese lacquer it resembles a small Victorian 'what-not' stand. An assortment of fruits to include black grapes, cut water melon, aubergines, red peppers and oranges are grouped in three dishes of Oasis by impaling them on wooden cocktail sticks. Be sure everything is firm as the finished piece has considerable weight.

The flowers are deep ruby 'Bladon Red' dahlias, sugar-pink nerines, vibrant orange 'Clemantine' gerberas, with cerise and tangerine-orange carnations. A few blooms of the scarlet Kaffir Lily, *Schizostylis coccinea* add late garden flower interest. These South African flowers last a long time in red or pink and bloom up to Christmas in mild seasons. The foliage is dark red azalea and orange skeletonized magnolia leaves topped off with a cut rosette of *Cordyline terminalis* in cerise and dark red. Placed on a boule table and backed by a large pastoral scene this vibrant colour combination is foiled by deep russet-red walls. Its effectiveness lies in the total absence of green which would dilute the impact of the orange reds, pinks and purples. The darker touches of foliage prevent it from looking garish and add depth.

A TABLE PLATEAU WITH A PAINTING AND SCULPTURE

To arrange flowers with existing works of art such as sculpture and paintings requires restraint in order to achieve a balanced harmony between the two. With this large painting by Sawrey Gilpin I have selected light-coloured flowers to contrast with the dark canvas and mahogany-topped breakfront table. The subject is *The Election of Darius*, 1772. In the centre of the table stands the bust of John Carr 1723–1807 one of the most important architects in the North of England. His design for the Grandstand at York Racecourse

70 *An Elegant Drawing-Room, Sutton Park*

71 *A Crashing Red Centre-Piece*

72 *A Table Plateau*

brought him to the attention of the Yorkshire gentry and a fine example of his work is the stable block at Castle Howard.

In Illustration 72 the style of arrangement is a departure from the traditional massed triangle with emphasis on strong vertical and horizontal lines. Majestic spikes of cream pampas grass, *Cortaderia selloana* gathered at the silky green stage soar above spears of variegated New Zealand Flax, *Phormium tenax* 'Variegatum' and dark brown fruits of wild Reed-Mace, *Typha latifolia*. This armoury of spikes and spears echoes the vertical columns in the picture and the staves and standards carried by the horsemen in this romantic history painting which tells the story of the election of the Emperor of Persia.

Arranged in a horizontal plane are the massive leaves of *Mahonia napaulensis* with up to fifteen pairs of glossy evergreen leaflets. A native of Nepal, it is second only to *M. acanthifolia* in stature. These leaves came from the sheltered garden of Trengwainton, Cornwall. Three large flower heads of *Mahonia* 'Charity' create varied levels of interest with their spiky leaves and upright racemes of yellow flowers. Sadly it does not inherit the fragrance of its parent *M. japonica*, but puts forth a wonderful display in the dullest days of November.

To the right a cluster of creamy yellow red hot pokers continue the vertical theme. *Kniphofia* 'Little Maid' is a most desirable plant, but will only flourish in full sun and rich soil. It should be divided only in spring to give it time to re-establish itself by September.

The many rounded-shaped flowers include 'Apricot Julie' chrysanthemums, 'Bingo' gerberas and yellow carnations grouped in blocks of colour running from front to back and end to end of this eight-feet by three-feet table. Right of the bust a cluster of 'Tynwald' roses introduces focal interest and fragrance together with the curious compact heads of ginger gold cockscomb, the velvet textured *Celosia cristata*.

Tinted paeony foliage, cream ivy *Hedera colchica* 'Dentata Variegata' and *Bergenia cordifolia* under plant this garden effect. Note how large areas of polished wood are left to suggest a reflecting pool.

A PAIR OF WALL TROPHIES FOR A SOIRÉE

Created for the entrance hall of the Art Gallery, the pair of wall decorations in Illustration 73 and Illustration 74 are reminiscent of trophies carved from wood or moulded plaster. Set against deep terracotta walls and spotlit they glowed their welcome across the city square for a large evening party.

To make something similar, ensure that you have a plain expanse of wall with a stout rawl-plugged hook to take the weight. The foundation is a hexagon of wood ten inches across. A slim batten of wood forty inches long is added to support the ribbon bow and tail. These are false appendages, not intended to carry any actual weight.

Cover the wooden foundation with a layer of designer's foam soaked lightly with water. This consists of a layer of Styrofoam for strength with Dryfoam on one side and water retaining foam on the other. It is obtained from good florists, but is expensive. Two bricks of Oasis could be used as an alternative, but are not as strong. Cover the entire wet foundation with cling food wrap or thin polythene with an extra layer at the bottom where water will accumulate and perculate downwards. Over wet foam will result in dribbles down the wall, so be prepared! Encase all this carefully in a cage of one-inch mesh wire netting. This extra precaution will take the strain of heavy fruits and thick-stemmed flowers.

Fix the foundation board firmly to the wall hook with stout poker wires. Work *in situ* to create the design in order to achieve the right placement angle at or above eye level. It is easy to develop an arresting design as each item is seen in profile against the wall.

These examples were created for an autumn party so the outline materials of dried seedheads and leaves are appropriate. Select well-conditioned flowers of sturdy texture that will last without too much moisture. Begin with the outline developing two diametrically opposite movements top left to lower right and visa versa. All stems should appear to spring from the central feature, in Illustration 73 a large turban squash, *Cucurbita turbaniformis* which is anchored with wooden skewers set at an angle into the netting.

In Illustration 73 the flowers top left are *Heliconia humilis* backed by dried reed-mace. These strange Parrot's Beak flowers came from the famous Mandai Gardens, Singapore. To the right are scarlet gerbera 'Joyce' with seedheads of *Allium bulgaricum*, pleated Chinese Fan Palm, *Livistona chinensis*, and reversed leaves of *Rhododendron sinogrande*. These foil clusters of 'Doris Ryker' roses and sprays of the hot Chilli Pepper, *Capsicum frutescens* with a variegated pineapple. Flamingo carnations and sprays of albino ivy develop the downward cascading movement.

At the lower centre tufts of reindeer moss are used to conceal any gaps in the mechanics with sprays of wired red skeletonized leaves. Scarlet red roses 'Gloria Mundi' spring out over glistening black grapes with *Allium aflatunense* seedheads. Above and to the left are sprays of orange *Euphorbia fulgens*, a native of Mexico, sold as a cut flower imported in winter. Removal of surplus leaves increases the intensity of the orange flowers. Singe the cut ends in a flame or boiling water to seal the milky sap it exudes. Two bold heads of *Kniphofia* 'Prince Igor' contrast with magenta crested cockscombs. More ivy and magnolia leaves frame the scarlet crystaline flowers of *Nerine sarniensis*. Named after the water nymph Nerine, they are also known as Guernsey Lilies although they are native to South Africa. Scarlet

73 *A Pair of Wall Trophies for a Soirée*

square peppers *Capsicum annum* and rosy red apples complete this clockwise description.

The ribbon bow and tail are added as separate pieces top and bottom. Here I have used broad Belgian wreath ribbon of watered silk moiré. The overall measurements are five feet long by four feet wide and would create a talking point at any party. Fixed above eye level they create visual impact in a crowded room.

Illustration 74 has the same construction, but the materials are slightly varied thus avoiding the monotony an exact copy might produce. A purple cabbage *Brassica capitata* is substituted for the turban squash, but is smaller and therefore less effective. For floral decorators working against time this type of design has many possibilities especially where furniture and floor space are at a premium. For more permanent display they can be made of preserved leaves, gourds and seedheads as in Chapter 8, or holly and fruits for Christmas.

Castle Howard is the palace of Yorkshire, yet still the home of the Howard family. Built for the first Earl of Carlisle by Vanburgh, it is breathtaking in its site and scale. The television adaptation of Evelyn Waugh's *Brideshead Revisited* has implanted it in the public's imagination on both sides of the Atlantic. We were fortunate to decorate it with flowers in 1971 and 1984. My arrangement in Illustration 75 dates from the second festival. A massive wine cooler of black bog oak is filled with the flowers of high summer. Long branches of Mock Orange stripped of their leaves cascade on all sides. Philadelphus 'Beauclerk' has large single white flowers and stamens with prominent yellow anthers, coupled with a delicious fragrance. Cream 'Tynwald' roses, 'Mont Blanc' lilies and ivory gladioli give focal impact and height to this fountain of green and white. The variegated foliage of acer, whole plants of pineapple and dark green Cycas palms add to the dramatic effect. An all-round arrangement is never easy, but this had to form the centrepiece of the Long Gallery. Cool and imposing it concludes this chapter of flowers in the grand manner.

74 A Pair of Wall Trophies for a Soirée

75 A Wine Cooler, Castle Howard

76 *An Easter Garden*

CHAPTER 6

FLOWERS FOR
WORSHIP

For many people arranging flowers in church is an act of worship in itself. It is certainly a peaceful place to be, given time to enjoy the flowers and to reflect upon the reason for placing them there.

Each religion has its own particular calendar and within the Christian faith we observe the church's seasons, some more important than others to the flower arranger. The festival of Easter is symbolic of rebirth and new life which coincides with the awakening forces of spring in the Northern Hemisphere.

AN EASTER GARDEN

At one time every church and chapel had its Easter Garden no matter how simple or elaborate. Made by children from the church primary school it taught the bible stories more vividly than any scripture lesson. My own hesitant efforts began this way at an age too young for ridicule. Illustration 76 is an evocation of childhood efforts assembled by eager hands and nimble fingers. This example is out of doors built on a fine stone table at the entrance to Heslington Church. Protected from wind and weather by the angle of the porch and tower this south-facing tomb commands a fine view of meadows and the great hall of the Barons Deramore, now the University of York.

A quantity of river sand from a builder's merchant makes a clean basis for the garden. Piled up at one end of the slab it is set with rocks to create the tomb of Joseph of Arimathea. A smooth round one should be placed to one side to suggest the stone that was rolled away on the first Easter Sunday morning. Jam jars and smaller jars filled with crunched-up wire netting are set in the sand and firmly wedged with rocks or large pebbles, then filled with water. This can be done in readiness before Good Friday with a sombre tree of yew

placed at the back on a heavy pinholder. This was gathered from the fastigiate Irish Yews which flank the church path and possibly predate the present Victorian church.

The flowers cannot be arranged until Easter Saturday as most incumbents insist quite rightly on a total ban on flowers during Lent and on Good Friday in particular. To consult your vicar and know his wishes is only courtesy, they all have their foibles, but can usually be persuaded to let you create something worthy of the setting and occasion.

These flowers all came from our garden, but if yours is a community effort with mixed offerings, they should be conditioned well in advance. Most have soft stems and tender new growth which wilt easily. When all are collected together sort the colours so that they can be grouped in one variety rather than a haphazard mixture. Pieces of carpet or bun moss should be tucked between the jars as work progresses so that all the sand is covered except for the path to the tomb.

These flowers run through the spectrum starting with wide open early tulips on the left. These are the rock garden variety *Tulipa kauffmanniana* 'Shakespeare' backed by bronze budding branches of *Spiraea japonica* 'Goldflame' also used in Illustration 31. Beside this is a Pussy Willow of striking appearance. Small blobs of cotton wool set neatly on dark brown stems make *Salix hastata* 'Wehrhanhnii' a desirable shrub where space is limited. Cut pieces root easily in water to share with friends. Clustered below are dainty greenish white and yellow *Tulipa turkestanica* with several heads to one stem; lovely seedheads follow.

In the left foreground are massed early pink Rhododendron, cerise Bergenia and wide eyed *Anemone blanda* 'Rosea'.' Deep velvety purple Pansy 'Lord Beaconsfield' commemorate Queen Victoria's favourite prime minister, these are grouped with *Iris stylosa* 'Mary Barnard', magenta *Primula × juliana* 'Wanda' and clusters of double pink daisies, *Bellis perennis* 'Dresden China'. Fragrant heads of Hyacinth 'Amethyst' are grouped with sprigs of pink heather to complete the group.

Behind the tomb with drooping heads as if in sadness are pink Lenten Roses *Helleborus orientalis* hybrids. Placed in deep jars of water they last better outdoors than inside. The cheerful yellow of forsythia and a mixture of narcissi tell us spring is really here. They are backed by the quaint blue, mauve and pink flowers of Lungwort or Soldiers and Sailors. Although the coarse bristly leaves of *Pulmonaria saccharata* do not last in water it has a quiet charm especially in the form given to me by Margery Fish. It makes fine clumps of silvery green foliage which remain attractive until autumn.

Ranks of blue flowers line the right hand side of the path with grape hyacinths, anemones, hyacinths, pansy 'Ullswater' and the 'Glory of the Snow' *Chionodoxa luciliae* a

dazzling blue. There is also a taller pink form included called 'Pink Giant'.

Bright yellow pansies hold the viewer's eye with variegated *Euonymus* 'Emerald and Gold' leaves and winter heather *Erica carnea* 'Springwood White'. This useful ground cover plant has white flowers set off by brown stamens. Between these is a plant of double white primrose, a special treasure.

Between the plants of primroses and cut *Tulipa praestans* 'Fusilier', a name which describes its scarlet flowers, is a green hellebore purchased from that specialist, Miss Elizabeth Strangman of Hawkshurst, Kent. It is a cross between the Christmas Rose *Helleborus niger* and the Corsican Hellebore *H. corsicus*. With finely chiselled blooms of apple green this aristocratic cross is *H. nigericors* 'Alabaster' a name which says it all. Leaves of the Italian Arum and Irish ivy complete this little landscape garden.

77 An Easter Garden in York Minster

AN EASTER GARDEN IN YORK MINSTER

For several years the garden in Illustration 77 was created by me and my helpers at the invitation of the Dean of York, The Very Rev Dr RCD Jasper and Chapter of York Minster. Six-sided it measures twenty feet by twelve, a daunting expanse of sand at the outset. The foundation frame of wood, rocks and a tomb lit from within were constructed by the dedicated team of cathedral stonemasons. Backed by the arcading of the North transept wall the area is dwarfed by the massive lancets of the Five Sisters Window. This world-famous expanse of early grisaille glass, awe inspiring in its height and magnificent detail, casts an eerie light. Thousands of pieces of greenish grey glass are intermittently studded with red which shine like jewels the longer you look at them.

The flowers are similar to those used in the previous plate: it would be repetitious to list them. Assembled and constructed under the gaze of hundreds of visitors who throng the Minster it provoked countless admiring comments and one or two amusing gems like 'Do you do this every week!'

We used countless jam jars and many flowers to fill the space. As a human tide flows about one it becomes imperative to concentrate the interest by blocking the colours and group similar flowers to give maximum impact. A difficult object to photograph, Illustration 77 gives some idea of the finished effect.

On the left a large branch of weeping willow gives height, with conifers in tubs to suggest a sombre grave. The purists will say that Christ's resting place was a barren rock cave, but even the most inhospitable places shall 'like the desert blossom as the rose'. This carpet of flowers symbolizes the risen Christ and the new beginning of the Resurrection.

As this display had to last for about two weeks, vigilant topping up was necessary; for even in the sepulchral chill of York Minster the flowers are thirsty subjects. Many of the plants were lifted from the garden in late winter and potted up to be brought on in a cold greenhouse. This gives sufficient protection to guarantee that they are in full bloom and unblemished by the weather. An alternative would be to buy pots of bulbs, primroses and cinerarias. I was always impressed by the generosity of those who gave gifts of money in remembrance of loved ones.

The garden was surmounted by a huge cross of wood fixed in the central lancet. Painted a soft vermillion, a colour we call York Red, it was draped with a long white cloth to represent the shroud. This effective idea by Charles Brown, the Surveyor of the Fabric, lent a theatrical touch dramatically lit by spotlights concealed in the Chapels of St Nicholas and St John.

FLOWERS WITH A CRUCIFIX

The decoration in Illustration 78 tells the Easter story with the minimum of material. It is greatly enhanced by the fifteenth-century polychrome crucifix which is an inherent feature of the design. This object of veneration unites the two halves of the arrangement so forming the focus of our attention. I have often stated my dislike of taudry accessories used as extraneous additions, but here is an example of a beautiful artefact which improves the composition.

On the left anguish and cruelty are expressed through curving pieces of sharp palm husk. A warm reddish brown they reflect the flesh tones of the wooden effigy. Enclosed within their arc branches of Thorn Tree suggest the crown of thorns. This species of Acacia protects itself from grazing animals by these barbarous projections. Only the giraffe has adapted to feed from these flat-topped trees which are so typical of the East African landscape.

Dry brown fungi suggest death and decay and conclude this design abruptly so that our eye is drawn to the shadow of the nail. The container filled with Dryfoam is a stoneware pottery chalice. It suggests the 'cup that could not be taken away', Christ's allusion to his agony and death upon the cross.

The lower placement has a more joyous message. Brown palm husks painted black on the exterior repeat the colour and texture of the chalice. Placed in a coffin-shaped vase of lilac-grey pottery they represent the breaking open of the tomb. An upward sweep of Easter Lilies, *Lillium longiflorum*, rises triumphantly from their midst. The two containers are unified by a soft blue altar cover in harmony with Christ's loin cloth.

This powerful interpretation of the desolation of the crucifixion and the hope of the Resurrection expressed through flowers employs line, form and texture with a colour restraint that befits the subject. The crucifix belongs to Mr Roy Grant and was photographed at his home St Oswald's Hall, Fulford, formerly a church.

FLOWERS IN WESTMINSTER ABBEY

In recent years every church and chapel seems to be having a flower festival to the extent that they have become commonplace in the public eye. Truly great festivals are few, but over the years there have been some significant highlights. One of the earliest was the decoration of our national shrine, Westminster Abbey in May 1966. I was invited to represent the North East Area of the National Association of Flower Arrangement Societies of Great Britain, which was to stage this grand event. My pair of large arrangements was at the entrance to the nave and had to be created the night before, the prototype for the rest of the nave. Pairs of vases in graduated colours from magenta, red, rose-pink to cream being the final effect, set against each pair of nave pillars. Illustration 79 shows one of my finished groups.

A pair of massive lead vases filled with sand ensured a stable foundation, but the mechanics are all important and those provided presented one or two problems. Set inside the top about nine inches down was a six-foot pole attached to a flat board weighted with bricks. Spirals of stiff wire held

about thirty large trumpet-shaped cones of green plastic. Filled with Oasis these elevated the flowers and branches to a total of twelve feet from the floor. The vases had been lined with thick polythene and extra bricks of foam were packed around the neck of the vase. Upon reflection, the whole contraption was extremely Heath Robinson, but at the time, I thought they were marvellous. The problem was they were not entirely watertight much to the dismay of the topping-

78 *Flowers with a Crucifix*

up team who spent much of their time with mop and pail amidst the throng of visitors on viewing days.

There is much to be said for working once a cathedral is closed as during the day much aggravation can result between arranger and visitor who consider it their right to be there and question the arrangers on all topics both horticultural and otherwise. To ignore them is to invite trouble!

A box of red rhododendrons from Sir Alex Douglas-Home, the then Prime Minister, had been sent from his Scottish estate, The Hirsel. Crushed stems in hot water soon revived this invaluable gift. I was amused to discover a note which said 'I wish these could have been any colour but red!' Presumably the packer feared that they might have some political significance. Long curving branches created the outline augmented by those sent by Lady Stoddart-Scott from Creskeld Hall in Yorkshire. These all-round arrangements swallowed quantities of flowers including long red Torch Gingers, *Alpina purpurata*, seen at the top. Tropical red *Ixora coccinea*, brick-red Amaryllis, scarlet gladioli, carnations and ixias, shading from deep magenta and crimson through every tint of vermillion, scarlet and flame created a warm welcome. Returning the next day for the Service of Dedication the Abbey presented a memorable and breathtaking sight.

YORK MINSTER FLOWER FESTIVALS – 1967 and 1972

It was the experience at Westminster Abbey which prompted me and my co-designer Brian Withill to suggest to the Dean and Chapter that we should decorate York Minster in September 1967. Our team of two hundred and fifty arrangers was drawn from the clubs of the North East Area of NAFAS. Fate dealt a sudden blow as the foundations of this massive building were declared unsafe and quite suddenly there was an urgent reason for our efforts. It must be the only flower festival in the world to have had a huge excavation in the middle of its design, crossed by scaffolding bridges. These carried many thousands who came to see this spectacle and by voluntary donations produced a profit of £8,000, at that time a record figure and a handsome sum to raise in three days.

We had the opportunity to mount a second festival with a new design in July 1972 to celebrate the completion of the five-year programme of restoration. Happily this coincided with the 500th anniversary of the completion of York Minster in 1472, a mission which had lasted 250 years. Visited by over 70,000 people in four days it raised a further £12,000 profit from public contributions and the sale of

79 *Flowers in Westminster Abbey*

brochures, as admission was again free of charge. None of this would have been possible without hours of voluntary committee work, a zealous chairman, the dedication and artistry of the arrangers and the support of the clergy and cathedral staff – in all a great team effort.

The decoration of the Screen of the Kings is shown in Illustration 80. Eight slender spires of flowers about nine feet high marked the position where the Gentleman at Arms had stood during the wedding of Their Royal Highnesses The Duke and Duchess of Kent in 1961. These beautiful arrangements, the work of the Sheffield Floral Art Society, were one of the highlights of this second festival. Their mechanics and construction are described in Illustration 89.

Following the success of these early festivals many other churches and ecclesiastical foundations have sought my help. To be invited to do an arrangement at an event organized by others is usually a pleasure, leaving one free to enjoy the task without responsibility and pressure. Unless you have been involved in a major festival it is hard to imagine how much concentrated effort goes into its production. Months of planning must suddenly blossom in a matter of

hours created from a delicate and perishable medium. Co-ordination and co-operation in every department is vital with good communication between clergy, arrangers and staff. This is a topic that could fill a separate book!

A PAIR OF AUTUMN PEDESTALS AT RIPON CATHEDRAL, YORKSHIRE

The pedestal design is still one of the most popular ways of decorating a church, despite the fact it is somewhat hackneyed. Let us consider the actual stand or pedestal itself. This must be in harmony with its surroundings and of a material sympathetic both to flowers and the church furnishings. The ubiquitous wrought-iron pedestal consisting of tripod feet, a straight rod, a bowl on top and decorated with fiddly curlicues is not the ideal. Dumped at random at chancel steps or beside an altar with flowers perched on top it can look out of place, like a cross between a coloured lollipop and a floral windmill. Do not use wrought iron if no iron work exists nearby. Try to seek out attractive pedestals

80 *The Screen of the Kings – York Minster*

81 *An Autumn Pedestal in Ripon Cathedral*

of polished wood, torchères, columns of painted wood, gilded candlesticks or whatever is most sympathetic to the immediate decor. Obviously every setting is different: an ancient Saxon crypt will require something solid and simple; a Gothic or Early English church forged iron; a Tudor or Perpendicular style carved wood; a light Georgian building a plinth of painted wood the colour of the neo–classical wood-work. These are only examples, a knowledge of architectural styles will guide you to select the right pedestal type. When possible use the existing furniture and adapt it to your pur-pose. This requires permission, explanation and faith on both sides in order that you can convert a candlestand into a pedestal. This successful solution utilizes fittings which were designed *en suite* with the reredos, dorsal posts, etc. The pedestal in Illustration 81 illustrates this effectively.

A pair of fine painted wooden candlestands were con-verted to hold these massive displays in Ripon Cathedral for its 900th anniversary celebrations. Because the top is only nine inches across, it would be impossible to balance such a large decoration without a specially designed support. A steel plate ten inches in diameter was welded to a steel pin six inches long. The stand is already drilled with a hole in the top to support a copper pin and candle sconce. It is vital that the steel pin is a snug fit and the plate sits flush to the wooden top. If not the entire weight of the decoration will exert a bending action on the union between plate and pin.

Four holes drilled in the steel plate are then threaded with strong wire. Once the metal bowl that holds the flowers is set on the plate these wires can be threaded through holes drilled in the rim of the tin or firmly attached to a covering of wire netting placed over the Oasis. A three-foot rod full of plastic cones is then placed inside the tin supported by the method described in Illustrations 41 and 61. An assembly of cones elevated the flowers five feet above the stand making an overall height from the floor of twelve feet. Each wooden stand is raised on a wooden dais covered with stone-coloured hessian visible in Illustration 82. They improve the propor-tion and balance the visual effect of a large display poised on a slender blue and gold stand.

The background foliage consists of large sprays of green

82 Overall View of High Altar – Ripon Cathedral

beech preserved in glycerine solution until dark brown: see Chapter 8. This dark background sets off the cream, yellow and gold flowers and separates them from the stone behind. A fountain-shaped group of twenty ivory gladioli is combined with variegated New Zealand Flax to create an elegant top to the design. The delicate arching seedheads of Venus' Fishing Rod, *Dierama pulcherrimum* quiver at the slightest movement, a home-grown addition of unparalleled grace, especially when it flowers.

Golden 'Harvest Moon' carnations, daisy-eyed single-spray chrysanthemums and chrysanthemus 'Apricot Julie Ann' all give downward transition. Cream and brown are combined in *Lillium* 'Sterling Star' grouped on the lower left. This lily has a branching head and star-shaped flowers as its name suggests. Large gold to primrose decorative *Dahlia* 'Rustig' give focal strength a satisfying match to the altar frontal and reredos in Illustration 82.

An entire plant of *Diffenbachia picta* 'Camillo' was removed from its pot, placed in a polythene bag and then lashed to three canes. This tripod of sticks enables me to place the rosette of foliage without impeding the passage of other stems in the foam. Every placement appears to radiate from a central point with downward graceful movement. This effect is accentuated by the drooping cream leaves of a hybrid phormium placed asymmetrically.

Illustration 82 gives a general view of the overall effect with the decorations in perfect scale to their setting. Note how the flowers are clearly visible from a distance yet they do not overpower the elaborate reredos or obliterate the presiding effigies of St Wilfred and St George. Ripon Cathedral is an intimate gem not to be missed with or without flowers.

Ripon Cathedral possesses a pair of the most beautiful and practical pedestals I have ever seen, bought as a military memorial. The three separate iron legs are joined by fine scroll work and terminate in a circular frame holding a separate bowl. They are much heavier and more stable in consequence than the usual tripod foot type with single stem and bowl, which are easily overbalanced. The separate liners are of polished brass, easily removable for cleaning. Iron pans corrode and rusty water is no good for flowers whereas brass, like copper, has fungicidal properties. They do not, however, possess tubes and rods for cones but that is a refinement that could be added. They were kindly loaned to us for a special occasion in York Minster.

THE VISIT OF THE DUKE AND DUCHESS OF YORK

In July 1987 the Duke and Duchess of York received the freedom of the City from the Lord Mayor in York Minster. This was an occasion of great pageantry for both Church and City unparalleled since the visit of Her Majesty the Queen to distribute Royal Maundy in 1972. The ceremony took place before a congregation of several thousand people at the nave altar. I was asked by the Dean and Chapter to decorate the raised dais backed by the Screen of the Kings and the trumpeters' gallery. It has to be remembered that York Minster is the largest Gothic cathedral in Britain and the sixth largest church in Christendom. The help and encouragement of the Chapter Clerk and Minster staff made this special occasion a great pleasure for me and my team.

Three pairs of pedestals welcomed the royal visitors beginning at the Great West Door with the white roses of Yorkshire, and white and pale pink mixed summer flowers. The progression down the nave was to deeper pink, coral and cerise in the second pair of pedestals. Flowers of quality and impact were chosen, in particular lilies, paeonies, sprays of roses and chrysanthemums with beautiful gerberas in assorted pinks. I could not have been happier with the lovely flowers created by the Minster Flower Guild throughout this magnificent building. My own brief was to create something of majestic proportion to flank the altar visible to all, yet unimpeding to clergy, choir and civic dignitories. From the pictures in Illustrations 83 and 84 it is hard to grasp the scale. The nine-foot gilded candlesticks normally positioned in the sanctuary at the High Altar were moved to the first step of the dias. Even when empty they balanced well with the long free-standing altar draped with a soft green festal frontal worked in coral and gold thread and presented by the Women's Institutes of Yorkshire.

The mechanics are a larger version of those used at Ripon the previous autumn. Steel plates two feet wide with welded steel pins nine inches long were lifted in place by two men. From four equidistant holes in each plate, guy ropes of steel wire were attached to stout eye hooks set into the square plinth of the candlestick. This was an extra precaution to allow for the tremendous weight of tin, water and flowers. Custom-made tins three feet wide and one foot deep were then wired to the plate. From these rose a six-foot rod covered with cones. Even when empty they looked enormous viewed from specially purchased step ladders. They absorbed sixty blocks of Oasis between them including the cones. Stout two-inch mesh wire netting covered the foam to ensure that it did not break under the weight of long branches.

The outline branches are of grey-green White Beam, *Sorbus aria* 'Lutescens' and a variegated Norway Maple of great beauty *Acer platanoides* 'Drummondii' selected for their reliable lasting qualities. Chinese fan palms and sago palms brought from Bermuda were in scale. Over 350 flowers were used and having no head for heights, I was alarmed to find I could barely reach the top-most tube on the newly purchased step ladders.

The overall dimensions were eighteen feet high by ten feet across. To make an impression from a distance the indi-

83 *Visit of the Duke and Duchess of York – July 1987 – York Minister*

vidual flowers need to be as bold as possible. For this reason I chose red anthuriums, open gladioli, trusses of salmon-pink 'Doris Ryker' roses and huge sprays of 'Cerise Bouquet' roses. This shrub is armed with vicious thorns and I had decimated our bushes before for the High Altar in 1972. Gerberas, carnations, 'Firecracker' lilies with pendant Parrot's Beak flowers, *Heleconia rostrata* added to the interest. The mixture of all these crashing reds was effective against the beige stonework which absorbs colour like a sponge.

Illustration 84 shows the completed effect with the unifying mass of the carpeted dais. It was because of this that I chose red flowers instead of white. It is evident from the photograph that the dais, painted screen and flowers form a complete composition. The foreground table was used for the ceremony of the scroll. A splendid decoration for a truly memorable occasion.

A HARVEST BASKET

Fortunately not all church decorations are as demanding so it is with relaxed pleasure that we can visit neighbouring villages to see their architecture and explore the district. Stillingfleet, situated south of York, is a charming village set around water meadows. The ancient church has a canopied lych-gate through which a path leads to the splendid Norman door. In Illustration 85 a basket of autumn flowers and fruits rests upon a tombstone beside this path. Shafts of afternoon sunshine steal across the churchyard transforming the decoration with a golden light. In the distance the River Ouse meanders through lush pastures.

The outline of the arrangement is of wheat gleaned from field edges, hedgerow blackberries and clusters of glistening elder. The pendant fruits of Pheasant Berry, *Leycesteria for-*

84 *Twin Pedestals for Royal Visit – Nave Altar – York Minster*

mosa, look more graceful stripped of their leaves. Lower left is *Cotoneaster frigida* 'Pendula' with red berries on stiff weeping stems. Above the grain is White Baneberry, *Actea alba*, with white berries made conspicuous by reddish brown stalks, an unusual but poisonous plant.

The focal area features some lovely roses with that intensity of colour so especial to the second crop. Deep cream 'Tynwald' and silvery orange 'Iced Ginger' are both my favourites together with 'Apricot Nectar'. Deep red decorative dahlias 'Blaydon Red' lend depth and shadow.

Two bulbous plants that flower in autumn are Colchicums and Schizostylis, sometimes called Autumn Crocus, though incorrectly, or Naked Ladies. Both single and double varieties are included here. They sprout up suddenly each year in turf never failing to surprise and delight, followed by glossy leaves in spring. Less easy to suit, the Kaffir Lily, *Schizostylis coccinea* 'Major', likes a warm sheltered site in full sun, but not too dry. Summer rain and frequent redivision ensures plenty of their slender stems with red cup-shaped flowers which continue to appear till late November. A few windfall apples completes the scene gathered from an old 'Improved Cockpit' tree. This informal basket of local willow is ready to be placed inside the porch or on a coffin stool beside the chancel steps. A tinge of sadness fills my mind as the last flowers of summer go to adorn the harvest festival. Can it be another year has passed?

A HARVEST DOOR WREATH

Of the two ancient doors to Stillingfleet Church this is the smaller. Built of magnesium limestone it is carved with chevron moulding and studded with floral bosses. I pass it often, deriving pleasure from its robust simplicity whilst wondering who was the Norman mason was who fitted this sturdy arch so long ago.

Set upon a fine oak door bound with iron hinges is a wreath of unstripped osiers hung like a sanctuary knocker. The basket makers of Stillingfleet still practise their craft where gnarled willows lean over the banks of the River Ouse between here and Ulleskelf, Norse names established before the conquest. It would be romantic to think that this lovely wreath was woven here about but in fact it was bought in a snooty London store in Sloane Street.

On to this foundation is taped a half brick of Dryfoam shaped to fit the curve of the wreath. A sheaf of dried Lyme

86 *Harvest Door Wreath, Stillingfleet Church*

85 *A Harvest Basket, Stillingfleet Lych Gate*

Grass *Elymus arenarius*, is set diagonally across the design. This grey-blue grass of sand dunes, too invasive for most gardens, dries an attractive soft buff. Ears of wheat gathered and dried whilst green are wired to give a second more horizontal line. Clusters of stalks gathered into bunches give a strong continuation line. Each straw has an internal wire to ensure it radiates in the desired direction, but such perfectionism is not essential. Rich brown and fawn Areca Palm leaf sheaths follow the line of the grasses.

Cobs of Indian Corn, *Zea mays*, with multicoloured seeds came from New England. The first settlers survived on this native crop and to this day hang corn cobs on their doors as a token of thanksgiving. Two pieces of beige oyster fungus have an even more remote origin. They were a gift to me in Monterrey, north Mexico and I have treasured and used them countless times. Clean, dry and hard they have never deteriorated as more local products do. Three gourds of creamy yellow were given to me by Elsa de Jaeger, the brilliant South African abstract arranger. You do not need to travel the world to find substitutes for such an eclectic mixture.

Curving sprays of orange-berried Fire Thorn, *Pyracantha crenato-serrata* 'Orange Glow', add a note of cheerful colour together with brilliant tinted leaves of Chinese Vine. Although these are not in water they will last in the misty autumn air. One plant I am not successful with is the Chinese Lantern, *Physalis franchetii*. Perhaps I do not give them a sunny enough spot to flower well. These came from that green-fingered gardener Beatrice, Lady Graham of Norton Conyers. Her nursery is crammed with rarities and her borders abound with old-fashioned plants like this. Gathered on the turn from green to orange and stripped of their leaves they should be hung up to dry. When fully ripe the Italians dip the Cape Gooseberry fruit into chocolate leaving the pulled back papery seed cases as decoration, a bitter sweet confection.

Windfall apples impaled on wooden skewers concentrate the focal interest. The decoration is finished with a bow and streamers of natural burlap ribbon. This stiffened hessian associates well with such rustic companions. Placed on the door on harvest Sunday, it welcomes the parishioners to church.

A HARVEST SUPPPER

The harvest home supper may be almost a thing of the past, but Illustration 87 shows a still-life group on this traditional theme. This large scale decoration is in St Oswald's Hall, an ideal setting for such an occasion with a fine floor of encaustic thirteenth-century tiles from Jervaulx Abbey. Converted from a disused church it now has a new life and is frequently used for medieval feasts.

Arranged on a six-foot sixteenth-century oak table is an analogous colour harmony of fruits, flowers and foliage. It ranges from orange through yellow to green with an interesting variety of shapes and textures to interpret the theme. Outline height and depth come from large pieces of Royal Palm sheath used to suggest a vellum scroll and following the line of the curtain of unbleached linen. This dry material is mounted on to canes to ensure it is held firmly and clear of moisture. Two big pottery bowls concealed by vegetation are filled with foam covered with wire netting. A heavy iron bouquet stand supports the tallest palm and the five-foot branch of pyracantha laden with berries.

It is common sense to fix the heaviest items first. You will then have confidence to experiment with the juxtapositioning of the varied elements of the composition. This is no haphazard jumble as careful study of the overall effect will show. Much thought has gone into the balance and proportion of each element. Note the pottery flagon, pumpkins and cauliflower used at the end. All are embraced by the horizontal line of beige palm sheath.

A deliberate change of form and texture comes right of centre caused by the vertical red hot pokers. These are the monumental *Kniphofia* 'Prince Igor' with six-foot torches to light the autumn border. Bleached cream and dark green shreaded palms erupt from the diagonal flow of lemons, oranges and pumpkins which lead down to a platter of green and yellow peppers. Matt-textured Heleniums are recessed behind.

The central pivot of the whole design is an ornamental squash *Cocurbita turbaniformis*, shaped on the underside like a Sultan's hat, hence the name Turban Squash. A lucky find in the local supermarket, this native of warmer climes will keep until Christmas if left dry and unpunctured.

Lemon yellow 'Gloria van Heemstede' and burnt orange 'Ormerod' dahlias are backed by tinted paeony leaves and bergenia. Their strength of colour outweighs more subtle inclusions in this visual banquet. On the left velvety heads of Crested Cockscomb have dried to the ox-blood red of the background seat cushion. The decoration ends with a burst of yellow peppers on branching stems. This exuberant example of still-life art may seem far removed from the white bread sandwiches and weak tea of after church school hall suppers as it aims to evoke the hospitality of a bygone age. A much simpler version can be studied in Illustration 100.

IN QUIET CONTEMPLATION

In contrast with the rich bavaura of the previous plate the arrangement in Illustration 88 has a subdued effect. It has a quiet charm full of subtle inclusions worthy of consideration. The setting is a window at St Oswald's Hall.

87 Harvest Supper, St Oswald's Hall

Arranged in a brass chalice are a connoisseur's collection of autumn flowers with a scheme of white and deep maroon. On the right is the filigree outline of the Threepenny Bit Rose *Rosa farreri* 'Persetosa'. It makes a dainty bush studded in June with exquisite buds and miniature pink flowers. In autumn it is hung with brilliant red hips set against bronze purple foliage. Above and to the right are the pink-tinted porcelain-white fruits of *Sorbus hupehensis*, a rowan of distinction. This native of China is found in various forms, some having more crimson fruits, stalks and berries. It is a desirable small tree with elegant glaucous foliage more refined in every way than its relation the red-fruited Mountain Ash. Sprays of purple-leaved vine complete with bunches of black grapes lead the eye to the alms dish of 1480 with an embossed design of vines and grapes.

A note of contrast comes from the blue-green leaves of *Hosta* 'Halcyon', bred and given to me by the late Eric Smith, that pioneer of hosta popularity. A few spotted leaves of Pulmonaria lead to the central rosette of *Phlox paniculata* 'Norah Leigh', the gift of Mrs Joan Elliot of Broadwell after whose mother it was named. Sadly it does not have a strong constitution, probably caused by the large proportion of white to green in each leaf. It needs a rich diet in semi-shade and looks effective with the compact white and grey-green Cocksfoot Grass *Dactylis glomerata* 'Variegata' and variegated oak leaved *Pelargonium* 'Lady Plymouth'.

The elegant white Japanese Anemones continue to open for many weeks with a purity accentuated by golden stamens and a lime green ovary. With them are the wide eyed daisies of Osteospermum, a South African flower previously known as Dimorphotheca, an even bigger mouthful. This tender perennial is over-wintered in the greenhouse from cuttings taken in September. It has clammy leaves of no account with dark-centred chalk-white flowers backed with blue which only open in full sun.

The star of this little show is undoubtably the deep

88 *In Quiet Contemplation*

maroon *Cosmos astrosanguineus*, aptly named from the Greek word for beautiful. The velvety flowers have photographed like black blobs which is not true of their wonderful texture. This choice plant emits a strong scent of chocolate and requires a sunny border and some winter protection for its tuberous roots, being a native of Mexico.

The other curiosity is the White Baneberry mentioned in Illustration 85. The crimson stems and fruit stalks are a striking foil for the white berries each punctuated with a black dot. There is also a red variety *Actaea rubra* with the same fine cut foliage and glistening red berries, equally tempting to the unwary for both are poisonous. Two spikes of white liatris, white colchicums and a dusky mauve border carnation complete the mixture.

The carnation came from a cottage garden nearby. Try to cultivate the habit of looking at friends' and neighbours' gardens, there you may find many desirable plants which can frequently lead to an exchange of cuttings. This is how

that doyenne of gardeners, the late Margery Fish, made many of her discoveries so rescuing plants for posterity.

Placed with the platter is a French Book of Hours dated 1470. This beautifully illuminated prayer book suggests quiet contemplation with the staff of life nearby to accompany this food for the soul.

A CHRISTMAS WEDDING IN YORK MINSTER

It would seem that all the world loves a wedding, especially when it is a really grand affair, then the interest quickens. Illustrations 89 and 90 show some of the flower arrangements created for the marriage of Lord and Lady Grimthorpe's only daughter, The Hon Harriet Beckett at the High Altar of York Minster. Solemnized shortly before Christmas, the flowers gave the cathedral a festive air and for the

89 *The High Altar, York Minster*

90 *A Christmas Wedding in York Minster*

guests and many hundreds of visitors a rare opportunity to enjoy the rose-pink festal frontal embroidered with gold and crystals. The bride wore a dress of cream wild silk encrusted with pearls. Her cathedral train was carried by young attendants in cream dresses tied with deep sashes of ruby velvet. With this overall picture in mind, I decided that two imposing obelisks of flowers were sufficient to frame the altar. Their scale and general location may be judged in Illustration 89.

Steady mechanics are vital when working on this scale and help to inspire confidence for all concerned throughout the ceremony. Two eighteen-inch square wooden plinths are placed right and left of the dorsal posts and flank the magnificent Persian carpet. On these stand heavy base boards into which screw a six-foot iron rod. About thirty cones are strapped to each rod with waterproof tape. Start at the top and work downwards with clusters of three at nine-inch intervals so that the front back and sides are covered. An eighteen-inch diameter metal bowl sits in front of the rod, filled with Oasis and weighted at the back with bricks. It is then covered with wire netting. Working on a step ladder place wedges of Oasis in each tube, tape in place and fill with water. It is much easier to top up at this stage than when the tubes are masked with vegetation.

Once confident that all is stable, the creative process becomes a pleasure. When working on any pair or arrangements it is helpful to have an assistant to hand up branches and flowers and to anticipate your requirements. They may also protect you from the curiosity of onlookers who unintentionally will distract your attention and spoil your concentration.

Long branches of gold and green variegated holly *Ilex × altaclarensis* 'Golden King' form the outline. I was fortunate to have access to some large overgrown trees for this purpose together with glossy laurel. Three generous plants of ivory white poinsettias are secured to canes then placed alternately down the arrangement. The flowers consist of long-stemmed single *Lillium longiflorum*. They rise nine feet in the air like a fanfare of trumpets to welcome the bridal party. Bold white chrysanthemums give focal weight with white carnations and daisy spray chrysanthemums. A ribbon of pink and cerise carnations runs diagonally down each arrangement chosen to match the sashes of the bridesmaids. The cream spider chrysanthemum 'Tokio' lightens the effect added last like the bride's veil of silk tulle clasped by a diamond tiara.

These two massive groups were flanked by two further pairs of urns placed at the Choir Screen entrance and the steps of the sanctuary. Arranged by Mrs John Foster, a friend of the family, they shaded from ruby red, cerise and pink then graduated to paler tints so forming the completion of a carefully planned and dramatically staged event. The sun shone, everyone smiled and as on all such occasions, the flowers expressed the happiness we felt. Flowers arranged in places of worship, whether simple country churches or glorious cathedrals, are a token of our faith in the living spirit and bring life to the building.

91 *Oceania*

CHAPTER 7
EXOTICA

This chapter is of decorations inspired by some of the countries where I have been invited to give lecture demonstrations. It is not comprehensive for with only fifteen plates at my disposal and twenty-five countries to choose from I am likely to cause offence by omission where none is intended. To be asked to contribute to the development of an art appreciated and practised by cultured people is a great privilege. I have derived tremendous pleasure and knowledge from these overseas visits. We now have a world association of flower arrangers which fosters greater communication, exchange of ideas and international understanding of the subject. I have been fortunate to play a small part in pioneering this development.

Mankind is separated by many self-imposed boundaries, yet the more one travels the less they seem to matter for a love of flowers is universal. It can be your passport to a world rich in vegetation and cultural and ethnic differences. The world has shrunk due to the magic of television and ease of communication. We can all be fireside travellers able to experience the beauty of nature and the mysteries of far away places without any inconvenience. To do it alone with only a suitcase of containers has been another story, at times frightening and rigorous, fraught with regulations and customs officials. But at my destination I always found kindness and richly rewarding experiences. It is not possible to convey adequately the debt of gratitude I feel to all those who put their faith in me and who forged friendships through flowers in distant lands where I was made to feel at home.

OCEANIA

As one third of the world's surface is covered by water, most of my travels have involved crossing great expanses of sea by air. In particular I recall my visit in 1977 to the lovely country of New Zealand for a six-week tour of Floral Art Societies. This entailed a complete orbit of the world with stops along the way.

The decoration in Illustration 91 is for such a flight of fancy, designed to depict an imaginary underwater world. A fantasy of coral gardens, shell-encrusted grottoes inhabited by a myriad of multicoloured fish. The stand is a free-form piece of blue Perspex (Plexiglass) cut and moulded like a wave to display three beautiful shells. These chambered nautilus have been polished from their natural white and brown to reveal the under surface of mother-of-pearl. Exchanged for a pair of sneakers on the beach in Bali, I have drilled two small holes near the rim to enable them to be wired to corresponding holes in the Perspex (Plexiglass) mount.

The outline of the design is of lacy sea fan, a form of black coral from the Indian Ocean, sprayed with aqua paint to highlight the edges. Preserved and coloured leaves of Camel's Foot Tree are wired and taped into sprays then placed in a horizontal plane. The Bauhinia is also known as the Orchid Tree on account of its white and pink flowers veined with magenta. They do not last long as cut flowers, but a tree in full bloom is one of the sights of tropical Africa and Asia.

The pastel-tinted Moth Orchids are so called because of their mimmickery of their pollinator. The Phalaenopsis is an epiphytic species clinging tenaciously to trees with strong roots and thick leathery leaves. The arching flower sprays are by contrast the epitome of elegance. In the wild they are mainly white, lilac and mauve with a contrasting throat of red or yellow. The modern hybrids have many exquisite colour combinations. As cut flowers they can be temperamental, wilting for no apparent reason. To revive recut under water and then float on tepid water for an hour or so.

Two tufts of wispy grey air plant, a species of Tillandsia, suggest seaweed. Their muted colour is repeated by the

125

lilac-grey heads of *Allium katrataviense* massed to resemble coral. To find the right plant material to interpret your theme may require many hours of searching as well as a good botanical knowledge. However, there is great satisfaction when it turns out right.

THE TEMPEST

To be cast upon the jagged reef of some coral atoll is for tales of piracy, treasure and shipwreck. In real life a terrifying experience for Sir George Somers and his men when their ship the *Sea Venture* floundered upon Bermuda in 1609. My arrival in 1965 was less traumatic and began a life-long love affair with this isle of enchantment. Annual visits are for me a keenly anticipated highlight and I am proud to be an honorary member of the Garden Club of Bermuda.

This underwater fantasy in Illustration 92 was inspired by Shakespeare's immortal play *The Tempest* based on the wreck of the *Sea Venture*. The airily poised shells and driftwood are firmly supported on a steel pin ten inches long welded to a heavy steel plate nine inches square. I was given this fearsome looking object as I left Guatamala with the admonishment 'Don't sit on it!' – not an easy travelling companion. It has proved invaluable for supporting heavy objects such as driftwood. Each item is drilled with a hole and then threaded on to the spike. The iron plate is concealed by a base board covered with coral-coloured fabric. A pair of heavy clam shells from Mombasa appear to rest on a delicate rosette of coral. Drilled with a masonry bit they are actually held by their own off-centre weight as they rest snugly against the pin.

Angular sun-bleached wood, a remnant of Bermudian Cedar, was collected on a rocky island in Hamilton Sound.

92 The Tempest

Drilled and impaled on the spike it forms a natural cradle for a chambered nautilus shell. Though not native to this northern atoll their beautiful form and colour tie in well with sea fans and rust-red fungi intended to imitate coral, all are secured in Dryfoam segments.

This watery grotto is inhabited by star fish of aqua-grey air plants, the extraordinary Tillandsia. As grotesque as Caliban these epiphytes will live attached to coral if sprayed regularly with rainwater. Blue-grey Echeveria rosettes nestle in the shell and on a branch resembling sea anemones waiting to open their tentacles. A change of form comes from trumpets of Sarracenia with fine red veins and fluted profiles, a perfect complement to the wavy shells.

Inspired by the sea gardens and strange rock basins of Bermuda's reefs, I hasten to say that this lovely island is not as sinister as this arrangement, conjured up from the silent world of the deep.

A SUBTROPICAL WALL VASE

Of the many houses I have stayed in none seems more like home than Mount Pleasant, Bermuda, scene of many happy holidays. In the drawing-room of this elegant eighteenth-century house is a silver wall vase shown in Illustration 93. Converted from a meat cover, half of it hangs above the fireplace on pale coffee-coloured walls. Two wall screws slot into holes in the back which is set flush to the wall. It holds plenty of water and strong crunched wire netting.

With several acres of gardens and woodland this property is an arranger's paradise. Both wild and cultivated plants inspire, seen with the fresh eye of the visitor. The outline is of sweeping Bamboo Palm, *Chrysalidocarpus lutescens* with light green leaves and yellow stems it is one of the many species found in the grounds. Central height is fixed by 'Green Woodpecker' gladioli and sword-shaped green and

93 *A Subtropical Wall Vase*

127

yellow leaves of Mother-in-Law's Tongue. How *Sansevieria trifasciata* 'Laurentii' got this name I am too tactful to speculate, but it is tough, sharp pointed and almost indestructable, despised by gardeners I love its sculptured curving form. Beside it are two yellow leaves of a climbing cactus *Hylocereus undatus*. The Night Blooming Cereus has three angled fleshy leaves more curious than beautiful and fantastic white flowers that appear after dark. These grew over rocks deficient in nitrogen, a common complaint on coral soils, and they turn this jaundiced yellow. A colour appealing to the arranger if not the gardener.

Spikes of yellow *Aloe vera*, an easy succulent, lead down to the focal placement of purple cabbage. To the right a cluster of croton leaves add a splash of yellow. Sometimes called the South Sea Island Laurel, the brilliantly coloured *Codiaeum variegatum* exudes a sap when cut like so many of the *Euphorbia* family. Undetectable at the time of picking the juice leaves a black stain after clothes are laundered. Whole rosettes of cut foliage are prone to wilt unless their stems are scraped and then dipped in boiled water for a few minutes.

On the left a dried Chinese Fan Palm picks up the colour of the walls and chintz curtains. Clusters of the blue-green fruits of *Livistonia chinensis* hang down on the right like polished pebbles of malachite. Dark green aspidistra and pale leaves of the Shell Plant, *Alpinia speciosa*, curve gracefully to the right to balance the long trails of Spanish Moss draped over the mantel lower left. Old bottles retrieved from the sea and Bristol blue decanters complete the composition.

AMERICANA

The United States of America has two national women's floral organizations: the Garden Club of America and the Federation of State Garden Clubs, both with a wide spectrum of activities of which flower arranging is only a fraction.

I have on many occasions had the pleasure of presenting programmes at national and club levels, all received with kindness and rapturous appraisal. With so many highlights over twenty years it would be difficult to list them all: I recall in particular the Williamsburg Bicentennial Garden Symposium at the restored colonial capital; the De Young Museum of Fine Arts, San Francisco with galleries of English antiques which I decorated with my flowers; lecture tours of the Deep South to the universities of Alabama, Georgia and Mississippi. Atlanta has one of the finest auditoriums and it is quite something to arrive on a moving stage before a thousand ladies! I hold the key of the City of Savannah. Nashville, Tennessee and delightful Knoxville, the Mid West and Cleveland, Ohio all hold special memories. Winters at Florida's exclusive Hobe Sound and elegant Palm Beach opened some rarified portals. When I recall my visits to New Jersey, New York State, Maine and Massachusetts I am reminded of so many transatlantic friends. It has been said I have seen more States than many Americans, but there is still a lot more to do.

It has to be admitted that because of the limitations of climate and life-style there are fewer dedicated arrangers than in Britain, but I have been lucky to meet the best. Sadly I have often heard it said 'I daren't arrange flowers, there are so many rules'. Who makes something simple into such a science, not me I hope? The commercial designers I have met are truly innovative, probably because they dare to be themselves. The result of this is twofold: if you want an arrangement you buy it; if you want to arrange you enter a flower show, but go armed with a set square and rule book.

Their style is severe and linear with a sparseness that stems from the Orient. One of America's greatest exponents was the late Gregory Conway, a Japanese-American. His visit to Britain in the Fifties came as a revelation. The arrangement in Illustration 94 owes much to his influence with two sophisticated black Perspex (Plexiglass) containers he would have enjoyed.

Brown coconut spathes are linked by curlicues of black sea kelp. Set against a violet background the pale pink Anthurium hybrids show up well arranged in a linear pattern with pink pineapples. Strong focal impact comes from a complete pineapple plant, returned to its pot when the flowers had faded, backed by variegated ivy.

Touches of pale green are added by the forced blossoms of the Snow Ball Tree. *Viburnum opulus* 'Roseum', also known as 'Sterile', has full globose heads of pale cream, but no luscious red berries like the wild Guelder Rose. In the garden it needs plenty of room and rewards with autumn-tinted foliage.

HOMAGE TO A PRINCESS

I first met Her Serene Highness Princess Grace of Monaco on a wet and windy March morning twenty years ago. Invited to give lessons to her Garden Club I little thought that she would be attending. Suddenly my few flowers and leaves seemed totally inadequate for the occasion as I recalled the profusion of garden flowers I had used at Versailles the previous June. It was because her friends had seen me there that I had been invited to Monaco. Never have I felt so self conscious and ill prepared. But sensing my discomfort, the Princess soon put me at my ease with her genuine interest and kindness. In her presence even the flowers took on a new radiance and my confidence returned.

The first of many visits, it was a love of flowers that brought us together. I felt priviledged to know her, not as a film star or a regal consort, but as a human being the world at large would never know. Her qualities were manifold, most of all her ability to make us want to be better people, more loving and more lovable. To every situation she brought her practical common sense, a touch of humour and sensitivity to others. Her own high standards demanded an equal response yet if we failed her she was always forgiving.

A life that illuminated so many will never be extinguished and she lives on in the hearts of all who knew her. Each May flower lovers from all over the world are drawn to the International Concours de Bouquet which she founded. To those of us on the panel of judges our annual visit to Monaco has become both a pilgrimage and a tribute to this very special lady.

The arrangement in Illustration 95 is dedicated to her memory. The Italian vase is similar to ones I have used in Monaco. The four tiers of alabaster are lined with foil to prevent the wet Oasis damaging this porous stone. Peach 'Sonia' roses, one of her favourites, 'Apple Blossom' gerbera

and 'Flamingo' carnations cascade downwards with rhythmic movement. White dendrobium orchids add a balletic quality she would have appreciated for her Ballet School was dear to her heart. Red-edged white spray carnations and red Schizostylis combine the national Monogasque colours. Arranged in the style of the Belle Epoque, tinted foliage adds a touch of individuality with variegated fuchsia, red mahonia and variegated ivy. A lovely fern, the Cornish Polypody, introduces a note of green. The Common Polypody is a fern widespread in the damp western British Isles, in the Cornish variant *Polypodium vulgare* 'Cornubiensis' the fronds are finely subdivided giving it a lacy appearance. It is also known as *P.v.* 'Elegantissimum', a name which aptly fits this context.

The decoration is topped with a pink pineapple fruit the symbol of hospitality, repeated on the mirror. *Ananas cosmosus* 'Variegatus' is a popular house plant, but it requires

94 *Americana*

129

95 Homage to a Princess

heat and sunshine to make it flower. This was imported cut for decoration and completes an elegant tribute to a lady who loved flowers and like them was greatly admired.

TROPICAL MAGIC

This predominantly foliage arrangement in the classical triangular style is typical of my work for the Garden Clubs of Mexico, Panama and Venezuela. The ingredients are to them commonplace, but what would we give for them here at home?

The outline contains three spiny leaves of Sago Palm, a species of Cycas. These primitive plants once prolific in primeval tropical swamps also grew in Britain millions of years ago. They survive only endemic to South Africa where they are protected plants. Their ability to withstand

unfavourable conditions such as fire and drought is on account of their woody root stock. This will sprout again once danger has passed. Hard and shiny they last for many weeks as cut material eventually drying to a sepia brown. Two are used top right, the other lower left.

In a monochromatic design contrast of form and texture become even more important. Here broad pale leaves of *Diffenbachia* 'R. Roehrs' contrast with yellow edged mother-in-law's tongue, aspidistra and feathery palms. They are backed by glossy rosettes of *Pittosporum undulatum*, a useful and fragrant flowered shrub.

Two fronds of the compact Cat Tail Fern sweep in an arc from the extreme left to lower right. This is not a fern at all, but a relation of edible asparagus. There are several forms but *Asparagus densiflorus* 'Meyers' is the most arresting. I grow it in a cool greenhouse where it flowers and bears red berries.

96 *Tropical Magic*

Near the centre of the design and in the lower placement are the strange fruits of the Screw Pine, *Pandanus utilis*. Not a pine, it gets its name from the spiral motion of the tufted leaves which grow on gaunt stems propped up by stilt-like roots. These vicious saw-edged leaves dry off and fall to the ground. Tinged with pink they make good dried material used upside down. A more delicate species is *P. veitchii* with white margined leaves. The club-like fruit, resembling a medieval mace, makes a striking addition to this group of apples, grapes and avocados. The green cups of Lenten hellibores are temperate zone additions.

Sprays of primrose yellow *Nerium oleander* enliven the central area, gathered from the middle of a variegated bush in the way that we search out all cream holly. It is not always appreciated that Oleanders are poisonous. Food cooked on wooden skewers, flowers eaten and leaves grazed by animals, have all proved fatal.

A note of complementary colour is introduced by rust-red croton leaves, fabric base and dark background. The container is the bronze Baccus covered with verdigris described in Illustration 26.

THE LATIN TOUCH

You are never far from nature in the tropics, with the jungle at the bottom of the garden. Most of us hope for fairies, but I have encountered huge spiders, snakes and even a crocodile. Forays into the undergrowth to gather material can be fraught with danger as one becomes absorbed by the fascination of strange sights and sounds.

Illustration 97 was inspired by my visit to the Garden Club Convention of Latin America held in Panama City. Six hundred ladies from Costa Rica, El Salvador, Guatamala,

97 The Latin Touch

98 Kenyan Safari

Honduras and Nicaragua were hosted by the Panamanians. Some had risked real danger to be there. Resplendent in fabulous evening dresses these glamorous ladies danced to hypnotic Latin rhythms under a moonlit sky. With partners at a premium I have never worked so hard!

From the jungle interior of Panama came gifts of plant material, orchids, rope vines and startling bromellias. With dexterous ingenuity they assembled outdoor decorations on huge tree trunks which rose from pools of floodlit water. These were for the folklore evening when dressed in national costume we banqueted under the stars. A week of spectacle and colour I shall never forget!

Illustration 97 is a tame version of their creations. Impaled on the spiked steel plate is a lattice of driftwood. Two colourful plants of *Neoregelia carolinae*, once called *Aregelia* are wired top and bottom their roots in polythene bags covered with moss. The family of *Bromeliaceae* has over a thousand species distributed between fifty-one genera. Their often showy flowers rise from or nestle in the rosette of leaves. Perched like nests they grow in trees catching rainwater and debris for nourishment.

Companions from the old world are the epiphytic Dendrobium orchids grown on similar conditions. As cut flowers they are available everywhere – even in chain stores. Their grace and lasting quality acount for their popularity. Here they are arranged in packets of wet Oasis wrapped in cling foil covered with moss. This colourful quick design relies on the invisibly supported wood and dramatic plant material for its effectiveness.

A KENYAN SAFARI

I first saw these striking Yellow Arums growing in a garden in Kenya. Although native to the Transvaal they will grow in any hot climate. They require marshy ground enriched with copious animal manure. The leaves of *Zantedeshia elliotiana* are typical of the arum family, smooth, green and the shape of an arrow head with one distinguishing feature – curious transparent blotches. They are rarely cut commercially because this weakens the plant. The stem sap is injurious to clothes.

More widely known and easier to grow is the White Arum, *Z. aethiopica*, sometimes called Lily of the Nile which is misleading as it comes from South Africa. Like its yellow and a pink relation *Z. rehmannii*, it likes a rich diet. It will survive out of doors in the milder parts of Britain and the slightly hardier variety 'Crowborough' we grow in pots, placing them in shallow water outdoors all summer. I used to have a green one called 'Green Goddess' with a spathe liberally brushed with green shading to white in the throat. There are now some lurid hybrids with almost fluorescent colours which I saw at the Chelsea Flower Show.

These strong-textured classic flowers remind me of my visits to Kenya in the early Seventies to teach the ladies of Nairobi. They used the yellow and white varieties to good effect. I recall those delightful safaris to see giraffe grazing and lakes fringed with pink flamingoes, visits to the Great Rift Valley and the steamy coast of Mombasa.

The highways and parks of Nairobi were planned by Peter Greensmith, a master of the art of planting. Bouganvillias in every tint of pink, orange and magenta were trained horizontally on wires down the central median. Large and numerous traffic islands were massed with spiky succulents and ferocious prickly cacti, the best deterrant ever to reckless drivers.

In Illustration 98 a piece of mossy wood forms a natural container supported by the metal spike described in Illustration 92. Sitting in a brown pottery bowl it has floral foam-filled saucers top and bottom. Curving pleated leaves resembling a palm cascade from the upper placement followed by the three yellow arums.

Clusters of yellow spray peppers introduce a different texture, but strenghten the yellow content. A foliage which incorporates the flower and leaf colours gives good transition, in this case *Euonymus* 'Emerald and Gold'. Like the bronze bergenias it is not tropical, but readily available throughout the year. The design relies on dramatic use of space plus strong forward movement, an effect partially lost by the camera.

ANTHURIUMS AND PROTEAS

To the majority of people these tropical flowers will appear exotic yet they were purchased in York. I have gathered such beautiful material in East and South Africa and had the thrill of arranging them before audiences to whom they appear as every-day garden flowers. I think in particular of a jungle garden in Mombasa where anthuriums grew in the shade of great trees which dripped orchids from their branches. In another lovely garden at Umhlali, Durban, on the beautiful South African coast, they grew not far from the proteas, the national flower.

Proteas take their name from a versatile sea-god Proteus who could change his form to escape capture. They are found in a wide diversity of shapes and colours. *Protea barbigera* has white to pink flowers surrounded by a mass of silky feather-like bracts which give the inflorescence its regal distinctive character. Their natural habitat is on rocky terraine close to the sea where full sun and perfect drainage make them natural companions for scrubby heather-like plants. They associate well with driftwood which suits their strong form and angular habit of growth. As imported cut flowers they last a long time eventually drying out to grey and fawn.

The anthurium is a large and showy perennial native to tropical America. Its flower consists of a shiny bract-like spathe from which rises a cylindrical tail or spadix housing a mass of tightly packed florets. Once fertilized the spathes turn from pink or red to green with many wonderful variations. Shining jewel-like seeds appear spasmodically along the spadix giving it a grotesque beauty rarely seen except in cultivation. Many species are native to Columbia. The most exciting I ever arranged were blackish maroon. Grouped on a stone altar with white and green vegetables, purple aubergines and tropical leaves it made a memorable combination not only for me but also the Garden Club of Guatamala.

They are known by many common names around the world – Flamingo Lily, Painter's Palette and Chinese Heart to name a few. Some have gorgeous foliage, in particular, *Anthurium crystallinum*, with glistening velvety shield-shaped leaves furrowed by white veins.

Three pieces of silver-grey driftwood are combined to form the support for the upper placement of the design in Illustration 99. A metal cup is attached by a right-angled screw attachment obtainable from driftwood specialists. These three pieces appear separately in Illustrations 7, 48 and 92 illustrating their versatility. They rise from a hand-thrown pottery bowl and rest on the table to ensure physical as well as visual balance.

The circular movement of the design is accentuated by albino sprays of ivy selected from a large plant of *Hedera colchica* 'Dentata Variegata'. They sweep upward on the right and cascade downward on the left picking up the colour of the anthurium's spadix. Two plants of a variegated succulent *Sansevieria hahnii* 'Golden' give interest planted in apertures on the wood. This dwarf rosette form of the mother-in-law's tongue is sometimes called the Bird's Nest plant. It grows slowly in hot arid conditions and is more

99 *Anthuriums and Proteas*

135

attractive than the better known tall sansevieria. Two pieces of grey moss add textural interest and in the case of the lower section help to hide the pinholder used to support the heavy flowers.

OUT OF AFRICA

Only once in my life has the name Smith been an advantage to me and that was in Rhodesia, during Ian Smith's regime when everyone assumed we must be related. Now Zimbabwee, this colourful country has left me with several favourable impressions, most especially the wide streets of Bulawayo. Designed by Cecil Rhodes to allow a full team of oxen to turn, they are lined with Jacaranda trees, a mass of violet blue against a cloudless sky in October, their spring.

The carved head in Illustration 100 is an example of their tribal art, worked by a native carver. The gift of the Judges Panel they also sent me by air to visit the Victoria Falls, a unique experience. A spectacular sight from the air, the mile-and-a-half wide Zambeezee river plunges over a rift in the earth's crust. As I paused beside these boiling torrents and staring into the chasm below a voice behind me said 'You won't jump will you Mr Smith?' Startled I looked round. 'You see,' said the lady by way of explanation, 'I'm the secretary of the West Essex Flower Club and you're due this year, I'd hate to have a gap in my programme!' I resisted the temptation to say 'Mrs Livingstone, I presume'. The world of flower arrangers is a very small one.

The carving featured in the centre of this design is com-

100 *Out of Africa*

bined with dried and fresh material and suitable for a buffet table. Orange gerberas and Pin Cushion Proteas, *Leucospermum cordifolium*, lead down to oranges, coconuts and mangoes. Although the proteas are more typical of South Africa they look well in this context, backed by apple-green leaves of *Fatsia japonica*, variegated aspidistra and spikes of New Zealand Flax for a colour contrast.

The outline of dried material has two Date Palm flower husks of a rich tobacco brown with the flattened and contorted stems of fasciated willow, a form of *Salix matsudana*. This is a home-grown addition from a contorted shrub which yields good outline material covered with silvery catkins in spring. Dyed orange pods of Flamboyant, *Delonix regia* have curious corrugations where the oblong seeds once sat.

On the left a winnowing basket from the same region extends the decoration, its woven pattern repeating the natural colours. A wide arc of royal palm sheath creates an all-embracing line.

The cloth of ribbed cotton suggests the red-brown earth of Africa. Once between your toes they say it calls you back with a yearning for those smiling faces and flashing white teeth.

SPIRITS OF SOUTH AFRICA

The vast size of South Africa is unknown to those who have never been there and whose knowledge is based on political reports. It has three different provinces, the Transvaal, the

101 *Spirits of South Africa*

137

Cape and Natal, each with its own identity moulded by topographical, historical and ethnic differences, many predating white man's arrival. The legacy of art left by these indigenous people deserves a wider appreciation.

I was delighted to receive these exciting masks, the gift of the Floral Affairs Club of Johannesburg. Partly intended to frighten they are also tremendous fun and have been used by me at my multinational presentations in South Africa and elsewhere. They convey the spirit of South Africa with its cultural heritage of hypnotic music, dance and tribal costume.

Given two accessories of equal size and uncertain of their gender, I have made the handsome fellow on the left – the container fitted with a dish behind his chevron crown. His equally delightful consort is placed further back to reduce her size. Carved wood and dried plant material have a natural affinity even without the enlivenment of fresh flowers. As all are arranged in wet foam the dried items are mounted on sticks to prevent them absorbing the moisture intended for the flowers.

Giant leaves of Leather Coat Tree *Coccoloba pubescens*, were first soaked in water to make them malleable. Moulded into interesting shapes they are dried and then placed top left and lower right. Curving sections of Royal Palm are looped at the top to repeat the consort's head-dress and continue the movement down and forward. Contrast of form and texture comes from eruptions of silky pink and cream grasses. Their delicate form like a head-dress adds movement with any current of air.

Two very different seed pods add focal weight and interest. Long corrugated pods of Flamboyant stand upright and curve forward resembling carved wood. Also known as Poinciana which explains the corruption to 'Fancy Anna', *Delonix regia* comes from Madagascar. Now widespread throughout the tropics, a mature tree in full bloom is a spectacular sight. The perforated seed pods of Lotus, described in Illustration 52, accentuate the dark bown of the masks.

Fresh flowers, including pink anthuriums, direct our eye inwards, with a shiny texture that enlivens the design. Two variegated pineapples repeat the stylized decorative carving with their tufted tops and criss-cross fruit. At the centre of each group are pink Waratah, *Telopea speciosissima*, an Australian member of the Protea family. Even without these fresh materials the decoration would be effective and could be used in an area where constant maintenance was absent.

SINGAPORE BAMBOO

Singapore is a garden city. In spite of its density of population and high-rise modernity flowering shrubs abound. Tree-lined streets clean of litter and with only restricted traffic make walking down town a pleasure. I am an honor-ary life member of its flourishing Gardening Society and have picked from its world famous Botanical Garden.

One of my more challenging assignments was to lecture each day at the Asean Orchid Congress, held by the five countries of Asia interested in commercial orchid cultivation. Imagine having as many orchids as you wish in all shapes and colours. A dream for any arranger, but one soon realises the necessity for foliage and rounded forms such as fruit. Solely spiky flowers can become boring design material. As on previous visits I am indebted to John and Amy Ede of the Mandai Gardens for mouth-watering exotics and foliage. They have created a paradise of tropical planting and an orchid farm second to none on the island.

The bamboo construction in Illustration 102 is typical of my work in the Orient. A shallow silk worm tray holds a thick block of wood with three circles of six-inch nails resembling a fakir's bed. Three poles of different heights and thickness are gripped by the nails. A second basket hangs at the back. Fine rattan hand fans used to combat the heat and humidity are placed in an asymmetric grouping. This simple foundation needs very little plant material to embellish it.

A diagonal curve of Sago Palm, *Cycas revoluta* inscribes an arc that balances the vertical parallel bamboo. A second smaller arc repeats the effect incorporating the upper basket. Hand-like leaves of dainty Rhapis Palm are long lasting here teamed with mottled Diffenbacia. The broad blades of black ribbed green Bird's Nest Fern, *Asplenium nidus*, have a long cut life. Small leaves of heart-shaped gold streaked *Scindapsus aureus* help to cover the mechanics together with a speckled rosette of Bromeliad. Although the design is five feet high, with such lovely leaves it needs few flowers. Ten Apple Blossom gerbera and five sprays of magenta Dendrobium are enough to complete the design. This multi-level decoration has many adaptations and being light and airy it 'leaves plenty of space for the butterflies'.

A DUCK FROM BALI

Bali is the only Hindu island in the vast archipelago of Indonesia. The sarong-clad Balinese have a natural grace and beauty and a willingness to please as yet unspoilt by tourism. Artistic in all they do, music, dance and drama are important to their daily life. Deeply religious they delight in festivals and processions to the countless shrines and temples that ornament the land. Each village specializes in a craft with fine metal work, jewellery, fabric printing and carving practised in family communities. These almond-eyed, bronzed and smiling people love to adorn themselves and their guardian statues with fresh flowers each morning; for them life is a celebration of nature's beauty.

This animated duck was carved by the shepherd who tends his duck flocks in the rice paddy fields. The decoration

102 *Singaporean Bamboo*

of fruit and vegetables is inspired by the lovely buffet table arrangements the Balinese make. French beans, lemons, courgettes and wrinkled avocados contrast with the shiny red of peppers and the startling form of Chinese Cabbage. All are secured in Oasis by wooden cocktail sticks.

Orange gerbera 'Clementine', 'Belinda' roses and 'Tangerine' carnations all pick up the colour of the bird's beak and feet. Although the Slipper Orchid is not a native to Bali, I could not resist including these blooms with waxy petals and white standards which look as jaunty as the bird.

When the Balinese arrange these containers they give them fanciful tails of fresh plaited palm. Used here instead are three maranta leaves shaded like feathers. Dark green camellia adds another glossy texture complementary to the

red lacquer base. This amusing container and collection of material would make an effective buffet table decoration that would raise a smile as infectious as those that greet you everywhere in Bali.

PAGODAS AND PARASOLS

From Bali to Thailand is not a long flight. In Bangkok I saw some of the most elaborate and beautiful floral decorations ever. This city of splendour and squalor set on a wide river is a metropolis of teaming life, not all of it to my liking. But set like an oasis amidst the most horrendous traffic is the Oriental Hotel. This haven of peace is a mecca for world travellers

103 *A Duck from Bali*

with impeccable service beyond compare. The flowers are changed in the early morning long before the guests appear. Special effects involving armfuls of orchids are prepared each evening for receptions and banquets. Knowing I liked flowers the valets brought to my room everyone's flowers as soon as they departed – I soon had a bathroom like a conservatory.

Colours in the tropics are more brilliant, but in Thailand they assume almost jewel-like intensity apparent in silks, parasols and highly decorated pagodas. The Thai people are gentle and artistic with a flair for presentation. This simple decoration in Illustration 104 captures in a rustic way this land of orchids.

The container is a plank of Bermuda Cedar, *Juniperus bermudiana*, cut in two. Rare since the blight of 1944, the upper piece slots into long nails driven into the horizontal section. A saucer of foam hides this union whilst a parcel of

wet foam is attached to the upright board by wire and staples. By the same method the Thai decorate whole tree trunks set in concrete bases with orchids. They seem to have limitless flowers where in England it is necessary to make a few go as far as possible. These lime green Dendrobiums sprout from the wood rather in a way they grow in the wild.

Lime green Chinese Fan Palms are split lengthways to reduce their bulk then trimmed into interesting shapes. Rusty bronze rosettes of Screw Pine are young self-sown seedlings. In the centre of each group are red and green Gusmannia plants with showy bracts around the inconspicuous flowers. Native to Colombia, Peru and Equador I have used them to effect in Caracas, Venezuela. The root ball is carefully removed from the pot and enclosed in a plastic bag.

A gentle syringing with a fine mist will help to freshen the arrangement. With clear cut shapes and the minimum of

105 Chinese Fruits with Jade

exotic material, this piece of natural wood makes a little look a lot. Despite my dislike of using accessories, imaginative additions work well in exotic designs.

CHINESE FRUITS WITH JADE

My visits to the China Floriculture Research Association in Taiwan and the Hong Kong Flower Club have given me an opportunity to visit these fascinating islands. Described as a shopper's paradise they are outlets for fine *objets d'art* as well as mass-produced exports from mainland China. I am always impressed by the Chinese love of commerce, their bustling street markets each with a special flavour. Displays of exotic fruits, strange roots and vegetables fire the imagination.

It is not necessary to travel to China to find the ingredients of Illustration 105. The local green grocer now stocks an exciting selection for a fruit and flower arrangement. The container is a bowl of avocado-green china raised on a base of padook wood. A heavy pinholder placed under the Oasis compensates for the forward weight of the fruit and vegetables. A purple cabbage is cut in half to expose an interesting pattern of leaves and stalk. Smooth purple aubergines repeat this colour with kidney-shaped mangoes and pinky brown litchi with contrast of texture. *Litchi chinensis* comes from southern China where its sweet white flesh is much appreciated. It is closely related to Euphoria which sounds like a state of mind, but is the Indian Rambutan. Waxy golden green Star Fruit accord well with the texture of the mythological jade animal bought in Hong Kong's famous jade market.

Two blooms have been cut from the main stem of gold Cymbidium orchids to make the spray less crowded, placed in tubes of water. Rosettes of a purple-flowered bromellia offset the heaviness of the composition with yellow-green leaves of *Fatsia japonica*. Three stems of Cat Tail Fern lead our eye to the secondary placement and relate to the animal's tail.

All the heavy items are secured by two split bamboo cocktail sticks obtained from a Chinese delicatessen. When flowers are few or expensive such a decoration can have two lives: one as a visual feast then the other to be eaten.

CHAPTER 8

DRIED BUT NOT DULL

IN THE PAST

The use of dried flowers is not new, their popularity swings with the pendulum of fashion in interior decor. Their greatest vogue, born of leisure, was in the Victorian era with over-stuffed vases and elaborate creations protected by glass domes. Since then they have come and gone as a reaction to that period; Art Nouveau vases of pampas grass, honesty and reed-mace may still linger in seaside boarding houses or shabby stately homes. But the lean years of the Second World War meant that all such embellishments were pushed aside.

The post-war years witnessed a tremendous upsurge of interest in all aspects of home decoration. After years of austerity and 'make do and mend' the women of Britain needed flowers on all their forms. Dried, preserved and artificial flowers are a matter of personal taste and I would hesitate to be an arbiter. I am pleased that the predictions of my first book have come true. In my second book I wrote in great detail about the various methods of drying and preserving so some of this is repetitious. Dried flowers in some form are here to stay, chiefly because we lack the time or means to maintain fresh flowers on a constant basis. Improved central heating is also an important factor.

In recent years up-market interior decorators have looked with favour on massed heads of deads, beginning with David Hicks. At present, on both sides of the Atlantic, the 'English Country House' look holds sway. Frocked tables and flounced draperies of patterned fabric mean that any flowers must be plain massed solids if they are to hold their own. Bowls brimming with fresh roses would be the ideal, but in their absence baskets of desiccated buds must serve. Certain talented London decorators have brought massed natural dried flowers back into favour, often selling at exorbitant prices for the best creations.

AIR DRYING IN THE GARDEN LOGGIA

This chapter has fourteen different illustrations of ways in which dried and preserved material can be used to decorative effect. Illustration 106 shows our garden loggia in August, the peak month for this process with a variety of plant material harvested from the garden. These will be placed carefully in clearly labelled cardboard boxes ready for storage in my granary studio overhead. Good storage space is important and I am fortunate to work with such ideal facilities. With a large store of both home-grown and imported material I have all the ingredients for designs created in late autumn and winter.

Two methods of preservation I favour are by air drying and glycerine solution. Choose a warm dry place with good air circulation free from direct sunlight. This loggia, once the cartshed, is perfect. Gather the flowers to be dried when they are dry, strip off surplus foliage and tie firmly in small bunches, then hang from a washing line or rafters. You will need to check these ties periodically as the stalks will shrivel and the contents could fall to the ground.

Some seedheads will dry partially on the plant and because of their brittle nature should be put in weighted jars or buckets – alliums, poppies and grasses are examples. I prefer seedheads to mummified flowers, enjoying their architectural forms as they near the conclusion of their natural cycle. Keep a watchful eye for vermin, field mice in particular can decimate cereals, poppy heads, etc.

Some flowers need drying fairly quickly and a capacious airing cupboard is a boon, ours still bears traces of Nina de Yarburgh-Bateson's nylon fishing lines used to dry delphinium, larkspur and hydrangeas. Hydrangeas picked when crisp and metallic dry quickly standing in jam jars of shallow water. Experience, and trial and error will guide you as even the plants themselves vary depending on the season.

Preservation of foliage by glycerine solution is a good way of ensuring a supply of dark brown pliable leaves which can be used in sprays or wired individually. Green beech branches *Fagus sylvatica* should be gathered in July. Prune away blemished leaves, crush the stems and stand them at once in a solution of one part glycerine to two parts hot water. It helps to brush this solution on to the tips of slow absorbing subjects such as fatsia, aspidistra and laurel. *Magnolia grandiflora* and glossy camellia are both tough and reliable subjects.

Large beech branches will take about two weeks to turn colour and absorb the solution. This should be topped up with more hot water if the level falls low. When dark brown and silky to the touch they are 'cured' and ready for use. Store in a dry, clean place as over-soaked material will absorb moisture from the air and 'weep' in high humidities. If dye has been added, as is the case with commercially prepared eucalyptus and beech, damage may occur to upholstery fabrics.

There are other methods of preservation such as pressing between newspapers, but this gives a flat effect only suitable for pictures under glass or collages. Preservation by freeze drying produces wonderful results, but is not readily available. Quick drying in a microwave deserves more study. Flowers carefully buried in drying powders, sand or borax are fine for a time, but must always be in a dry atmosphere if they are to retain their form and colour. I recommend the many books devoted to this single subject for one never stops learning tips from someone else's methods.

A WINTER BOUQUET

This decoration in the entrance hall of Middlethorpe Hall, shows how effective a bouquet of dried and artificial materials can look. Built as an elegant country house in the reign of Queen Anne, Middlethorpe has had a chequered history, now beautifully restored it is one of York's finest hotels. Guests from around the world like to be warm and appreciate open fires and central heating. But these high temperatures spell death to cut flowers. Potted plants and dried arrangements provide the touches of life and colour so essential to rooms in winter. Illustration 107 and the four succeeding illustrations are all designed for this chapter and I am grateful to the hotel management for allowing me to use their lovely settings.

The foundation to this decoration is a bundle of lime twigs, but because they would scratch the antique table, they are mounted on a base board. A disc of wood three quarters of an inch thick and nine inches in diameter is pegged centrally with a twelve-inch long dowel rod. This stand is painted matt brown and has felt glued to the bottom side to protect the table. With the dowel now upright a third of a

brick of Dryfoam is impaled on the top. Handfuls of twigs are then bound firmly with reel wire to the dowel until it resembles a sheaf or bundle. The stalk ends radiate outwards cut to just clear the table.

This seemingly casual sheaf of twigs with its foam centre becomes the container stabilized by the disc base. For larger designs the disc foundation should be weighted. Influenced by the deep-red walls I have selected pale seedheads for contrast. The outline is of Bear's Breeches, the statuesque *Acanthus spinosus*. The purple and white flower spikes appear in late summer and dry well, if mature, hung upside down. (See Illustration 106.) They smell faintly of sweet peas even when dry but do not bend too close as they have spiny sepals. The arching delicate seedheads of Venus' Fishing Rod, *Dierama pulcherrimum* are full of grace, glycerined to increase flexibility. Round heads of *Allium aflatunense* and spiny heads of Sea Holly, *Eryngium giganteum*, lead our eye to pale celadon green ballota. *Ballota pseudodictamnus* is worth growing for its leaves alone, but the flower spikes are most attractive composed of whorls of woolly bracts. Nip off the leaves and tips when harvesting and air dry. Glycerining will make them less brittle but not such a pleasing colour. Glycerined aspidistra leaves add a honey tone on the left with dyed red millet grass and three maroon reed-mace.

The focal area consists of velvet-textured Cockscomb dried to an ox-blood red, dried gourds and three artificial apples. These hand-painted and waxed fruits are so realistic as to deceive the most observant. A rosette of fabric Dracaena and three begonia rex leaves are such a good colour blend that I felt I could bend my principles and include them here. Although not a lover of fabric flowers, these foliages printed from photographs of real leaves can be very deceptive. They also introduce colour which enlivens the neutral tones.

Tied with a lavish bow of lichen green ribbon this large bouquet of winter blends happily with fine pictures, a log fire and general air of welcome.

A CONICAL DESIGN IN A BROWN STUDY

The small sitting-room at Middlethorpe is an intimate setting ideal for reading or writing. This conical design of dried materials shown in Illustration 108, a study in browns, blends happily with its decor adding a note of quiet elegance.

The container is one of a fine pair of bronze Regency mantel vases with an ormulu collar and sienna marble plinth. A slender cone of Styrofoam is wired firmly to the rim. Retailed at florists in assorted sizes these cones are intended to take only dried or wired stems. Start with a smaller shape than the overall dimensions bearing in mind that they increase in volume as items are fixed in place. Usually

brown, they can be green or white so it may be necessary to cover them with crepe paper to match your colour scheme.

The materials wired and pressed into the foam are a mixture of matt and shiny textures which become more noticeable when working in a monochromatic scheme. Rich brown watered silk ribbon begins with a bow at the top and spirals down from right to left like a sash of honour, terminating in a bow on the right. This is a handy way of covering the base whilst introducing some plain areas to offset the more fussy fillers. Clusters of pecan nuts, raphia palm cones, fake acorns and strawberry corn are all fruits with shiny brown textures to contrast with small beige gourds, clusters of poppy heads and a creamy Australian bush flower. The spiny bracts of Miss Willmott's Ghost, *Eryngium giganteum*, commemorate a great gardener who was reputed to scatter its seeds when on visits to other gardens so perpetuating her presence. They dry on the plant turning a gun-metal grey in dry weather, or they can be air dried.

Clusters of fabric croton leaves relate in colour and texture to the glossy tan lampshade on the desk, backed by orange skeletonized magnolia leaves. The top three spikes of grass from Panama add a flourish teamed with the supremely graceful Squirrel Tail Grass, the annual *Hordeum jubatum*. These were glycerined for me by that consumate floral artist Lilian Martin of Edinburgh. They remind me of the egrets of feathers worn by ladies of the Prince Regent's Court, adding movement with the slightest breeze.

FOR A GUEST ROOM

No guest room is complete without flowers, but providing fresh ones in a hotel with several suites is quite a chore. Illustration 109 shows a *petite* decoration about twelve inches high suitable for a dressing or occasional table. Muted apricot, gold and aqua echo the colours of the curtains. The container, also used in Illustration 9, is a choice bronze tazza in keeping with the tinted engraving of *Le Repos de Mars*. Even the god of war would be able to rest in this lovely bedroom at Middlethorpe Hall.

Dryfoam holds an outline of home-grown poppy heads,

108 *A Conical Design*

109 *For a Guest Room*

dyed peach glixia daisies and fawn wild Barren Brome Grass, *Bromus sterilis*. All grasses should be gathered before they flower and shed their fever causing pollen. Preserved in glycerine solution they will last many years, silky and pliable. The shining pointed leaves of Silver Tree, *Leucadendron argenteum*, were pressed in my suitcase as I left Cape Town. Their unique silky silver texture was also appreciated by Princess Grace of Monaco who mounted my pressings in her flower pictures. Here they are wired and taped with gutta-percha into short sprays. A few dyed and glycerined bought eucalyptus leaves add a depth of colour.

The focal area has three fantasy flowers made from a brown Tithonia head with a corolla of petals cut from pieces of dyed maize husk glued in place. These contrived flowers were made in Kenya by Safari Flowers. Dating from the Seventies they were exported in all colours together with other styles putting judges in a quandry as to how they should be classified. Flowers made up from plant material have now been ratified in competitive work.

Pink protea cones, gold achillea and seedcases of honesty add depth and interest. This type of small decoration makes a charming present, not intended to last indefinitely. Tiny parcels of pot-pourri packed in muslin may be added to impart fragrance. A regular blow of breath helps to dislodge dust. I was once commissioned to decorate a stately home, its lovely chatelaine cleaned her arrangements with a hair drier, a compliment to both me and them.

A STUDY IN MONOCHROME

This study in monochrome in Illustration 110 employs all the tints, tones and shades painted on an Italian table. The embroidered picture of classical figures with an urn inspired my choice of an alabaster vase. Originally a lamp base and found in a flower club sales table, it is heavy and stable. A piece of Dryfoam is bound firmly to the narrow neck.

Designed as a drooping triangle, the decoration accords with this elegant sitting-room at Middlethorpe. Bleached clusters of a species of helichrysum contrast with tan dried fungi and parchment-coloured gourds to hold central attention. Curving pods of Flamboyant, both natural and bleached, graduate outwards together with spiralling wisteria vines stripped of their bark. Although it is possible to experiment with bleach I prefer to buy them ready prepared.

Dyed and clipped fan palms define the outline, with curved sprays of glycerined *Magnolia × soulangiana* leaves introduced to soften the effect. This deciduous shrub bears erect branches which would look gawky here so the individual leaves have been wired, taped and mounted. Use natural gutta-percha to cover the wires, it is a rubber tape and looses its elasticity so test before buying. The tapered

triangular pods of *Tulipa kaufmanniana* are home-grown favourites, with buff Lyme Grass and shredded palm they add a graceful note.

Close to centre is a contrived flower made from the scales of Cedar of Lebanon cones glued into a teasel head, a precious souvenir of my visit to the Green Finger Club of Beruit in 1974, alas no more. Pendant sprays of eucalyptus and cream aspidistra flow down to the right of polished Raphia Palm cones. This native of the Mascarene Islands also produces raffia twine. The enormous hand-like flower stalks are festooned with cones that look like grenades. Used individually the beak-shaped end can be drilled and the nuts mounted on wire.

A FRIVOLOUS PAGODA

The colourful decoration in Illustration 111 owes its inspiration to the beautiful curtains, one of the features of Middlethorpe Hall. Give me a piece of glazed chintz and I'm away because some other artist has already provided me with a colour scheme. Intended for a boudoir, this arrangement in a pagoda of red tolé has a note of frivolity which is carried through in the coroneted bed draperies not shown here.

The metal container is French and a great favourite as it looks good with a lot or a little. In a more rustic vein five terracotta flower pots of graduated sizes could be constructed to give a similar effect. In order not to hide this container four separate placements held in Dryfoam burst from the top and sides linked by shot silk ribbon and clusters of helichrysums of peachy pink. Groups of artificial cherries contrast with loops of dark pine-green ribbon adding a rhythmic movement.

In order to give unity the same materials are grouped alternately and opposite including blue-green, pale-pink and bronze-red grasses. Note how they are placed in bunches, not mixed up together. Delicate skeletonized Banyan leaves dyed deep turquoise are teamed with shaded fabric leaves of Maranta. Curving sprays of red dyed and glycerined leaves of eucalyptus add to this colourful display.

In the centre of each group peach-pink teasel heads take the place of flowers. This light-hearted affair is not my usual style of decoration but it suits the romantic mood of the room.

A BLACKAMOOR PEDESTAL

Arranging flowers each day throughout the open garden season means I am rather relieved when August comes and I can rely more on dried materials in keeping with autumn days ahead. This handsome blackamoor in Illustration 112

has a curious history and makes an ideal pedestal for an imposing display to the ceiling. He stands in the drawing-room at Heslington lit by a concealed spotlight.

Strapped to the wooden tray he carries a brick of Dryfoam. Thus his weight counterbalances the plant material, some of which is many years old, which when washed periodically in soapy water looks like new. Afraid of weeping dye on to the carpet, I use fabric eucalyptus bought in Montgomery, Alabama long ago. I have never found its equal; the same can be said of controllable wire stems which curve to any desired shape. Dark brown leaves of cycas palm and cream aspidistra both take a long time to glycerine and change colour. But once preserved they will last indefinitely with a grace and movement that is hard to improve upon.

The begonia rex leaves of printed fabric were bought as a fake plant, pulled apart and then remounted on long stub wires taped with gutta. They add a dash of colour found in the scatter cushions. Although expensive, these fabric leaves are washable and can be used in a variety of ways over several seasons. The purist may eschew them and prefer dried leaves in their place, but that is a matter of taste.

Leading to the focal area are the dried heads of dyed pink Banksia, a family akin to Proteas. First found in Botany Bay in 1770 there are over fifty species. Whisps of pink grass and black fake elderberries lighten the design which concludes with a central rosette of fabric dracaena.

The painting of fruits on a brocade-draped table is entitled *Champagne and Oysters* by Gottfried Schultz. A fine French clock and bronze pastille burners complete the composition.

111 *A Frivolous Pagoda*

112 *A Blackamoor Pedestal*

A FLORAL FIRESCREEN

One advantage of dried material is that the arranger is free to experiment unhampered by the limitations of keeping it alive in water or water-retaining foam. This gives scope for wall plaques, collages, trophies, swags and other decorative designs. Pressed flower pictures under glass I will leave to such specialists as the late Princess Grace in *My Book of Flowers*.

Illustration 113 shows a firescreen made for the morning-room in Illustration 21. When the fire is lit it hangs on an inside door. The antique oval frame measures thirty one by thirty five inches. Those more patient than me will be able to produce smaller versions as wall plaques. At our national shows I marvel at the skill of such gold medallists as Elizabeth Tomkinson who has developed the technique of pressed material gummed to a background combined with the three-dimensional effect of collage. Had these labours of infinite patience been in embroidery they would have endured longer, for this is an ephemeral medium. However,

it is a comfort that our mistakes can be more easily rectified or abandoned.

The background is of a fibrous composition board used for partition panelling. Avoid wood as it is too hard to take stainless-steel pins. Choose a fabric to cover the board which will enhance the setting, this aquamarine silk is also used for cushions and picture mounts. Your choice of frame and fabric will influence the character of the finished design, experiment with hessian, velvet, linen or felt. Whatever you select must be applied tightly, crease free and secure at the back first with drawing pins and then with glue. Never use glue on the front as it will produce an uneven tension and even soak through. On an oval or circular panel, gussets of surplus fabric must be cut away at the back to reduce bulk. Once secure cover the back neatly with brown paper and fix ring hooks to the frame.

A small half sphere of Styrofoam or Dryfoam should be attached, secured by long pins a little below centre. The smaller the foundation the easier it is to conceal later. Begin with the outline of fine material, grasses, tulip and poppy

113 *A Floral Firescreen*

153

pods, etc wiring the weaker stems, if necessary. This could become a manual on floristry, but let it suffice to say choose the lightest gauge wire for support as too thick wires will look clumsy and heavy. Larger items like the maroon fabric leaves could be gummed, but once done you cannot change your mind. Fake dianthus, tiny dandelion clocks and helichrysum lead to the centre backed by red grass and millet.

A bow of ribbon may be introduced secured by tiny pins. Salvaged from an old bonnet this malachite green silk adds a touch of quality. As observed earlier the ribbon says a lot, just as sometimes the envelope tells more than the letter. Graduate to bolder items such as dried gourds, shining seedheads of Centaurea and contrived flowers; the latter are made from melon seeds and teasels, see Illustration 129. Rounded Bay Grape, *Coccoloba uvifera*, and skeletonized banyan leaves help to finish the posy. As the finished screen will be propped up it pays to secure heavier items with small pins to prevent forward movement.

A RECTANGULAR COLLAGE

Illustration 114 is a rectangular collage made in the same way as Illustration 113 with a tied bunch design mounted on bronze silk in a seventeenth-century style frame. By now you will be able to identify most of the material with seedheads, grasses and sprays of fabric leaves. The exception could be the central orange flowers made of dyed Sisal hemp glued in a fringe around a helichrysum. Sent by the Judges Council of Peru to York Minster for the 1967 Flower Festival, I used them in a multicoloured modern design to complement a patchwork cope as amazing as Joseph's coat of many colours. On the final day because of evensong they were forced to close the door against a long queue. A voice cried out 'Let me in, let me in'. The last person to be admitted was a beautiful girl who told me 'I come from Lima, I read about this in the newspaper at home, where is our exhibit?' I showed her, both humbled and shaken that she had come so far and almost missed the experience.

114 *A Rectangular Collage*

Diagonal movement comes from pale green ballota to counterpoise the ribbon. Fabric croton leaves, wood roses, orange contrived flowers and skeletonized magnolia leaves all supply changes of form and texture. Little material is needed, but it must stand up to close inspection. A tropical butterfly salvaged from a Victorian collection is attached as my signature.

A HARVEST TROPHY

I am not certain where a collage ends and a trophy begins, but the decoration in Illustration 115 is unframed so maybe there lies the difference. Designed for the kitchen wall it has a stylish yet rustic simplicity as the eye explores the sculptured forms and textures of mainly neutral material. It is inspired by the Spanish Barley fork which I was obliged to carry the length of the King's Road, hardly the pastoral idyll that the implement evokes.

A flat basket of bleached osier is firmly fixed to the wall. Do not rely on a nail, rawl plugs and screws are needed. Over this is placed the fork, also secured to the wall with a tiny eye hook to ensure stability. A brick of Dryfoam with a groove cut out sits snugly across the handle, wrapped in brown paper to make it less visible from any angle and firmly wired to the basket.

The effect of a wheat sheaf is made by bunches of bearded wheat wired into the top. The cut stems are added at the bottom of the brick. Aqua grasses following the line of the fork handle are placed horizontally. A bleached Flamboyant pod split in half runs diagonally forming a visual link between the fan palm top right and a second one wired to the basket lower left. Rust dried fungi give contrast of both colour and texture together with tropical pods of *Aspidosperma verbascifolium*. The woven corn dolly is an accessory in keeping with the theme.

Five yellow gourds give strong focal interest and the whole is tied up with a bow of turquoise blue burlap ribbon.

115 *A Harvest Trophy*

Simple yet effective, each item shows clearly against the terracotta wall. Two stone jars suggest the harvester's reward and complete the country atmosphere.

A TROPHY IN THE GRANARY

The trophy in Illustration 116 consists of a collection of antique wooden implements displayed on the gable wall of my granary studio. Oak beams, polished copper and agricultural bygones add to the air of rusticity. The base of the design is a large dough trough used originally in bread making; bound with iron, its concave shape adds depth to

the composition. I have resisted the temptation to fill it devising a more interesting design by placing the hay rake and maltster's shovel off centre lower right. These heavy items are all suspended on nylon thread from sturdy rafters as well as eye hooks in the wall.

Three blocks of Dryfoam covered with wire netting are wired behind the blade of the shovel; with these secure mechanics we can create with confidence. Two dry stalks of Giant Cow Parsley, *Heracleum mantegazzianum*, are mounted on canes and placed to continue the line of the handle. Beware, this mammoth biennial can cause horrible blisters if gathered when still green. Three corn dollies woven by Brian Withill are mounted on canes, radiating

116 *A Trophy in the Granary*

from centre left. Their beautiful spiral motion adds to the interest.

A cascade of bottle gourds gathered in Cyprus form a strong focal movement. *Lagenaria vulgaris* will grow on an arbor in warm climates: the curiously shaped fruits were once used for water and gun powder. Two Cardoon heads display a boss of silky seeds and lead to two tree cucumbers from Florida. At the top teasels and giant poppy heads radiate upwards with an explosive line.

To add too much could spoil the group which is highlighted by a star burst of *Allium christophii* with sperical heads as large as a football. The silvery lilac flowers on purple stems dry in the garden and retain their colour.

Diagonally opposite spirals of dried asparagus fern and pendant heads of Dierama create downward movement. This international mixture is completed by glycerined leaves of a tropical tree given to me in the Transvaal as yet eluding identification.

A HARVEST WHEAT SHEAF

The theme of harvest is continued in Illustration 117 with a small and easy-to-make wheat sheaf suitable for home or church decoration. The foundation consists of a disc of wood seven inches in diameter pegged with a dowel fourteen

117 *A Harvest Wheat Sheaf*

inches long. A sphere of Dryfoam is impaled and then firmly strapped to the top of the dowel. These dimensions produce a sheaf twenty-two inches high with a head twelve inches across, so you must scale them down if you require something smaller. I weighted the base to make it more stable. The foundation will now resemble an old-fashioned hat stand.

Gather the wheat, oats or barley when ripe, but still green and lay it on a rack of wire netting so that it dries flat. Grain left until golden as here is inclined to shed. Never pick without permission to glean. Cut the ears from the stems with about two inches of stalk attached. Clean the left over stalks of surplus foliage to expose their shining stems. With an eighteen gauge wire, wire the stalks into small bunches ending with a double-ended mount wire like a hair pin end. Insert these bunches into the bottom of the sphere pointing downwards. Trim the ends so they are flush with the table.

The head is composed of small wired clusters of wheat ears inserted all over the remainder of the sphere. Start at the bottom next to the stalks and work upwards adding until you reach the top and back. It takes a lot of wheat so do not be too ambitious. If your sheaf is to be any larger it is advisable to strengthen the sphere with wire netting and use a cement filled pot as a base, see Illustration 15.

The finished sheaf may be decorated in any way you choose. A tie of red or blue ribbon for poppies and cornflowers looks attractive. My example has a plait of raffia tied neatly with a knot and held in place with hair pins of wire to prevent it riding up. The decoration is enhanced by the potato riddle, strawberry basket and old sickle which together create an evocative composition.

WINTER FRAGRANCE

Trees made from a variety of materials have been described in Illustration 15 with further examples in Illustrations 45 and 126. They have countless adaptations, one of the

118 *Winter Fragrance*

prettiest being a fragrant lavender tree. The example in Illustration 118 was photographed in the lovely home of Isobel, Lady Dunnington-Jefferson. Made as a winter decoration it picks up the colours in her Andres Vermeulan painting of *Skaters in a Dutch Landscape.*

Gather your lavender before it is too open and loosing its essential oil. Dry on flat racks of wire netting or open wicker trays out of the sun.

Select an attractive tree trunk; this one is cherry and set in a flower pot of cement. Attach a four-inch Dryfoam sphere bearing in mind the larger the foundation the bigger will be your tree. This example is thirty inches high and twelve inches across overall. Mauve statice and looped bows of aquamarine ribbon help to bulk out the lavender and introduce contrast. Placed in a porcelain cache pot the cement is hidden by reindeer moss.

Placed beside it is an ironstone bowl of pot-pourri and a Spode botanical plate, part of a choice dessert service. In recent years pot-pourri has enjoyed a revival together with many nostalgic reminders of a more gracious age. Each great house had its own recipe of home-grown ingredients. The following recipe was given to me by that great flower arranger Anne, Countess of Rosse. She credits Lady Sykes of Sledmere with the original dated 1820.

'Pick roses at midday when dew has gone and remove stalks. Spread to dry on sheets of paper but not in the sun. When they are dry, mix them with any other dry flowers you like, clove pinks, violets, orange flowers also lemon verbena, sweet geranium, bay leaves with Balm of Gilead and dried lavender. Then add spices: one ounce each of cloves, mace, cinnamon with half an ounce of borax, allspice and gum benzoin, put in some thin slices of orange and lemon peel and a handful of rosemary. Mix it very well.'

Today it is difficult to find orange flowers or Balm of Gilead *Commiphora opobalsamum*, a Middle Eastern shrub with aromatic berries related to the plant-yielding Myrrh, the third most costly gift of the Magi. She also mentions that a small packet of orris root may be added to oils of lavender, geranium and verbena together with attar of roses to revive this concoction. A frugal footnote states that as the latter is hard to come by it may be dispensed with; what a relief and a winning touch.

The present-day equivalent can be bought in all sorts of blends together with a bottle of essence that I prefer not to describe. Like most things today, one can settle for the quick and easy and inferior or work at the laborious and individual. I know which I prefer.

A GARLAND FOR AN ALABASTER VASE

The elegant garland in Illustration 119 shows the versatility of dried plant material enhanced by a beautiful alabaster ewer. Lent to me by Di Fargus, it once belonged to Eleanor Shaw who inspired so many of us in the early days of the flower arrangement movement. One of a pair, it stands thirty-one inches high.

The foundation is a stiff plastic-coated wire bent so that it grips inside the neck of the vase. This inverted crescent ends in a second placement which balances the design. This is my method of assembly. First cover the wire with neutral gutta-percha tape, this ensures a firm grip and blends with the brown dried material.

Select an interesting mixture of shapes, to include pointed seed pods, flat leaves and the rounded forms of flowers, cones and gourds. Make a mock-up design with these to ensure variety of colour and texture. Ribbon may also be included to give the impression of binding up the garland and continuous movement. Here the contrasting turquoise velvet is chosen to match cushions in an otherwise cream and brown room.

Mount each item on suitable wires and cover these with tape reassembling the mock-up design to help you visualize the finished effect. Most of these previously used materials you will recognize with two exceptions. The long sinuous cones of Norfolk Island Pine, *Araucaria excelsa*, used at each end and like cord near the plinth and, in the focal area, two contrived lilies made in Kenya from agave leaves grouped round a furry palm spadix.

Start at one end and bind on each item firmly with reel wire so that they overlap each other sufficiently to cover the foundation frame yet still show their own value, foiling the larger items with solid and skeletonized leaves. When the focal area is reached begin at the other end so that all items appear to flow away from the centre. There are many variations of this style of decoration which is inspired by the wood carving of Grinling Gibbons. For further descriptive instructions see Illustration 125.

A THANKSGIVING WREATH

The North American custom of Thanksgiving dates from the Pilgrim Fathers who celebrated their first harvest at Plymouth Colony with a feast of wild turkey and cranberries, in mid November. The decoration in Illustration 120 would suit this occasion inspired by Della Robbia wreaths, see Illustrations 122–124.

The foundation is a sixteen-inch Styrofoam frame intended for wires or wooden picks. A wire wreath ring of dry moss could be substituted. Cover the frame with a bandage of brown crepe paper to blend with the materials.

119 *A Garland for an Alabaster Vase*

The majority of items will last indefinitely except for the clusters of kumquats, red apples and fresh cherries secured on cocktail sticks or wired in clusters. For a permanent effect these could be replaced by cones or seedheads.

To make something similar wire flat leaves such as bay grape, magnolia or preserved laurel. This process is called 'mounting up'. Take an eight-inch long stub wire of suitable thickness or gauge and bend it into a hair pin with one end slightly longer than the other. Hold the stalk and wire loop between the thumb and forefinger and with the other hand twist the longer wire round the leaf stalk and the shorter wire. Close the two wires together to form a double wire. This sounds complicated but with practice you will be able to do it automatically ending up with both ends of wire parallel and the same length. This double mount is used constantly in floristry designs to lengthen short stalks. Ingenuity will be needed for stalkless objects such as nuts and gourds. A small drill with a fine bit will solve the problem but take care of your fingers. Once drilled the walnuts, brazils and pecans can be wired with fine gauge wire into clusters. Time consuming yes, but long lasting and effective.

Arrange the wired materials in a mock-up pattern to get an idea of the design you wish to make, then assemble. Start with a collar of flat leaves adding the larger items placed equidistantly. Clusters of wheat and grasses break the formality and balance the diagonal movement of two tones of burlap ribbon. Finish by filling in with bunches of nuts and fruits. It can now be hung on a wall or door or used on a dining table with chunky candles as a table centre-piece.

120 *A Thanksgiving Wreath*

121 *A Christmas Lantern*

CHAPTER 9
CHRISTMAS DECORATIONS

A CHRISTMAS LANTERN

The feast of Christmas is celebrated world-wide with the addition of festive trimmings in homes, churches and public places. Each country adapts what is available both real and artificial, for this is the season when flower arrangers allow themselves the freedom of mixing fake with real. For me nothing can improve upon fresh materials. However, it must be admitted that with central heating and open fires the latest artificial materials are so realistic as to deceive even the keenest eye. By judicious mixing many effective decorations can be produced. The style and construction will vary according to what is to hand, the function and purpose dependent upon individual taste and circumstances. I once saw a pedigree herd's cow shed decorated with shining milk bottle tops, nothing could have been more ingenious or effective. Certainly a stable fit for a King!

In Illustration 121 this antique brass lantern with its shining candle welcomes guests to our home at Christmastide. A symbol of a Greater Light, it expresses goodwill, peace and happiness to all who enter. Placed on a slice of yew wood it is enhanced by fresh flowers and foliage.

The outline is of Blue Cedar, *Cedrus atlantica* 'Glauca', with additional snippets of Blue Spruce, *Picea pungens* 'Koster's Blue', two of the best conifers for blue-green foliage. The pure yellow holly was culled from the centre of a large bush of *Ilex × altaclarensis* 'Golden King', it lights up the decoration and foils the flowers. Red is one of the most welcoming of colours and complementary to green, it has become a favourite for festive decorations. Wide-eyed anemones and scarlet carnations are an obvious choice, but cut poinsettias would be equally effective. Three slender reed-mace coated with red flock give height and balance the curving placement lower right.

A wall wreath of artificial blue spruce and fresh holly is hung on the crimson wall to balance the visual effect and add depth. Soft blue-green moiré and bronze velvet ribbons are looped amidst clusters of baubles of bronze silk and red glass. Details of how to make such a decoration are described in Illustrations 122, 123 and 124.

A CHRISTMAS DOOR WREATH

This is the season when we welcome friends and acquaintances to our home and nothing says this better than a door wreath. Provided the door is not too exposed, most such decorations will stay fresh and attractive until Twelfth Night.

Woven wreaths of vines, grasses and willow osiers are becoming increasingly popular as well as the traditional holly wreath sold by florists for cemetaries. It is perhaps this latter association which causes some people to be reluctant to adopt what is a popular holiday custom throughout the United States of America.

Illustration 122 shows the front door of The Manor House decorated with a circular design of fresh garden materials. The shape echoes the form of the half standard box trees and contrasts with the vertical line of the slender columns. The curving fanlight and polished knocker heighten the effect.

The foundation is a shallow plastic trough filled with Oasis sixteen inches in diameter. These wreath frames are available in several sizes from most florists. Lightly soaked with water they make an ideal support. Oasis will crumble if oversoaked so it is advisable to wrap the ring with a three-inch bandage of thin plastic cut from dry cleaner's polythene. It is through this that the stems are inserted into the Oasis.

First place an overlapping fringe of dark evergreen yew,

fir or spruce sprigs around the inner and outer perimeter, short pieces gleaned from the Christmas tree might suffice, but the effect should be thick and luxuriant. A selection of wired fruits is added next. Three rosy apples equidistantly placed give focal interest. They are secured by a double-ended poker wire passed through the core or a tripod of wooden cocktail sticks. Clusters of rose hips, pine cones, green quince, pecan nuts and iris pods add cheerful colour and variety. These are backed with ivy leaves, *Hedera helix* 'Buttercup' and rosettes of *Euonymus fortunei radicans* 'Emerald and Gold'. Tufts of grey lichen moss fill in the ground work whilst sprigs of yellow winter jasmine, *Jasminum nudiflorum*, add a cheerful note. The generous bow of red velvet with ribbon streamers helps to balance the composition. Red bows are added to the box tree stems on Christmas Eve.

A PINE CONE WREATH

If because of the fear of vandalism or the vicissitudes of weather an outdoor wreath is impractical, interior doors or walls lend themselves to this formal treatment. A simple wreath of pine cones, saved from the garden, is amongst my favourites. Economy of materials and quiet understatement are its distinctive features.

The example in Illustration 123 was constructed on a sixteen-inch diameter ring of Styrofoam. This hard material is for wires and dry stems only, and is stronger than Oasis. Cover the frame with a bandage of brown crepe paper to tone with the cone colour. Five concentric circles of dry pine cones are used starting at the outer ring first. Each cone is firmly wired by passing a gauge wire half-way around the lower scales. Bring the two equal ends together twisting the wires tightly towards the cone's stalk. The two wires can then be pressed together to form a straight double-ended mount to insert into the frame. Save your best cones for the middle circle so that the smallest cones will graduate neatly to form the inner-most ring. In a warm room the cones will expand and cover any gaps.

Additional decoration is a matter of personal taste and it is fun to experiment. Here an asymmetric sash of red ribbon with a small bow top right is balanced by a larger one and tails lower left. Scot's pine boughs, *Pinus sylvestris*, golden berries and variegated holly complete the effect. If I could grow only one variety, *Ilex × altaclarensis* 'Lawsoniana' is

122 A Christmas Door Wreath

123 *A Pine Cone Wreath*

the holly I would choose. My plant came from stock sold at the Saville Gardens, Windsor. The leaves are larger, flatter and less spiny than the common holly and the central golden variegation overlaps with brighter green the deep green margin. It is apt to revert to the all-green parent, so these portions should be removed. Variegated hollies are slow to establish, but are amongst the hardiest and most attractive of our native evergreens. It is not surprising that the Druids of Ancient Britain attached great importance to holly, ivy and the parasitic mistletoe.

A DELLA ROBBIA WREATH

The inspiration for the wreath in Illustration 124 came from the ceramic garlands produced by the Della Robbia family in fifteenth-century Florence. Made of glazed and coloured pottery they frequently surrounded a blue and white bas relief of the Madonna and Child. The foundation is a fourteen-inch wire wreath frame bound with dry moss. The moss is covered with bandages of gold metallic foil paper chosen to tone with the basic foundation cover of gold plastic rose leaves. Long pine cones mounted on poker wires create the main feature. The dried gourds resemble carved wood in muted shades of brown. These are hard to find as they usually rot off before drying out completely. Silk covered baubles could be substituted like the three lime green ones here. Clusters of pecan nuts – drilled and wired individually

– small protea cones and polished raffia palm kernels all add variety of texture and form. Russet and lime green silk leaves lend sparkle and tone with the lime velvet and brown silk ribbon. It hangs above a mantel flanked by bronze caryatid candlesticks. Carefully stored, such a dry decoration will give many Christmases of pleasure.

A WALL GARLAND

Garlands, swags and wreaths owe their origin to classical antiquity and have great appeal to flower arrangers. Their revival in the furniture and plaster work of the eighteenth century is a source of inspiration to us today. The example in Illustration 125 is in five sections on a stiff wire frame. A firm foundation ensures that the whole hangs evenly linking picture, light brackets and carved chairs in one rhythmic composition. First create the wire sections on the spot so visualizing the finished effect and measure accordingly. Small hooks and eyes of wire ensure that the separate sections will fit together easily, cut one crescent to arch over the painting, two for the dip of the swag and two separate tail pieces.

Next select the ingredients to include background, focal and filler materials. Here fir, rose and galax leaves all of gold plastic, unite the ormulu brackets to the gilded picture frame. Green plastic camellia leaves, shiny red berries and lime green fabric leaves give contrast of texture to bows and

124 A Della Robbia Wreath

streamers of velvet ribbon worked carefully through the design. A judicious inclusion of tinsel sparklers twinkles in the candlelight.

Begin by laying all the ingredients on a large work-table or the floor to make a mock up of the design. This also ensures that you don't put all the best bits in one end only to run short at the other! Cover the strong wire support with gutta-percha, a rubber tape, or a narrow bandage of crepe paper. This will ensure a firm grip as items are bound on with a reel of iron wire. Begin by binding from the tip allowing each item to overlap, creating the design as you work. This is a satisfying process but it requires concentrated effort to keep everything firm and secure. Pull the reel tightly around each placement but do not twist wires around each other as this makes any future dismantling much harder. Careful observation will show that the separate sections each work to a focal area backed by an emphasizing bow, one at the crown

of the swag and at each lowest dip. This tapering and full-ness is hard to achieve, but adds to the interest. To assemble, attach the top crescent over the picture first. The two end tails are wired to the brackets then the two dipping swags to complete the whole. After Christmas it is carefully dismantled and each section placed between dust sheets in the chest below.

A MANTEL SWAG

The overmantel in Illustration 126 shows a similar treatment inspired by the drawing-room colour scheme of peach-pink and lime green. This swag is also made in five sections for easier storage. The materials include artificial fabric roses, red velvet vine leaves, bunches of irredescent grapes, fabric leaves and gold foliages. Crystal beads with creamy

125 *A Wall Garland*

127 *A Pair of Swags with Drops*

pink pearl drops create a richly jewelled effect. Individually wired sequins could be substituted at less cost. The classical fireplace is carved with a panel of two putti playing with a lion surrounded by a garland.

The handsome ormulu urns with siennese marble plinths hold a pair of topiary trees. Twenty-inch dowel rods sit in plastic flower pots of instant cement to support Dryfoam spheres. These are covered with copper foil paper and then interspersed with grapes, leaves and some much-prized frosted apples. Peach-pink bows and tails link with the ribbon used in the swag. This artificial decoration will withstand the heat of the fire whereas fresh evergreens would quickly wither.

A PAIR OF SWAGS WITH DROPS

A third and easier-to-make type of swag is illustrated in Illustration 127 in the dining-room. Strong screws are set into the wall just below the cornice. A long lathe of wood forms the back support for a streamer of maroon velvet topped with a bow. These are the mechanics used in Chapter 3, Illustrations 36 and 37 with blue moiré ribbon. Two groups of artificial materials are used on each swag to resemble carved drops. They are arranged in Dryfoam strapped to the lathe over the ribbon. It is an easy and economical design created *in situ*. Doing them on the ground and then hanging them up rarely works as the viewing angle is different.

The artificial materials consist of silver fir branches, grapes, cerise pink leaves, aquamarine foil flowers and a pair of turquoise birds. The colours accord with the curtains, place setting and Oriental carpet. The scene of many elegant dinner parties, the circular table is of veneered rosewood with six solid rosewood chairs. The highly polished table reflects the sparkle of crystal and silver; six Spode plates depict the carols of Christmas.

The table centre-piece is an Irish dish ring of Dublin

128 *Still Life with Fruit*

silver with a glass liner. Sprigs of jasmine, spray chrysanthemums, apricot and cream mini-carnations, berries and cream ivy complete this low all-round design. Real flowers with their light fragrance can be appreciated at close quarters. They are the final compliment to the guests with good food, fine wines, gentle candlelight and genial company.

STILL LIFE WITH FRUIT

On the sideboard a still life of fruits and flowers makes an important statement. The room is dominated by the portrait of Isabella, Duchess of Grafton by Sir Godfrey Kneller. Born Lady Isabella Bennet she was the only daughter of the Earl of Arlington and lived at what is now Buckingham Palace. Her ambitious father married her off, aged five, to the illegitimate son of Charles II, Henry Fitzroy, first Duke of Grafton. The decoration below (Illustration 128) is amongst my favourites because it allows considerable scope for the mixing of colours, forms and textures.

The container is a silver tureen with liner. It stands on an oval silver tray for added importance. The galleried edge of the tray is a useful boundary for fruits grouped at the base. With moist Oasis firmly taped into the liner begin with the outline. The top left branch of berries is a deciduous holly from North America, *Ilex verticillata*, stems of colourful chilli pepper, *Capsicum frutescens*, combine with sweeping sprays of *Euphorbia fulgens* at lower right. This tropical shrub belongs to the same family as the poinsettia. It exudes a milky sap when cut and should be sealed in a flame to make it last. Two flower spikes of *Kniphofia snowdenii*, a native of Uganda, amazed me by flowering so late with the slender tubular florets of scarlet coral. The orange carnations, croton leaves and clusters of iris berries lead to the focal oranges. All the fruits are impaled on cocktail sticks resting clear of the Oasis to prevent rotting. Several varieties of home-grown apples, lemons and cut kiwi fruits are topped off with a variegated pineapple. Purple grapes and a cabbage complete this triadic colour harmony of orange, green and purple. To the left an arching stem of albino ivy, *Hedera colchica* 'Dentata Variegata', narrowly misses the cutlery drawer. Yellow jasmine and the papery seed cases of honesty complete the group. The elegant Regency candelabra frame the decoration adding height without obscuring the portrait. This is a colourful yet less expensive decoration than an all-flower piece and suggests an abundance and richness associated with entertaining.

THE CHRISTMAS TREE

Few of us would wish to forsake our traditional Christmas tree, yet for certain practical reasons, such as lack of space, there are many attractive substitutes to make at home. I always stand our real tree in water to prevent needle drop. The bucket inside the terracotta pot is firmly packed with logs and heavy pebbles. It drinks copiously through the festive season. The tree in Illustration 129 is an eye-catching alternative and can be made to any size. It appears conical, but is constructed from a flat sheet of moist Oasis backed with strong Styrofoam. This is sold by the sheet and cut with a knife to size. First make a slender triangle of wood, the one illustrated was thirty-six inches high, nine inches wide using wooden lathe two inches deep of quarter-inch thickness. The sandwich Oasis sheet is cut to fit this casing, moistened and then wrapped in cling film. Some water will drain downwards, but enough should be retained to keep the greenery fresh. Occasional spraying or resoaking will help. However, if you are able to find the blue-green fir *Abies nobilis* this will not be necessary as it lasts almost indefinitely. Its unique colour and strong form make it much sought after by Continental florists.

This design can also be done with boxwood, ivy leaves, as in Chapter 1, spruce or cuppressus evergreen. The tree trunk is firmly set in a pot of cement or plaster. This is covered by a basketry cache pot and topped with pebbles. Fix the wood frame to the trunk with a dowel rod, peg or nails. The Oasis sheet is quite heavy when wet so the mechanics must all be firm to avert frustration later. Now slot the Oasis sheet in place and begin at the bottom of the frame with a fringe of greenery adding short sprigs to imitate overlapping growth. The stem ends should be cleaned and sharpened to pass easily through the film. This is a fragrant if somewhat messy task on account of exuded resin. The finished tree can be decorated in a variety of ways, but allow the beauty of the foliage to predominate. Dainty bows of red ribbon, small gold baubles and flowers made from melon seeds seem just enough. The flowers are Mexican and consist of six seeds glued into a dyed teasel. I have often wondered what might grow if these white and grey edged seeds were planted.

The little star came from a visit to Guatamala. It is made of straw and edged with emerald sequins. Sorting through one's treasures as Christmas approaches brings happy reminders of flower friends around the world.

A TRIANGULAR CEPPO

The tree in Illustration 130 utilizes the same pot, basketry cover and silver birch trunk. This time the base is an open triangle of wood resembling an Italian ceppo used to display the nativity; it measures fifteen inches wide, thirty-three inches high and three inches deep. Six small half sections of birch are glued equidistantly to the sides of the frame. A second section is glued on top with a half-inch hole drilled through it. These form the rustic candleholders. The top

candle is mounted on stiff wire passed through a hole drilled in the apex. A star of straw would look equally effective. A small section of birch above the trunk conceals the half-inch dowel rod peg which holds the frame to the base. It also supports a carved wooden angel from Oberammergau.

The garland is made on a separate triangular wire frame. It can be changed from year to year to give the basic frame a new look. Here I have used thirty sprigs of plastic fir, fourteen gold paper leaves, thirteen Japanese tinsel and pearl flowers, red berries and pine cones. About two yards of red lurex cord and parchment watered silk ribbon are worked through the design. As for the wall and mantel garlands it is advisable to lay out all the items in a pattern, taping each stem with gutta-percha. The frame could be made from dry cleaner's coat hangers or a similar gauge wire purchased from an ironmonger. Cover this also with tape to ensure a good finish. With the frame on a flat surface begin at the apex and bind on each item with reel wire. Secure the ribbon ends at the same time. Pass the ribbon and cord from right to left then left to right as items are bound on. Catch the ribbon with the reel as it crosses the frame in a rhythmic flow. This gives the effect that the garland has been bound up with the ribbons as well as adding movement to the finished design. The completed garland is then attached to the wooden frame. If you use lighted candles ensure that they are firmly fixed and never left unattended.

AN ABSTRACT TREE

The next tree shown in Illustration 131 owes as much to carpentry as it does to flower arranging, but it is not as complicted as it may appear. As with all decorations, simplified hybrids can be evolved, a slavish copy would be boring. The basic 'tree' consists of a fifty-inch long dowel fixed into some support. Mine is a root of beautifully sculptured and bleached wood from South Africa, the gift of the talented artist Elsa de Jaeger. A hollow tube, fractionally wider than

130 *A Triangular Ceppo*

131 *An Abstract Tree*

the dowel, is set vertically into the root. The dowel 'stem' will take in or out of this tube which facilitates dismantling and storage. The eighteen 'branches' are cut from slender lathes of wood with a diagonal point at each end. A small hole is drilled in the point through which a decoration can be hung. These sections begin at two inches length and each one is one inch longer so that the lowest branch is twenty inches long. A hole half-inch in diameter is drilled in the centre. All the branches are then spray painted. In this case aquamarine car paint, but dark green metallic paint would look attractive.

Now to assemble the tree. Slot the 'trunk' into its root or other support – a log of wood would suffice. Then slide on the largest branch followed by a section of tubing, as used to support the dowel. My version is cream to repeat the root colour. These sections should be about three inches long, but as the tree builds up and nears the top the space between each branch should be reduced to two inches. This will give a closer set and more realistic appearance. The branches can now be swivelled at angles to each other to give a three-dimensional look to the whole. The sections of snug-fitting tubing prevent the cross branches from all slipping together.

The easy part is to decorate the wooden-framed 'tree'. This example has crystal tear-drop baubles, irridescent grapes, pear and aqua balls and red flock apples. They are all suspended on nylon thread with a wire hook through the small hole in each branch tip. Aqua and mother-of-pearl leaves are intermingled with bows of red velvet. Stubby candles rest on the end of the branches. A less dangerous method of illumination would be to use metal-encased night lights covered with a strip of red ribbon. The crystal finial powdered with irredescent glitter completes the effect. My example was used as the centre-piece for a large buffet table and made a great conversation piece in an all red and white dining-room.

MADONNA IN A FROZEN GARDEN

Public exhibitions and competitions with a Christmas theme are always popular. The decoration in Illustration 132 was created for one of my demonstrations. The central feature is a Dutch crystal madonna from the Leerdam glass factory. Her simple lines set the theme for a crystal garden of frozen flowers. The first three placements are of coconut palm spathe silvered and mounted on false stems. These are firmly impaled on a pinholder secured to the glass brick. Five silver aspidistra leaves repeat their movement on the left interspersed with aquamarine plastic fir fronds. Dynamic movement is created by the swirling cane. About fifteen pieces of basketry cane of varying lengths are covered with narrow strips of aqua metallic foil paper. Each tip ends in a turquoise fabric leaf. This very pliable material can be

curved or interwoven as desired. The five barley sugar twist glass icicles are mounted on strong wires also covered with foil. A few pieces of rough glass waste are used to conceal the pinholder.

The focal area consists of three flowers made from metallic crinkle foil paper with silver holly berries as stamens. This paper is sold at good florists, art shops and flower clubs. It is most versatile and attractive and can be purchased in many beautiful colours. To make the flowers cut out two strips of foil three inches wide and eighteen inches long. Ensure that the grain or stretch quality runs across lengthways. Paste the back of the paper with glue and lay six inch-long stub wires of twenty gauge at one inch intervals across the paper. Then place the second piece of paper on top and press together. Smooth out any air bubbles around the sandwiched wires and leave to dry overnight.

Next day cut the paper into strips one inch wide, three inches long, with the stub wire trapped down the centre. The petals are cut out of these strips. I prefer to cut out free hand, but beginners may feel happier drawing around a templet to achieve uniform petal shapes. However, experience will show no two flowers are the same, so slight variations in petal size will look more natural. Any petal or leaf shape can be cut out, but a lily shape works well. The grain must be across the petal with the wire as the centre vein.

132 Madonna in a Frozen Garden

Shape the petal by gently curving the wire and modelling the glue-stiffened paper between the thumb and forefinger. Its stretch quality allows for expansion. Six shaped petals can now be assembled around a cluster of stamens, wired sequins or tinsel sparkler. Exotic effects with two tones of paper, jewelled stigmas and stamens can all be tried. Bind the six petals and centre together with silver reel wire. Mount on extra poker wires to extend the stem. Cover the stem with a narrow strip of foil, crepe paper or gutta-percha. These fantasy flowers will last many seasons and have countless variations and uses.

A MOSS TEDDY BEAR

As Christmas is essentially a festival for children, it is fun to make a decoration especially for them, though I find this one appeals to adults as well. The teddy bear is made of bun moss used to represent the fur of this well-loved animal. The body is a wire frame which I must confess was bought ready made. However, it is not too difficult to fashion one from crunched-up two-inch mesh wire netting. Remember whatever shape you make it will thicken up considerably once it is covered. Teddy has to start life looking very thin.

In Illustration 133 this model is about sixteen inches high. The wire frame is firmly stuffed with moist wreath moss bound in place with reel wire, paws and all. Then pin the bun moss in place with straight hair pins. Bent stub wires could be used, but they rust and discolour the moss. Bun moss is a special variety of carpet moss only found in wet acid woodland. It grows out of the ground in winter to form small rounded flattish buns. It is rare and should be picked very sparingly. An imported supply is available from good florists.

Once the foundation has been covered with pinned on moss the bear is ready to be trimmed with jaunty neck tie and jewelled eyes backed with white card. You will be surprised how many different facial expressions can be produced, for once the eyes are added he comes to life. His wooden spoon and Goldilocks porridge are whimsies of my own. Use a small steamed pudding basin filled with Dryfoam. Into this are wired clusters of white everlasting flowers, *Anaphalis triplinervis*. Little bows of ribbon and ivy leaves complete the decoration. Designs made of bun moss will last a long time and dry out to a soft grey-green colour. Periodic respraying with water will help to maintain the fresh look of ferny woods.

SLEEPING BEAUTY CASTLE

This fairy-tale castle can be made to any scale, this one is quite large for demonstration purposes. The towers are strong cardboard cylinders saved from metallic crinkle foil drums. Any type of stout tubing will do, such as discarded carpet rollers. Three tubes cluster together to form the lower section, grouped on an oval base. They should be cut to give a variation of heights. The two small side turrets are fruit juice cartons. The fine pointed turrets are cut from a glittering Perspex (Plexiglass) sheet. Stiff card gummed and sprinkled with glitter could be substituted. The base board and towers are covered with pale green metallic foil paper. Small lanceolate windows are cut from emerald green paper and glued in place, as shown in Illustration 134.

Having created the castle the enchanted forest is the next placement. This consists of an outline of contorted hazel branches sprayed black. Spider's webs spun from silver reel wire create an eerie effect, bespangled with cyrstal dew drops. Although laborious to make, the cobwebs have many uses and cost little but time.

To make cobwebs:

Open out a wire dry cleaner's coat hanger to form a circle. Attach about ten separate diagonal pieces of fine silver reel wire. Cross each one in the centre catching the end tightly around the frame at each side. The frame will now resemble the spokes of a bicycle wheel. With a separate piece of wire of manageable length catch together the central crossing wires

133 A Moss Teddy Bear

and attach firmly together. You are now ready to weave the loose end outwards in an increasing spiral pattern, looping the wire around each spoke as it crosses. The centre is the hardest part, but it gets easier as you progress towards the outer perimeter. Detach the complete web from the frame by untwisting the wire spokes. Paint the web with gum and sprinkle liberally with untarnishable nylon glitter. I once saw a Christmas tree entirely covered with glittered webs, an enchanting spectacle representing hours of patient work.

The other elements of the forest consist of jade green and tan fabric leaves with blue-green fabric flowers. Aspidistra-style leaves of aqua paper, made as for the flower petals, help to hide the pinholder and Dryfoam mechanics. In the centre three dried heads of an alpine thistle, *Carlina acaulis*, catch the eye. Their centres are spangled with emerald sequins. To the rear, tall jade grasses suggest an overgrown place balanced by sinister leaves of black glittered mahonia lower left. The entangled crescent movement of the design is in deliberate conflict with the vertical lines of the castle. This effect is used to illustrate the fairy story it symbolizes, the struggle between good and evil. Young children love a decoration made just for them, especially if the towers conceal sweets or other seasonal treats.

YORK MINSTER ANGELS

An interpretive tableau concludes this chapter with a pair of carved angels lent by kind permission of the Dean and Chapter of York Minister. Once the finials to the dorsal posts of the High Altar, they now reside in the wood carver's museum. I have use them for many years before countless hundreds of people for the finale of my Christmas demonstrations.

134 *A Sleeping Beauty Castle*

By raising one angel on its original post, space and height are added to the composition. Their outstretched wings of gilded wood are repeated by the placement of Chinese Fan Palms arranged in a descending rhythm. This movement is achieved by using an upper container attached behind the taller angel and a lower one on the left. Their haloes are gold and ox-blood red; touches of this colour appear in the moiré ribbon. The antique putty colour of their robes is picked up by curved strips of coconut spathe which add vigour and movement.

Fresh plant material is minimal, with three ivory-white poinsettias and five white gerbera 'Delos'. A few sprays of green and cream variegated ivy weave a path for the eye to follow. The whole is backed by a triptych of pale green wood piped with gold cord and bronze-red ribbon. This niche with its Gothic points helps to focus attention on the group and isolate these religious objects from the secular surroundings of my studio. They convey, with flowers and gilded leaves, a feeling of tranquillity in keeping with the true message of Christmas – Peace on Earth, Goodwill to all Men.

135 *York Minster Angels*

136 *An inviting glimpse of the formal garden seen through the terrace door, with a cascading arrangement of roses and honeysuckle.*

CHAPTER 10

INSPIRATION FROM THE GARDEN

This chapter illustrates the gardens of my home, The Manor House, Heslington, York, which are open to groups by prior appointment only. I am indebted to Allan Buckle, the gardener, for continuing the high standards of his predecessor the late Norman Puckering.

My special appreciation is due to my two friends, Brian Withill and David Gilkeson, who during the past decade have improved the design and added many notable features, including two ponds.

In 1968 we came to live at The Manor House; originally a farmstead it had been converted by Lord and Lady Deramore twenty years before. Surrounded by agricultural buildings with functional areas between, the four gardens take their names from these enclosures, protected by mellow brick walls. Each has its own character opening on to the next which helps to create an element of surprise.

The visitor enters the lantern gate along a path of York stone. To either side stretch herbaceous borders with the Georgian porticoed door ahead flanked by topiary. Tender plants enjoy this sheltered aspect running the length of the house.

Flag-stones give way to grass in the old orchard, where borders of blue, pink and mauve are backed by clematis. Ancient fruit trees play host to honeysuckle and golden hops entwined through their branches. In their dappled shade grow choice ferns, trilliums, hellebores and bulbs. This collection owes much to the generosity of gardening friends as these plants are rarely found for sale.

An eighteenth-century iron gate leads into the second garden with its spacious lawn and raised terrace created from the demolished cow shed. An old wisteria festoons the French window of the garden hall. *Magnolia grandiflora* 'Exmouth' and *Rosa banksiae* 'Lutea' enjoy this sheltered southern aspect.

Formal beds of white, pink and cream roses framed by obelisks of golden yew lead the eye to the centre-piece of this vista, a carved stone mask spouting water into a semicircular pool. Borders of mixed white flowers are backed by climbing roses, including 'Madame Alfred Carrière', 'Iceberg' and 'Paul's Perpetual White', with a double clematis 'Duchess of Edinburgh'.

The old granary with its first floor studio stands both as a focus and a vantage point from which to view the next and largest garden. Once the stackyard with stables, barns and horse pond, informal island beds are grouped in harmonies of colour, form and texture like large flower arrangements, but with an ever changing pattern.

The arches of the cartsheds form a rustic loggia for alfresco entertaining with a view of the smaller pond. This tranquil expanse of water is home to varied wildlife, its boggy margin fringed with king cups, primulas and iris. From this focal point meandering paths invite exploration of a shady glade. Bold plantings of hostas, foxgloves and dicentras enjoy the shelter offered by rhododendrons and azaleas in a spinney of birch and pine.

From the larger upper pond a garden seat provides a restful view across the three-acre garden. From here the path leads back through the old rose garden backed by a beech hedge whose maturity belies its young age. A brick path edged with herbs invites the visitor to linger on the way to the courtyard. Double wrought-iron gates lead into a yard of rounded cobbles and herring-bone brick. Clipped box trees, bay and ivy in terracotta pots, lend a formal air.

137 *Naturalized narcissi and forsythia herald the spring in what was once the stackyard.*

138 *Juniper 'Skyrocket' and cherry blossoms frame the south-facing
terrace with the stone troughs and colourful alpines.*

139 *A basket of rose 'Canary' Bird, azaleas and tulips gathered from
these borders and the glade beyond.*

140 *Flower-filled borders lead to the guest cottage which has commanding views of the four connected gardens.*

141 *In the glade colourful azaleas and rhododendrons lead to the upper pond.*

142 *Drifts of tulips are foiled by Bowle's golden grass and orange reed-mace euphorbia. Globe flowers and reed-mace fringe the pond's damp margin.*

143 *The upper pond transforms a once drab corner of this three-acre garden; home to fish and waterfowl it is a year-round attraction.*

144 *Dappled sunlight highlights the yellow double border leading to the lower pond and studio.*

145 *The lower pond is edged with candelabra primulas, variegated iris and an orange-barked willow, beautiful in winter.*

146 *A tapestry of hostas, ferns, dicentras and blue poppies indicate the wealth of planting in this flower arranger's paradise.*

147 *The terrace door festooned with wisteria planted after the house was converted from a farm in 1948.*

148 *The terrace gate leads to the old orchard with sentinels of iris, hostas and hebes.*

149 *The pink and white rose garden with the granary studio reached by an outside staircase.*

150 *White lights decorate a blue spruce growing by the courtyard gate. Terracotta pots of clipped box, bay and ivy formalize this cobbled area. A Christmas door wreath and lanterns offer a welcome.*

INDEX

Page numbers in *italics* refer to illustration captions

ACKNOWLEDGEMENTS

My sincere thanks are due to many people who have helped me, in particular Richard Webb and Delian Bower for inviting me to write this book. My thanks to their staff and to Alyson Gregory for editing my superfluity of words with tact and sensitivity; also to Peter Wrigley who designed the jacket and layout.

Tim Megson has by the brilliance of his photography captured the fragile beauty of my arrangements with skill and patience. I owe him and his assistant Adrian Forrest a great debt of gratitude. My thanks also to Allan Green.

On home ground a special thank you to my friends Brian Withill for deciphering my handwriting and transcribing it into immaculate typescript and to David Gilkeson who has made many helpful suggestions about the text.

My thanks to Allan Buckle who tends the plants that have provided such a wealth of cut material and for his help with preparation and mechanics. To my late gardener Norman Puckering for fifteen years of unfailing loyalty. Frank and Irene Bough of Ward's Florists, York, have obtained many unusual and exotic flowers for which I thank them.

To all those who have opened their lovely homes, churches and museums with unstinted co-operation and hospitality.

Finally to you my readers who by your encouragement and support over the years have helped me strive always for something better. I hope you will enjoy this book and find it a source of beauty and inspiration.

Picture Credits
All photographs by Tim Megson except for:
Illustrations 11, 18, 23, 95, 124 and 135 by Allan Green, York
Illustration 68 by Graham Powell, Harrogate
Illustration 80 by Woodmansterne Picture Library, Watford